THE LADY'S CHAMPION

HEARTS OF BLACKMERE
BOOK ONE

MARIE LIPSCOMB

ISBN 978-1-8382037-0-2

Violet Gaze Press

20-22 Wenlock Rd

London

DEDICATION

For Jake, who deserves to be a romance hero.

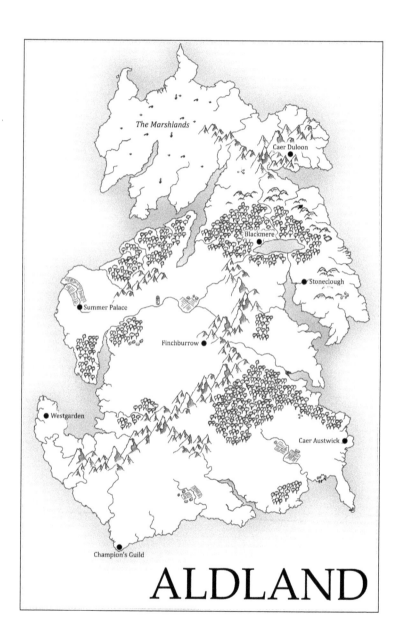

The Marshlands

Caer Duloon

Blackmere

Stoneclough

Summer Palace

Finchburrow

Westgarden

Caer Austwick

Champion's Guild

ALDLAND

CONTENTS

PROLOGUE

Centuries ago, Aldland was at the mercy of a cruel and tyrannical nobleman.

Every passing day brought him victories, and every day the people hoped for salvation. His influence spread across the kingdom, and any who dared defy him felt the full extent of his wrath.

Just when all hope was lost, a force arose in the south, an army, the Champions of Aldland. Driving him back to his last remaining stronghold, they defeated him, and took his castle for their own.

The champions were heroes.

From their base, the Champion's Guild, they dedicated their lives to the safety of Aldland's people, fighting to protect those who could not defend themselves. Soon, no one would stand against them. There were no wars to be fought, no tyrants to quell, and so, the champions took on a new purpose.

They fought for the pleasure of the people; the mightiest and most beautiful warriors in Aldland, displaying their strength and skill to the delight of the masses in contests and tourneys. And though their purpose changed, their legendary status never faded in the hearts of Aldland's people.

CHAPTER ONE

NATALIE'S HEART still raced from the excitement, and considerable stress, of the day's events. After twelve years of pleading, letters, and planning, the Grand Tourney had at last come to Blackmere. Aldland's finest fighters were just a stone's throw from the castle.

Though she was back in her bed chamber, the scent of combat lingered in Natalie's senses; the tang of sweat and adrenaline. The roar of the crowd still vibrated in her chest. Even while perched on the town's walls, where she was forced to keep a respectable distance from the violence, the curses and mud, she could taste the battle.

Jenny, the tavern's landlady placed her hands on her hips, her dark blonde hair swaying just above her shoulders. "I swear, Lady Blackmere, if you get me into trouble..."

Natalie, pressed her teeth into her lower lip and pulled

the gown's laces tighter against Jenny's slender figure. "I won't." She could not hide her grin as she threaded the final eyelets on the bodice. "This is my castle anyway. Who are you going to be in trouble with?"

Jenny sighed in defeat. "Well, what am I supposed to do all night?"

"Whatever you want. The castle is yours for the evening."

"It's awfully… dreary. No wonder you're so pale and pasty, hiding away up here all these years."

A huff of incredulous laughter burst from Natalie's lips. "Thank you. That's just what I needed to hear before I meet my heroes." She pushed her auburn locks over her shoulders to keep them out of the way of the laces.

Jenny turned her head. She pressed her lips together and cringed at her poor choice of words. "I only say it from a place of concern, Natalie. You were so bold and rosy-cheeked when you arrived at Blackmere all those years ago, and now—"

"I know." Natalie drew a steadying breath and offered her friend a reassuring smile. The past twelve years had been hard. Raw grief had dulled to numbness, then complacency, and finally comfort. But now, it was time for her to break out from her self-inflicted prison.

The champions had saved Aldland once, long ago. Perhaps they could save her spirit.

"Anyway, there's plenty to do tonight. You could

read?" Natalie gestured to the bookshelves tucked in the corner of the room. There were tales of epic battles and brave heroes, mythical creatures and indomitable heroines. Their spines were battered and bent out of shape by multiple re-readings.

"Is that what you do in here all day?"

"Among other things."

"Such as?"

Natalie chewed her lip in the heavy silence. If she was honest about what she really did for fun, it would only result in teasing. She smiled to herself as she thought of the scraped and chipped stones concealed behind tapestries, the places where she had gotten carried away with the blunted, decorative swords which hung on the castle's walls.

With a tug, she knotted the laces at the small of Jenny's back and stepped around the tavern landlady to admire her handy work.

Against Jenny's slight frame, the gown was loose and creased, and stopped four inches above her feet. The washed-out blue wool was cool against her pale skin, just as it was with Natalie's, but the gentle pink of the setting sun glowed through the window, and cast soft light on the landlady's rosy cheeks and freckles. Her blue eyes sparkled in the light.

At the sight of her, a sense of longing overcame Natalie. She could not remember the last time she had stayed outside long enough for the sun to warm her skin.

Lowering her eyes, Jenny stepped to the side, peering at her figure. She looked every bit as stately as the lady of Blackmere Castle should. "By the Goddess, I look like a queen."

Natalie could not help but smile. She would gladly give Jenny the castle if it meant she could take off in the morning, concealed among the ranks of the champions, and live among them at the Guild. "You look beautiful."

"Why do we have to switch though? It's completely normal for the nobles to meet the champions after a tourney. Just call them here."

"Someone has to stay here. If the castle looks empty, they'll know something's amiss. And if the champions come here and meet me as Lady Blackmere, they'll be stiff and formal and dull. I want to meet the *real* champions."

"Oh, you and your champions." Jenny rolled her eyes, smoothing the folds of fabric over her slender figure. She looked around Natalie's bed chamber, at the dark stone walls, fine—albeit dusty—tapestries, and the large, soft, canopied bed. The landlady smiled. "And what are you going to do while I'm locked away in a castle like a fairytale princess."

"Your job," Natalie grinned. "I'll serve drinks in the tavern."

Jenny cocked her eyebrow. "To the champions?"

"Aye, if they're thirsty."

"Lady Blackmere!" Jenny laughed, rolling her eyes. "If

the rumors are true, the champions are *always* thirsty."

Her racing heart pounded harder. "Oh, by the Goddess I can't wait, Jenny. I've wanted to meet them for so long. I wrote to the Guild every year from the moment I became Lady Blackmere, begging them to come here. I want to hear their stories, and see their battle wounds."

"You've heard their stories. The troubadours sing of them constantly."

"But I want to hear it from them!"

Jenny shook her head and gathered her own rumpled dress from the floor. "I suppose it won't be so bad. The feasts are over, and kitchens will have closed for the night by the time you get there. Just make sure you don't wreck the place."

"You have so much faith in me, Jen. It'll be fine."

The smile fell from Jenny's lips as she took Natalie's hands in her own. "You need to be careful though, a bonny woman like you. You might find the champions aren't so willing to talk as they are to show you their prowess in other ways."

Her concern made Natalie's heart squeeze. Jenny had been a good friend to her, ever since she had arrived at Blackmere. Grief had not driven the landlady away as it had with so many others Natalie had once been close to. If anything, the solitude of the castle seemed to be a sanctuary after a long day running the tavern.

"I'll be careful. And if it comes to that, I'll leave."

"And what? You'll close the tavern for the night?"

"Aye."

"And my staff?"

"Will be compensated."

With a huff, Jenny held her own simple dress aloft, and dropped it over Natalie's head. Lady Blackmere wiggled through the canopy of thin, taupe wool, pulling it over her figure. She winced at the tightness of the bodice. Her ample chest and full waist were packed into the pale wool, but she would manage. The generous flare of the skirt barely skimmed over her thighs and stomach, and did not restrict her movement.

Jenny screwed her face as Natalie rearranged her bosom. "I hope you weren't planning to breathe tonight."

"I'm sure once I see the champions, I'll be unable to anyway."

The landlady laughed as she rolled the sleeves above Natalie's elbows.

Unlike Natalie's fine gown, fit for a noble, Jenny's simple dress was designed to be laced at the front by the wearer. Natalie tugged at the laces, closing the dress as best she could and hoped she didn't look too indecent. At least the white cotton smock she wore beneath gave her some semblance of coverage.

"So, is there anyone in particular you fancy?" Jenny gave a sly grin. "A champion who caught your eye."

Natalie scoffed. "I could barely see their faces. The chamberlain insisted it wouldn't have been proper for me to sit close to the fighting. From what I saw, The Dragon fought well."

"Ah, yes, the Tourney's victor," Jenny smirked. "That chiseled jaw, the glistening muscles. I'm sure he's a great conversationalist."

Natalie rolled her eyes as Jenny stepped behind her and began to fuss with her long, coppery hair. "Who would you pick?"

"If I had the courage? Genevieve," Jenny sighed. "The Thorn of the Rose."

"Oh? She's intense."

"Wonderfully so."

"Agreed," Natalie laughed. "Are you sure you don't mind me taking your place at the tavern? Wouldn't you rather go to meet her?"

Jenny dismissed her with a wave of her hand. "I'm glad of the night off. I know how much this means to you Natalie. I'm glad to see you getting out and meeting people. It's been so long since—"

Natalie's throat clamped shut.

Jenny seemed to detect her sudden discomfort, and adopted a brighter tone. "Anyway, you have to do it. You've been pining after the champions since the day I met you and you missed most of the Tourney."

Natalie smiled and lowered her head. Her fingers fidgeted with the ends of the ribbon crisscrossing over her chest. "I did always dream of meeting Brandon—"

Jenny snickered as she tugged and braided Natalie's hair. "Brandon the Bear? The one in all the songs?"

"He was Grand Tourney Victor for six years."

"Aye, but... the way he fought today..."

Natalie would be bitter until the end of her days that her chamberlain had cornered her with her duties that morning. There had been disputes over farm borders to settle, funds to be allocated, letters to be sent to neighboring nobles—mostly apologies for not attending their events—and a seemingly endless list of repair work to be done to the castle. She had missed the melee, and barely made it in time to see the final round of the joust.

Jenny shook her head and restarted the braid. "He was out almost as soon as it started. He lost in the first round of the melee."

"He was unlucky."

"He's not..." Jenny's words faded behind a grimace as she placed Natalie's sloppily plaited hair over her shoulder. "He's not in the best shape, to put it kindly. His best days are behind him. People have taken to calling him Brandon the Boar."

"People can be cruel." Natalie grimaced and looked out of the window, at the dwindling sunlight. "Besides, my interest in meeting him is purely out of respect for his prowess in the Tourney."

"Aye, and I'm sure it has nothing to do with the songs they sing about the size of his *weapon*."

Natalie's cheeks tightened as she hid her grin behind a façade of outrage. "Stop it."

Jenny chuckled and placed a gentle kiss on Natalie's shoulder as she squeezed the top of her arms. "Just try not to destroy my tavern, my lady."

Natalie smiled and leaned back into Jenny's touch. "I'll try."

Her eyes drifted to a small crack, gleaming silver in the corner of the window. Frustration tightened her jaw. There was always something which needed to be fixed.

The crumbling pile of ancient stones was hers to fix. Hers alone.

She was isolated, a hundred miles from her mother and father, tasked with the responsibility of running Blackmere castle and the surrounding lands.

Blackmere was a grim and dreary place compared to the castle she had grown up in. Caer Austwick's white towers and legendary rose gardens had been her playground whilst growing up, but after the passing of her maternal grandfather, Blackmere became her home; *their* home. A home for Natalie and her newly wedded husband. A home to raise a family in.

No one, least of all Natalie, had intended for her to live

in Blackmere alone.

She had to get out, even if just for one night. Away from the empty corridors and endless unused rooms.

Natalie silenced her memories with a smile and turned to face Jenny. "How do I look?"

"Like a bonny barmaid about to burst from her ill-fitting frock."

"Perfect."

CHAPTER TWO

"*L*<small>ADY</small> *B*<small>LACKMERE?</small>"

Natalie closed her eyes and exhaled an exasperated breath as her name rattled through the air. Her fingertips rested against the keep's heavy wooden doors, agonizingly close to freedom. Slow, shuffling footsteps drew near and quelled her excitement.

Her shoulders slumped as she turned. "My dear chamberlain. You should go home for the evening. Enjoy the celebrations."

The elderly man hobbled towards her. His silver eyebrows, stark against warm brown skin, knitted together as his clouding eyes scanned her lowly garb. In his mottled hands he carried an open ledger, its pages crinkled at the edges. A brown and black speckled quill, and a pot of black ink sat upon the pages. "I have a few things I need to discuss with you."

"Can't it wait until tomorrow? We've both had an eventful day."

"It's about the Tourney, my lady. I need to fill the account books. There are gaps."

Natalie let her fingers fall from the door handle.

The chamberlain took his cue and began flipping through the pages of his ledger. His breath rattled in his throat as his eyes scanned the entries. "Now...The Tourney." He chuckled. "Oh Goddess, where do I begin?"

Natalie forced a smile. Every moment she lingered was time she could spend speaking with the champions—or rather pining after them silently and overthinking what she could say to them.

"Ah, yes." The chamberlain peered down his nose. "The Tourney Victor's prize money, and the Guild Master's cut. You made no mention of it when we were accounting for the expenses, and I noticed there was rather a handsome sum of gold handed over."

Natalie's stomach tightened at the mention of it. She had not looked forward to the conversation. "It was my own money. The money my parents gave me."

His eyes flickered towards her. "Your dowry? My lady, your mother gave you that money in the event that you remarry..."

A shrill ringing pierced her skull, muffling the chamberlain's words. Heat crept along her spine. Her muscles tensed, demanding she throw open the door and bolt outside. "Chamberlain, please."

He snapped his jaw shut and pressed his lips into a thin line. "My lady?"

"It was my money. It was given to me to use *if* I ever chose to remarry. I have no intentions on using it for its intended purpose."

The old man's eyes lowered as he moistened his lips with his tongue. "Very well, Lady Blackmere. I shall adjust the records of your personal account." He scribbled a note in his ledger and peered down his nose at the pages. "Oh, and one other, rather urgent matter."

Natalie pressed her fingernails into the palm of her hand. "Yes?"

"There have been reports of bandits spotted on the east road."

"Goodness, I hope somebody stops them."

The chamberlain raised an eyebrow and cleared his throat. "The aforementioned portion of the east road falls under the jurisdiction of Blackmere—your jurisdiction."

Natalie's smile tightened. A muscle beneath her eye began to dance. "Very well. Dispatch the guards."

"How many should I send?"

She stared at the grey stone floor, her mind racing. "A lot of people will be travelling the roads after the celebrations tonight, many with coin in their pockets and ale clouding their minds. They'll be easy targets, won't they?" She took a deep breath and gave an assertive nod. "Send every guard we have."

"All of them?"

"Yes. Let's get this dealt with as quickly as possible. I want my people safe."

"Very good, my lady. And how do you intend to pay the guards for the extra work? I do think it's time we raised taxes."

Natalie's eyes drifted across the hall as she searched for answers. The portrait of her mother and father stared back at her, their thin-lipped, disapproving faces watching her. "No. Take it out of my allowance."

A wave of satisfaction rolled over her as the chamberlain blinked in surprise, shrugged and made a note in his ledger.

She hid her grin behind a cough. "Will that be all?"

"Yes, my lady, for now. I'll dispatch the guard right away." A soft chuckle escaped his lips. "The castle will be very empty tonight, but I'm sure all will be well. All the best fighters in the land are down the road in the tavern anyway."

Excitement speared her chest. "Indeed, they are. Goodnight, Chamberlain."

"Goodnight, my lady." He turned to shuffle away, before casting a final confused look at her appearance. "Might I ask where you are going?"

Natalie turned on her heel and heaved open the heavy wooden doors. "Out. I'll be back soon."

Pulling the door closed behind her, she hurried across the castle courtyard, wishing she had her fine grey wool shawl to wrap around her shoulders against the bitter late-autumn wind. The green hills of her land loomed beyond the castle walls, speckled with tiny white bleating dots.

The guards were distracted, grumbling among themselves as they patrolled the castle walls. Blackmere's flag, a ram's head on a field of green, fluttered above the ramparts.

A satisfied smile curved her lips as she reached the castle gate unhindered. The cobbled road sloped down beyond the strong wooden gates, surrounded by rows of houses and shops.

Natalie turned and glanced up at the keep. Jenny stood in the window of her chamber, looking as radiant as the Queen of Aldland herself. The landlady waved regally, blew a kiss down to Natalie, and scrunched her nose in amusement. With a grin, Natalie bowed low, and turned back to the gate, relaxed her shoulders, and began her journey to the tavern.

Evidence of the Tourney met her at every corner; brightly colored bunting fluttered in the breeze above shop doorways, overly excited children chased each other through the streets with sticks, and the sweet scent of honey cakes baked for the spectators still lingered in the air. Natalie's stomach growled its lament; she had not had the opportunity to taste one.

As she passed the woodcarver's workshop, she caught the soothing scent of sawdust. She cast her eyes over the wooden swords and horses made for children. A grin broke across her lips. As a girl she would have rioted if not permitted to get one, and some part of her still felt that desire.

"Can I help you?" the carver called from the back of his shop. He was a small man, not a day over thirty. His rounded face was dusted white with wood shavings.

"I was just looking, thank you."

He wiped his hands on his dusty apron. "Did you watch the Tourney then?"

"Some of it."

"Bunch of posers," he griped. "Good day." He tipped his hat and turned back to his whittling.

She gave the back of his head a wry smile. Without her finery, none of the townspeople recognized her as Lady Blackmere. To them, she was just another commoner, dressed in plain brown wool, her hair pulled back into a simple braid.

The Knight's Rest tavern sat in the shadow of the grey stone outer walls of the town. It was the first thing greeting weary travelers as they passed through Blackmere's north gate. The sweet aroma of fresh hay wafted from the tavern's stable.

Natalie bade the stableman good evening as she passed. He squinted at her and wiped his sweaty brow on his arm before lifting the handles of a wooden cart packed with steaming manure. "Miss," he greeted her with a nod.

Her heart steadied a little. She was unknown to her subjects even just a few feet from her own castle, unlike her mother and father, who were omnipresent in Caer Austwick, always hosting some kind of event.

"Getting Natalie to talk to our guests at parties is like coaxing birds from the sky," her father would sigh.

She had no interest in their parties. Nobles were boring, stiff and conniving. Their company was like Westgarden silks; exceptionally fine, and more often than not, fake. She did not care to speak to them, and did not impress her company upon her own people. If the townspeople wanted to befriend her, she was willing, as she had been with Jenny, but she did not actively seek anyone's company. The anticipation of conversation tended to curdle her gut.

She reached the tavern door and froze at the sound of boisterous singing coming from within. The champions were inside, celebrating their victories and drowning their losses. She swallowed and took in a shaking breath.

"This is my only chance," she whispered as she pressed her fingertips to the door. "After this, I may never lay eyes on a champion again."

The steady, thumping rhythm of marching guards began at the top of the hill. In no time at all the bandits would be gone from the roads, and her people could celebrate in peace.

She braced herself and pushed open the tavern door.

CHAPTER THREE

E VEN AFTER an hour had passed, Natalie's heart still thundered. The tavern hummed with chatter. Barmaids hurried between tables, their cheeks flushed with exhaustion and heat, faces shining from exertion. The sour stench of ale, the sweet scent of fresh timber, and the musty warmth of excited bodies all clamored for attention in Natalie's senses. She wiped her fingertips on her apron and ran a cloth over the bar.

The victorious champions celebrated around a long table on the top level of The Knight's Rest. Their laughter and song drowned out the patrons and losers on the busy bottom level. Natalie's eyes flickered towards them at any opportunity she got. Their names, aliases, and stories of their deeds ran through her mind, though assigning a face to any of the legends was all but impossible. Still, there were some she would recognize in her sleep.

"Next year! Next year I'll beat you all!" Genevieve, the

Thorn of the Rose sang loudly from the balcony. She was tall, muscular and beautiful, her smooth, dark brown skin illuminated by candlelight. Long black braids swung behind her back as she tipped her head back and drank. She had excelled in the axe-throwing competition, and celebrated by working her way through a cask of honeyed wine. Natalie could not help but smile as the warrior smashed her empty tankard onto the table and roared. The other champions cheered at her triumph.

"Excuse me?"

Natalie flinched as a smooth, masculine voice called out to her mere inches from her ear.

A man with soft honey colored curls and warm olive skin, leaned across the bar, his hand outstretched towards her forearm to catch her attention. He was handsome by any measure. A golden sword was embroidered onto his copper silk tunic; the sigil of The Champions Guild. Natalie's throat tightened as he gave her a broad, inviting smile.

"May I have a drink, please?" He withdrew his hand and blinked up at the champion's table as they erupted into another song. "Sorry, it's awfully loud in here, isn't it?"

"Oh! Yes. Of course," Natalie stammered. She snatched a wooden tankard from the bar, and sent it clattering onto the stone floor. The man's soft chuckle fanned fire across her skin.

"Are you alright?" he grinned.

"I'm fine," she grunted as she bent over to collect the

tankard. She was rapidly beginning to regret forcing herself into the tight bodice of Jenny's dress. "What drink would you like? You would like a drink?" She cringed. "Wait, you said that, already…Goddess."

"Are you sure you're well?" The man flashed an easy smile. "You look as though you're burning up."

The room swayed around Natalie as her heart hammered against her sternum. "You're a champion." The moment she spoke she regretted it. His smile grew wider, and he pushed the hair back from his forehead.

"Robert Trevaryn, at your service."

She tightened her grip around the wooden handle of the tankard before she could drop it again. "Ironclaw?"

He raised an eyebrow and leaned on the bar. "So, you've heard of me?"

"Of course I have," she gushed, setting the empty cup down. "You were winner of the joust two years running, and the first man to beat Brandon the Bear in the melee."

"A fact he's still sore about."

"I can imagine." She gave a breathless chuckle and placed her hands on her hips. A voice in the back of her mind scolded her for her overfamiliarity. The voice sounded suspiciously like her mother.

"I take it you were a fan of his?"

A flash of pale blue silk appeared in Natalie's periphery. "Peacocking again, Rob?"

Her lungs turned to a solid iron mass as Henry Percille, the current Grand Tourney Victor, raked his topaz gaze across her. To describe him as handsome would be to describe a hurricane as breezy. His hair, as black and sleek as a raven's wing, was oiled back, showcasing strong cheekbones, a chiseled, smooth shaven jaw, and blush-pink lips.

In that moment, had he recognized Natalie as the noble lady of Blackmere, she did not doubt that Henry's full attention would have been devoted to her. However, the Tourney Victor had no time for a simple barmaid. He turned his back to Natalie, and rested his arm along the bar, creating a barrier between her and his fellow champion.

"Come upstairs with us, Robert," Henry purred. "You don't need to sit down here at the loser's table, chatting up plain tarts."

Natalie's heart leapt as a hand darted towards her. Henry reached over, and snatched a bottle of wine from behind the bar. Indignation rose in her chest and the smile slipped from Robert's lips.

"Excuse me," she snapped. Her hand darted out of its own volition and grasped the body of the wine bottle.

Henry turned to her, a look of revulsion twisting his handsome features as he held on to the neck of the bottle. "Are you speaking to me?"

"Yes, I am," Natalie frowned, tilting her chin to meet him. "You're being rude."

"Rude?" Henry looked to Robert in amusement before correcting his expression. He fixed his steely gaze on Natalie. "Are you aware whom you address?"

"Aye, I'm very aware, and you're welcome to drink and eat your fill, as is your right as a champion, but I'll not have you being rude. I don't care who you are or how many victories you've won, you treat this tavern, and this town's people, with respect."

Henry raised his eyebrows, and flared his nostrils. "It's customary for the champions to eat and drink whatever they wish after a Grand Tourney, at the expense of the hosting noble. If you have an issue with me taking the wine, I suggest you speak with Lady Blackmere."

His eyes burned into her, challenging her to argue with him. The urge to reveal her identity swelled on her tongue, pushing against her lips. Robert threw his arm over Henry's shoulders and gave him a companionable squeeze.

The gesture loosened Henry's grip, and Natalie withdrew the bottle from his hand as he turned to the other champion.

"Henry," Robert grinned as he ruffled the other man's hair. "Let's not sour your victory with unpleasantness. I'm sure you can find it in your heart to ask the lady politely."

Natalie's blood boiled as Henry sighed deeply and looked around the bar, as though conjuring manners took all his considerable strength. His throat twitched as he swallowed, and the muscles in his cheeks danced to the tune of his indignation.

"May I have the bottle?" Henry muttered.

Natalie fought to keep the smile from her lips as she handed him the bottle and gave a slight curtsey. "You may. Enjoy it."

The young champion turned his back to her once more. "I trust there will be no further issues. Robert, if you wish to join us upstairs, you are more than welcome." He bowed his head and stamped up the wooden stairs, back to his table.

Natalie's gaze followed him, to where Genevieve watched over the balcony. The warrior woman glanced at Natalie before wrapping her muscular arm across Henry's back and guiding him back to his seat.

Robert puffed out his cheeks. His eyes widened, as though venting the pressure from his head. "You're lucky he's in a good mood tonight. He'd be trying his hardest to get you turned out onto the streets otherwise."

"I'd love to see him try."

Natalie turned away, hoping the Ironclaw did not see the heat spreading across her cheeks, and the beads of sweat on her forehead. Her heart was a battering ram against her ribs. She took a deep breath and grabbed a bottle of honeyed wine from the bar, poured two tankards, and passed one back to Robert.

"Thank you," he called from behind.

She drank back the sour-sweet wine, cursing herself for the outburst. Stories of the champions were always of their great deeds, their beauty and charisma, not their egos. But she had insulted Henry Percille, the Grand Tourney Victor, and suspected he would ensure none of the other champions would speak to her; not with any courtesy anyway.

Behind her, Robert released a satisfied exhalation, and his tankard clunked against the wooden bar top. "Bloody Henry. They call him The Dragon. Well, at least, he calls himself that, narcissistic prick that he is."

Natalie snorted as she drank, sending a blast of air into the cup. The wine splashed up her nose, stinging the back of her throat and launching her into a coughing fit.

"I'm sorry," Robert chuckled. "I shouldn't have."

Natalie fought to control her breath, clawing at the tight bodice. She longed to go back to the castle, to get into her nightgown and hide beneath her bedsheets. Resigning herself to the likelihood she had destroyed her chances of meeting the other champions, she filled her cup again and raised it to her lips.

"So, anyway," Robert said with a broad smile as she gulped down the wine. "How would you like to meet Brandon the Bear?"

CHAPTER FOUR

SMOOTHING DOWN her apron with trembling hands, Natalie picked her way between tables and chairs. She followed Robert's lead, scooting by patrons who held out their empty tankards and called after her. If word got back to Jenny, she would tease Natalie, and say she was a better noble than a barmaid, and that was saying something.

Her pounding heart drove her through the crowd. She kept her breath measured, as she did when speaking formally before courts and kings, yet still her ears rang, and cold sweat pooled on her burning skin.

Despite the remote location, gossip did reach Blackmere, albeit somewhat delayed. What Natalie knew of Brandon came from whispers of his staggering height, his monumental strength, and his dark, brooding eyes. Troubadours came from neighboring lands to sing of his victories, his defeats, and even, when they suspected the nobility was out of earshot, the size of his manhood.

Robert leaned in close to her ear, the scent of honey on his breath. "He's in rather a bad mood today, on account of, you know… he did not fight as well as he expected. Some might call it a crushing defeat. He's over there, brooding."

She craned her neck above the patrons. Her gaze was drawn to a figure sat hunched over a table, nursing a tankard of ale and shrouded in shadow. He ran his thumb along the rim of the cup, and stared into the amber liquid. His warm, rosy complexion told of a life spent outdoors and physical work. Concern weighted his brow, and dark, sorrowful eyes were edged with fine lines. White hairs threaded through the otherwise thick dark brown of his beard, and his brown hair was silver at the temples.

Even sitting, hunched over his drink, he dominated the space.

"That's him, isn't it?" Natalie whispered. There was no mistaking a man that size. Lightning tingled along her skin. The sweet taste of the honeyed wine lingered on her bottom lip as she moistened it with her tongue, her legs solid rods of iron.

Her stomach lurched as she realized she was standing alone.

"Cheer up," Robert called to the man as he shuffled between tables.

The large man looked up with a start, and leaned back in the creaking chair. "Took you long enough."

The sound of his voice knocked the air from Natalie's lungs. She had imagined it smooth, poetic, like honey sliding from a warm knife, but his voice was thunderous and deep, as though it rolled from his chest rather than his tongue. His rough Marshlands accent was hewn from the rock and heather.

His eyes hardened as they passed over Natalie, as though trying to work out why she was standing there staring at him. Her body tensed.

Robert placed two full tankards on the table, and turned back with open arms towards Natalie. "Brandon, look, I made a friend. Be a good Bear and say hello."

The scrape of wood against stone set her teeth on edge as he stood from his chair, knocking the drinks on the table behind him.

"Oi!" a disgruntled patron called out as he wiped ale foam from his trousers.

Brandon turned and grimaced an apology, wiping his hands along his sides as he straightened his back.

He was taller than Natalie by more than a foot, though not the height of two men, as the songs claimed. He was the only one among the champions who was not clad in silk. The plain brown woolen tunic he wore was worn, frayed at the sleeves and around his hips. It clung to his heavy frame, the coarse wool stretched tight over his rounded chest and stomach. He tugged at it before offering his hand to Natalie.

"My lady."

Her stomach flipped at the use of her title. Panic quickened her pulse as she prepared to be ushered away from the tavern and treated as though she was made of crystal.

His eyes darted towards the bar, then back to her. "You work here, don't you? I saw you standing behind the bar."

"Oh…" With a start she realized his hand still hovered in the air between them. She placed her fingers across his waiting palm, her hand so delicate in his. He curled his hand around hers and brought his other hand up to envelop hers completely; a greeting for a commoner. Relief washed over her, and she found she could breathe once more. "Aye. Yes. I work here."

"Well, it's a pleasure to meet you." He smiled at her, and her heart skipped, bouncing between her stomach and her throat. Her hand grew hot, pressed between his broad, rough palms.

"She's a barmaid at this fine tavern. And she's a fan of yours," Robert smiled beside him, nudging the Bear's thick bicep with his elbow. "She's heard *all* the songs about you."

A soft shade of pink crept up from beneath Brandon's beard, as he dismissed Robert with a roll of his eyes. "Unfortunately, I haven't done anything song-worthy in a long time."

He turned back to Natalie, his eyes widening a little as he finally released her hand.

In the corner of her eye, Robert's grin spread. "Won't you join us?"

"Oh," Natalie breathed. The room around them tilted a little, as the honeyed wine snaked through her mind. She fidgeted with the seam of her apron, torn between the urge to hide, and the desire to talk to the champions.

Brandon shot his friend a wide-eyed look and smoothed a broad hand over his beard. The back of his hand was covered with small scars, some fresh and pink, others faded and silver.

"Now Rob, I'm sure she has a lot to do. It smells like something's burning in the kitchen."

Natalie sniffed the air. He was right, but the bitter tang of smoke was barely detectable above the sweaty stench of the tavern. But Jenny had assured her the champions' feast would have ended long before Natalie arrived.

"The kitchens are closed for the evening," she frowned. "Perhaps the chimneys need to be cleaned?"

"Ah, perhaps," Brandon raised his brow. He lowered his head and pressed his lips together. "I apologize my lady; I should not have brought attention to it."

"I'll have it cleaned in the morning, though I'm afraid you will have left by then."

"Aye. We leave first thing, back to the Guild."

Natalie's heart sunk. So many questions lingered at the back of her throat. For so long she had longed to ask him of his stories, of his countless victories in the Tourney, and bask in awe of his greatness, but now, standing before her, he was just a man.

"So, you'll join us?" Robert beamed. "The chimneys can wait, the night is young, and I know I can certainly speak for Brandon when I say that he would very much enjoy your company."

Brandon exhaled heavily. "You're drunk, Rob." He gave Natalie an apologetic smile, and placed his hand on Robert's shoulder, pushing the smaller man down until he sat laughing in the chair. "I apologize. He's an insufferable ass at the best of times, and a barely tolerable drunk."

"It's quite alright," Natalie smiled as the mighty Iron-claw chuckled and reddened like a schoolboy.

A cheer erupted from the table above, as a group drunken townspeople laughed and drank with the champions. Two women perched on Henry's lap, pouring wine into their mouths and kissing him deeply. The other champions cheered, and a chant spread around the tavern; "*Dragon, Dragon, Dragon!*"

Brandon gazed up at them, and for a moment, his lips parted, like a starved man watching a king at his coronation feast. He cleared his throat and raised his tankard to his lips, focusing instead on the amber ale.

Genevieve stood at the balcony, her eyes scanning the calmer drinkers below. When her gaze fell to Natalie, she frowned, drew back and rejoined the boisterous group.

"I never imagined the champions were like this," Natalie muttered.

Brandon chuckled softly and gestured for her to sit at the table, setting his cup down. "What did you imagine?"

Robert raised his eyebrows as he drank, and the corners of his lips spread out from either side of the tankard.

Ignoring Ironclaw's smirk, Natalie accepted the invitation to sit. Through the flimsy fabric of the dress, the wood was cool against the backs of her thighs. She leaned forward, and rested her elbows on the table. "I supposed I imagined champions as legends, warriors, more god than man."

"Ah," Brandon sighed. "Well I can see how you might be disappointed." He pulled out the chair beside her and squeezed by, tensing his stomach so he did not bump into her. The scent of salt and leather flooded the air as he passed. "We champions are just men and women trained to look pretty and fight for entertainment. No doubt I am the most disappointing of them all."

Cold dread dripped down Natalie's spine. Her eyes widened. "No! Oh, by the Goddess, I did not mean that you were less than…" She covered her face with her hands and looked at him through the gaps between her fingers. "Sir if I have offended you—"

He cut her off with a deep, rattling laugh and raised his tankard to his lips. "Sadly, my reputation has far outgrown me." He shifted in his seat as he took a drink, and his knee brushed against hers. He patted his stomach and smiled. "And I have far outgrown my legend. Don't fear, my lady, you've committed no offence."

Breathless from embarrassment, and the heat of his thigh against her leg, Natalie pressed her fingers to her lips. She looked into his eyes, and felt her pulse quicken throughout her body. He was not the chiseled warrior she had imagined, but as her eyes followed the curvature of his figure, her chest grew tight and her stomach tingled. "Please forgive me. You are in no way a disappointment."

Brandon's lips flickered into a smile, which sent wildfire through Natalie's veins.

"That's not what the last girl said," Robert snickered, glancing over his shoulder, clearly thinking himself inaudible. A swift kick under the table from Brandon bought his silence.

Natalie fought, and failed to keep her laughter locked behind her lips.

"I take it back," Brandon grimaced, rubbing his eyebrows with his thumb and first finger. "Ironclaw is the most disappointing of us all."

Sputtering laughter escaped Natalie's guard, and her cheeks grew hotter still as she covered her mouth

Robert raised his cup in silent salute to himself, and downed his drink.

Natalie's head spun. She found herself giddy, overwhelmed by the ease of their conversation. Her throat was parched, begging to be quenched by more of the warming, delicious honey wine. The thick scent of smoke stung her eyes as the champions upstairs sang and banged their fists on the table.

Brandon's eyes narrowed. "Are you certain it's the chimney?" He pulled himself to his feet and hurried over to the window.

"I'm… yes, quite sure," Natalie stammered, looking to Robert for assurance.

"He's just trying to impress you," the tipsy man grinned, winking as he set down his cup.

Natalie blinked as something warm splashed across her face. Robert's eyes widened, and grew dull.

She could only watch in horror, as Ironclaw slumped forward, slain by the crossbow bolt, protruding from the back of his skull.

CHAPTER FIVE

A CRY BEGAN in Brandon's gut, rolled through his chest, and burst from his lips with the violence and agony of a broken soul. Natalie blinked as Robert's blood dripped down her face, and spattered onto her breast.

Chairs scraped and clattered to the floor, tables crashed as they were flipped onto their sides, and the people in the tavern ducked behind them for cover. The stench of smoke, and the orange glow of fire, filled the tavern.

Natalie's view was blocked as Brandon leaned across the table and held his fallen friend in his arms. "No, no, please. Rob!"

"The castle is under attack!" someone called.

A ringing in Natalie's ears drowned out the sounds, swelling until her vision blurred. People ran, screaming. Someone grabbed her by the arms and pulled her to the ground. She searched, wide-eyed but unseeing in the panic and her own darkening vision. Glass shattered. Blood pooled on the floor as she pressed her body down against the cool stones.

Fingers gripped her underarms. "Can you stand?"

Stand? She could not move. Fear froze her to the tavern floor. She dug her fingernails into the cracks between the stones and closed her eyes. The hands released her.

"The guard will be here at any moment", she reassured herself, whispering to the ground. The tavern was close enough to the castle. The guards would hear.

The sounds of battle surrounded her, and time became measured, not by minutes, but by the moments she could cling to her life. She prayed to the Goddess they would not discover her, that a bolt would not snuff her life as it had Robert's.

Someone was barking orders, his voice clear and unafraid. The authoritative commands gave her something to anchor to in the chaos.

"Get up, Brandon," the man snapped. A glint of pale blue silk shimmered in the smoke. "We're losing."

"Losing? Henry, we've lost, they're dead!"

"Do you want to die too? As a pathetic old man?"

Natalie pulled herself from the ground, using the upturned table to support her shaking body. The tavern was dark, illuminated only by flickering firelight. Through the smoke, she saw Brandon stood facing Henry. The front of his brown tunic was black with blood.

She took an uneasy step towards them. "What's happening?"

"You're alive!" Brandon's eyes widened at the sight of her. He hurried to her side, and offered a hand to help her over the makeshift barricade. "We're under attack."

"Attack? Who by?"

"Bandits," Henry spat. His eyes were wide with panic, and his dark hair stuck to his sweaty forehead. "Common thieves who should have been no match for champions."

Bandits. The word gnawed at Natalie's conscience, taunting her. Her legs grew weak and shook beneath her as she thought of Jenny, unguarded in the castle, left to the mercy of cruel men in her stead.

A bloodthirsty roar put an end to her thoughts as a man, clad in black, stormed into the tavern. The spiked club in his hand was poised to strike, and his shoulders heaved with breathless excitement.

"Get back," Henry barked as he held his blade towards the attacker.

Weaponless, Brandon took a step behind Henry, shielding Natalie with his body. She closed her eyes and tried to process what was happening.

"Stay back," Henry bellowed to the bandit. "Stay back if you value your life. Do you know who I am?"

"You're dead." The bandit laughed, and the sound of his footsteps pounding the stones sent Natalie's heart into panic. She gritted her teeth as weapons clashed, metal striking metal with bone-shattering force.

The tavern fell silent.

Summoning the courage to look, she peered around Brandon's back. The bandit lay dead at Henry's feet as he cleaned off his blade. He shook his head as though he had just swatted a pesky fly.

"It's a good thing you brought your blade to the tavern." Brandon's breath came in short, panicked bursts as he hurried over to the window and stooped to look outside. "I think most people are hiding in their houses now. It's quiet out there."

Natalie looked around the tavern as tears streamed down her cheeks. Bodies lay across the floor, draped over tables and strewn across the stairs. Some of them were clad in black like the bandit Henry had slain, but many of them wore fine champion's tunics.

"Where are the castle guards? What in the Goddess' name is going on?" Henry gasped. His breath was ragged as his frantic eyes searched the empty tavern. "It shouldn't be this easy for common bandits to take the castle."

Realization burned in Natalie's temples. "Sent away." Her voice was barely audible, choked by fear and smoke. "The guards were sent away."

The champions turned to Natalie, despair darkening their eyes.

"There are no guards?" Henry frowned.

"What kind of a fool leaves their castle unguarded?" Brandon shook his head and ran his hands across his hair.

"We need to leave." Henry panted. His breath grew hard as he peered through the door.

Natalie opened her mouth to speak, but was silenced by the broken look on Brandon's face.

The man's eyes were unfocused, his lips parted and downturned. "I just watched my best friend die. All because some noble fool doesn't know how to run a castle."

Tears formed in Natalie's eyes as her mouth snapped shut. Robert, and who knew how many other people were dead because of her. Perhaps Jenny was dead too. If she had only stayed in the castle, if she had kept the guards in the town to defend it instead of sending them away…

Her throat tightened, there was no setting this right. The air was forced from her lungs as Brandon snatched her hand in his. "What are you—?"

"We're getting out of here," Brandon growled as he pulled her towards the door. "They'll find us if we linger."

As they stepped outside, she saw the full extent of the attack. The shops and houses nearby were ransacked, their contents strewn across the cobbles. Glass glittered between the stones. Tears stung at her eyes, and her lungs hardened as she searched, unsuccessfully, for signs of survivors. The keep was barely visible from the tavern, but in the darkness, fires burned atop the defensive walls. They had taken the castle.

"They've left the gate open," Brandon whispered as he turned towards the town's entrance. "Thank the Goddess."

She was numb, speechless.

Brandon ran, dragging her along as though she was weightless. Her hand ached in his constricting grip, and the tips of her fingers turned cold and numb. They sped towards the neighboring stables, not daring to look behind. Once inside, Brandon made a small growl of relief as they found the horses had not yet been cut loose.

They scurried through, searching each stall until they found Brandon's mount; an enormous grey horse with a thick black mane.

"Don't you dare leave me behind!" Henry hissed as he rushed towards them, keeping a firm grip on the hilt of his blade.

"Hurry," Brandon whispered as he released Natalie's hand and set to work saddling his horse. "We won't make it far on foot."

She swayed and steadied herself on the wooden pole of a pitchfork. Her fingers trembled as they recovered from Brandon's grip, though she was certain he had not intended to hurt her.

Brandon's mount stood patiently, ears flat and nostrils flaring as it listened and waited for signs of danger. It nickered as Brandon ran his hand along its muzzle, and lowered its head as he pulled on a bridle.

Brandon's eyes remained downturned. "Henry, if you don't want to face the bandits alone then you need to saddle your horse."

Natalie's veins filled with ice as Henry paced back and forth, his features twisted in disgust and frustration. He stopped and his lip curled into a sneer. "Those bastards. Treacherous mongrels and nothing more."

Brandon tightened the strap around his horse's belly and inhaled slowly through his nose. "Ready your mount, Henry."

"When did you become so weak?" The younger champion spat. "I used to respect you." He turned on his heel and marched off to find his horse.

Natalie closed her eyes and released a shuddering breath.

Her throat closed as Brandon turned to her and lowered his head. He opened his mouth to speak, but thought better of it. The moonlight darkened his eyes, turning them into bottomless black pools. She felt as if they were pleading with her to tell the truth, to accept responsibility for what she had done.

A thousand questions swarmed Natalie's mind, but every one of them seemed wrong. She had sent the guards away from the castle, and now she had lost Blackmere. People had died because of her.

Hay hissed and crunched beneath her feet as she stepped into the stall. The moon shone through a small square window on the far side, casting silver light over Brandon's features, and illuminating the plumes of their breath as they took a moment to make sense of things. She flexed her fingers on her aching hand.

"Forgive me, my lady." Brandon's voice was raw and shaking, and it shattered her heart to see a man as strong as the legendary Bear so broken. He took her hand gently and ran his thumb across her tender knuckles. "Did I hurt you?"

"It's quite alright." Tears fell down her cheeks as she forced a smile. The pain was fading, but the fear and shock of the attack was too much to bear.

He let go of her hand, his eyes shining with grief. "I let them take Robert, I won't let them take you, or Henry."

"I…" she tried to speak, but the words would not come.

"Forgive me, I did not ask your name."

"Nat—" She froze as her heart bolted. He would blame her. He would hate her and leave her behind if she told him who she really was.

"Nat?"

Her throat was too dry to form anything coherent. "Nat." Her heart thrummed against her ribs, seeking an escape from its confinement.

He nodded as his eyes glistened with tears. The sharp clatter of hooves signaled Henry was ready to go.

"Are we really taking her with us?" Henry sighed as he rode towards them.

"Aye," Brandon growled, stepping back to allow Natalie to place her foot in the stirrup.

She bounced twice and hoisted herself onto the gigantic steed, patting the grey hair of his neck as she settled into the saddle.

Her heart leapt as a bloodlust roar erupted in the opposite stall. A man dressed in black charged towards them, his blade drawn. Natalie clung to the horse as he stamped beneath her. She held her breath as Brandon whirred around, blocking the bandit's strike with the handle of the pitchfork. Henry unsheathed his blade and struck the bandit from behind. The scoundrel collapsed to the ground, and lay lifeless among the hay.

Heart pounding, Natalie steadied the horse, bringing him around to Brandon's side. With a grunt, Brandon climbed up behind her, enveloping her in warmth as the curve of his stomach pressed against her back. "We need to go, now." He reached around her to take the reins and urged his horse on with his heel.

They broke into a trot as they passed beneath the town's portcullis, riding into the darkness and the unknown. Natalie clung to the saddle, her mind and body numb, leaning back against the man she had always admired; the man who would despise her if he knew who she really was.

CHAPTER SIX

Dawn crept over them, bringing with it the grim realization of the night's horrors. The sky flushed lavender and pink as they rode through the forest at the foot of the hills, Blackmere's grounds fading into the distance behind them. The cool morning air chilled the tears on Natalie's cheeks as she and Brandon rode, their hips rocking from side to side in time with the horse's strides.

Natalie sighed as she wiped the tip of her nose on her sleeve. She was cold, and worn, and no matter how hard she willed them not to be, the events of the previous night remained a reality.

"Is there a village nearby where we can leave her?" Henry muttered.

She did not have the energy even to be riled by his comment. She stared ahead, her eyes glazing over, until the world was nothing but a purple and orange blur.

"Did you have family in Blackmere?" Brandon's chest rumbled against her back as he spoke.

"No," she whispered. "Just a friend."

His breath blew against the back of her neck. "I'm sorry I didn't fight harder."

"You did all you could."

"Did I?"

They followed a sparkling brook through the woods, heading upstream. The trees were crowned with gold and red leaves, which fluttered to the ground like confetti. Birdsong, and the cheery sound of splashing water filled the air. If not for the bitter sorrow in her heart, Natalie would have been enraptured by the mystical beauty of the woods. That there was still beauty and serenity in the world when everything she knew was in tatters, was salt to her wounded heart.

A broken sigh escaped her lips. Brandon took one hand from the reins, and ran it over the back of her hand, squeezing it gently. His touch brought some reassurance, but it was only a fragile, fleeting thing.

Henry rode behind them, his stony silence peppered by occasional curses. "This is ridiculous. We can't ride around directionless and moping forever. Let's just head back to the Guild."

Brandon cleared his throat and brought their mount to a halt. He placed his hand on her shoulder as if to steady her. "I'm going to get down and walk, give the horse a rest."

Natalie held on to the front of the saddle as he climbed down. The air at her back became cold and empty as she rolled her aching shoulders.

"I'll get down too." She swung her leg around and prepared to dismount. As she slid down from the saddle, she wondered if her legs would work at all. Her fears were confirmed as she stumbled across the forest floor. She barged into Brandon's arm as he held it out to stop her.

"Easy," he soothed. The muscles in his forearms flexed beneath her palms as she steadied herself.

A blush prickled at her cheeks as she waited for the strength to return to her legs. Her veins were filled with pine needles, and her feet burned as the blood coursed to them. It took all her will to ignore Henry's scoff at her back.

"Thank you," she whispered as Brandon held her upright. She wriggled her toes, wincing at the prickling pain.

"It's alright. It's been a long night in the saddle."

His gentle smile struck her like a kick to the stomach. If he only knew who she was, what she had done, he would not smile at her that way. As though she was one of only a few good things left in that harsh world.

When the vigor was restored to her exhausted limbs, they set off again. Henry remained on his mount, whilst Natalie and Brandon walked at either side of the grey horse. She smiled as Brandon pet the weary animal and whispered words of encouragement to him.

Natalie ran her hand through the waxy warmth beneath

the horse's mane as she walked. "Does he have a name?"

"He has two. In the arena he's Thunder. The rest of the time he's Big Lad."

Despite the raw ache in her heart, a soft laugh escaped Natalie's lips. "Big Lad." She patted the horse's shoulder and smiled. "It suits him."

Henry rode up alongside them, peering down from his mount like a king at a parade. "Sorry to interrupt this romantic leisurely stroll, but we do need to decide what to do."

Brandon groaned and released a heavy sigh. "I'm thinking."

Henry rolled his eyes. "By the Goddess, we'll be here all day. Allow me to make it simple. We'll ditch the girl, and head back to the Guild. We have champions' names to add to the list of fallen, and their replacements to train. We're due at the Midsummer Melee in Westgarden in less than six months, and it'll be a damn quick contest if you and I are the only competitors."

"No." Brandon's curt reply stopped Henry in his tracks.

The Dragon whirred around, glaring at the larger man. "What do you mean?"

"We need to do something. We shouldn't have run away and left those people."

Henry's brow creased. "Which people?"

"The people of Blackmere. In the town."

"I'm not risking my life for shepherds and weavers, old man. You saw those bandits cut through us. You saw them swarm the castle. There were hundreds of them. No, I'm not doing it. Too much risk, too little reward. Let's get rid of her, go back to the Guild, and move on from this mess."

Brandon lowered his gaze. The gentle splashing of the brook and the songs of the birds who fought their own battles high in the trees were the only sounds in the forest.

Natalie held her breath as she awaited their decision and watched as Brandon stared at his chest. The bloodstain had dried, turning dark, almost black, against the brown wool of his tunic.

His dark eyelashes fluttered against his cheeks, and the steady rise and fall of his breath measured the passing silence. "I—"

The clatter of approaching hoofbeats cut him off.

The slick swish of drawn steel set Natalie's heart racing as they peered through the trees. A rider came into view, trotting towards them, holding out a hand in a gesture of peace. The rider was heavily armored and armed with two throwing axes at each hip. Her braided hair swung behind her as she approached.

"Viv?" Henry frowned, sheathing his blade.

The rider pulled on the reins and pressed the back of her hand to her nose. She stopped to catch her breath, shaking her head. She finally found the breath to speak. "What's happening?"

"Viv! You're alive!" Brandon smiled. "By the Goddess, I thought we were the only ones who got out."

She shook her head and glanced over her shoulder as though confirming she had not been followed. Satisfied, her weary dark brown eyes turned to Natalie, looking her up and down. "You stole a barmaid?"

Brandon stepped up to her side. "She escaped with us. This is Nat."

"Gnat? Like a fly? Does she bite?" The woman grimaced, before jumping down from her horse, and patting it firmly on the shoulder. "Good horse." She held out a hand towards Natalie.

For a moment Natalie forgot their dire situation. She gripped the woman's hand in both of hers. "You're Genevieve! Thorn of The Rose!"

"I know, it's a bad name."

"No, it's wonderful. You're wonderful."

"The Thorn is easier to say."

"Very well," Natalie nodded eagerly. "The Thorn."

Genevieve's face brightened a little, though her dour expression returned as she turned her eyes to the other champions.

"Have you any news?" Henry's voice was weakened with exhaustion and waning adrenaline. The whites of his eyes were tinged pink, making his bright blue irises all the more piercing.

"What in the name of the Goddess is happening?" Genevieve shook her head. "I woke up in the tavern and thought the world had ended. I've been trailing you for hours."

"Were there any survivors?" Brandon asked.

Genevieve nodded sharply. "The people are hiding. Everything is broken. I did not stay long. There are bandits, crawling everywhere like rats. And the Lady. Lady Black-mere. She is a prisoner in the castle. People are whispering about a ransom."

The world fell out from beneath Natalie's feet, her head spun. "She's alive?"

"Last I saw her," The Thorn bowed her head.

Jenny was alive, and if the bandits wanted money for her, they would keep her that way. Breathless, relieved laughter forced itself from Natalie's lips.

Brandon ran his hand over his beard and his eyes grew distant.

"The Lady of Blackmere lives?" Henry gasped as he dismounted his weary horse. "How did she look?"

"She seemed well. She did not appear hurt."

"That settles it then," Henry announced. "We need to go back to Blackmere Castle, and rescue the Lady."

"You've changed your tune," Brandon frowned. "I thought you didn't want to go back there?"

Henry gave a lazy shrug. "Not for commoners."

"If we're going back, it's to save them *all*, including the townspeople." Brandon's voice rumbled at Natalie's side. "I don't imagine those bandits will be kind to the people in the town either." He turned to Natalie, a fire blazing behind his eyes. "I would never forgive myself if I didn't try to help. Lady Blackmere may be a fool, but she doesn't deserve that fate."

"Good man." Henry clapped Brandon on the shoulder and his chest swelled with purpose. "We'll storm the castle, and save Lady Blackmere. We'll be heroes."

Natalie took a steadying breath. The weight of her deceit lay heavy on her shoulders, but if the belief they were saving Lady Blackmere's life spurred them to save Jenny and the townspeople, then her lie could continue until they were safe.

"We're all tired, and the horses need rest." Brandon mused. "We'll rest up, and come up with a plan to save her."

"We can't do it alone," Genevieve frowned. "There are many bandits."

"Did you see how many?" Brandon folded his arms across his broad chest. Natalie tried not to look at the thick muscles in his forearms, or the way his tunic strained across his biceps.

"Hundreds?" Genevieve shrugged.

Henry huffed in frustration. "Three of us, versus hundreds of bandits? Not a chance."

"Blackmere has allies," Natalie said at last, choosing her words carefully. "Maybe we could ask for aid?"

Henry snapped his fingers. "Her family are in Caer Austwick. We could send word."

"It's a hundred miles away," Natalie said. Her hope dwindled by the moment. "It'd be a week before their army could get here."

"What about local allies?" Brandon shrugged and turned to Natalie. "Do you know their names? Any of them?"

Natalie closed her eyes and ran through the books and ledgers in her mind. The thought of her chamberlain, defenseless against the bandits, haunted her, but she tried to recall their conversations. There was a settlement southeast of Blackmere, a Lord who her mother had once coerced into offering masonry workers to repair the castle's walls in exchange for a reduced sum of gold. "Stoneclough! Lord Stoneclough, I think. It's at least a day's ride though."

"I'll go," Genevieve nodded. "Tell me where. We'll find somewhere you can set up camp and then I'll ride out."

"Excellent." Henry's cold gaze fell to Natalie. Her stomach slithered beneath his gaze, and his visible disdain for her. "And what do we do with the barmaid?"

The viper in her belly leapt to her tongue. "I'm going to fight too." Heat rose as Henry's laughter shattered the calm in the forest.

"With what?" he chuckled.

"With my bare hands if I have to! Blackmere is my home." Natalie glared after the man as he shook his head and rode away, guiding his horse further upstream.

"Ignore him," Genevieve sighed. "If you want to fight, fight."

Brandon grunted in agreement. "We'll get your home back." He clicked his tongue and led Big Lad along the riverbank.

Taking a deep breath, Natalie followed.

She trailed behind the champions, barely looking up from the banks of the brook as she ran over every conceivable scenario in her head. If they could only save her people, save Jenny. She would do anything she could to help them.

Tiny silver fish darted from where her shadow darkened the water. She trudged across the uneven ground, beads of sweat trickling down her back. At last, the rhythmic clip clop of Big Lad's hooves slowed up ahead.

In the distance Genevieve called out, "This is a decent place to camp."

"You have to be joking," Henry cried.

The constant gushing roar of a waterfall grew closer. Natalie hurried to where Brandon stood with his hands on his hips, peering through the trees. In the midst of a clearing, was a cottage. The tiny home seemed abandoned and in poor repair, grey stonework covered in dark green moss.

The slates on the roof were chipped and crooked.

Genevieve pressed her face to the dark, cobwebbed windows and nodded as Henry pulled a tangled web of vines away from the door.

"Cozy, isn't it?" Brandon smirked as he led Big Lad to a nearby pool at the base of the waterfall.

Natalie's eyes followed him as he crouched beside the drinking horse and cupped water in his hands, scooping it up to his own lips. Her eyes darted down to his thighs, thick and muscular, straining the thin linen of his breeches. He released a satisfied gasp, before splashing the water over his face and smoothing down the bristles of his beard, leaving the bare skin at his throat glistening.

Her heart quickened as he looked over to her and a smile softened his features. "Well, my lady, I suppose this is home, for now."

"I suppose so." Heat blazed across her chest as she lowered her gaze and hurried towards the cottage.

CHAPTER SEVEN

THE COTTAGE door creaked open on decrepit hinges. Natalie pressed her sleeve to her nose as she took a tentative step inside. Dust danced on beams of light.

"Disgusting," Henry spat, hovering in the doorway.

Natalie's footsteps thumped on the bare floorboards. On one wall, two murky windows permitted a meagre offering of fragile light. The sooty hearth gaped on the opposite wall, with half-charred blocks of wood still piled among the cold ashes. There was a rickety wooden table, a large stone trough and wooden bucket for washing, and a black iron stove. A dusty wooden staircase led to a loft, which covered half the cottage. The boards of the narrow staircase creaked beneath Natalie's feet as she climbed halfway up. The top floor was bare, but for a wooden bed frame, topped with a straw mattress, and a dusty wooden chest.

"Who do you suppose this place belongs to?" Brandon

frowned as he stooped below the low beams on the bottom floor. He wiped his hand across the window and peered outside. Absent-mindedly, he wiped his hand on his trousers, and left a dark grey stain.

"Whoever it is, they're probably long dead," Henry sighed. He drew an arc across the grimy floor with the tip of his boot. "And no doubt they'll come back to life in the night to cut our throats. Come. We'd be better camping out in the woods."

"Out in the open?" Genevieve raised her eyebrow at the young champion and shook her head. "Too cold for you, Dragon boy. You should stay here."

"Once we get a fire going it'll be fine," Natalie assured them as she stepped down onto the floor. She looked around for a broom to sweep the soot in the fireplace, and found one leaning by the stove. A flurry of woodlice scurried from its sparse bristles as she lifted it.

"Well thank the Goddess for commoners," Henry smirked. "You people are rather good at making the most of a bad situation."

Natalie fixed him with an iron stare, but bit back her retort. The thought of spending days cooped up in the tiny cottage with the unbearable man turned her heart sour.

"So, anyway, this Lady Blackmere," Henry muttered as his eyes trailed across the cobwebbed ceiling. "What does she look like?" He turned to Genevieve. "Was she beautiful?"

"I didn't see her face."

"Pity. What about the rest of her?"

Genevieve scowled.

Henry smiled slowly, and rasped his fingers against the light dusting of peppery stubble on his cheek. "Well, I pray to the Goddess that she's a stunner, because I can't stay here. I'll ride with you to find this Lord Stoneclough. The Bear and barmaid can stay here. We'll need to take Brandon's horse as a backup."

Natalie's heart seized at his suggestion. The ride to Stoneclough and back would take them days; days she and Brandon would be left alone. Heat fanned across her cheeks at the very suggestion.

"We have to wait here?" She turned to Brandon, who stared wide-eyed, a look of sheer panic on his face. "Alone?"

Henry's lips curled into a smirk. "Problem?"

Brandon cleared his throat and took a step forward. "We'll be fine. I'll train her to fight while you're gone. Just do what you have to do."

The young champion snickered as he stepped out of the cottage and into the fresh morning air. "Poor old Brandon. How the mighty fall."

Natalie's blood boiled as she went to storm after him. A voice in the back of her mind warned her not to rise to his taunts, but the wildfire flashing through her veins refused to stand for it.

"My lady." Brandon stepped away from the window

and reached out his arm, forming a barrier between her and the doorway.

Without taking her eyes from the door, Natalie stood, seething. She blinked rapidly as Brandon stepped towards her and cupped her shoulders, his touch firm and reassuring. "My lady. He isn't worth it."

"I'm not afraid of him."

Brandon lowered his head and whispered, "Nor should you be. But he's riding to meet Lady Blackmere's ally, and might be the only hope we have against those bandits. He's our best fighter."

Her breath shuddered out of her lungs as the fire in her gut diminished. He was right. Henry was an ass, but they needed him.

"Wait until after Blackmere is saved," Brandon smiled. The lines at the corners of his eyes deepened. "Then you can tell him exactly what you think of him. I might join you."

Natalie returned his grin. She imagined Henry's shock when he discovered she, not Jenny, was the true Lady of Blackmere.

Her enthusiasm dwindled as she realized there would come a time when she would have to reveal her true self to Brandon, and admit her part in Robert's death.

Betrayal weighed heavy in her heart, but to tell him now could jeopardize everything. For her people, for Jenny, she would lie to her hero.

"Is something the matter?" he asked. He stooped slightly, tilting his head to better look into her eyes.

"No. Nothing." She forced the smile back onto her lips. "You're right. Let him make his snide remarks if it means he will save my people."

"You're a stronger person than most."

Her skin tingled after he released her, and the sensation of his touch lingered as they walked outside together.

"You really ought to rest the horses," Brandon called as his boots crunched on the forest floor.

Genevieve was already mounted on her horse, and holding onto Big Lad's reins with her left hand. She scowled, resting her chin on her fist as she waited for Henry to stop preening himself in the reflection of the nearby pool. He side-eyed a patch of dried blood on his sleeve and turned to Brandon.

"Is this disgusting, or does it make me look battle worn?"

Natalie grimaced, and fought to hold her tongue.

"Easy," Brandon whispered out of the corner of his mouth, sensing her need to retort. He lifted his head and addressed Henry. "You look fine. I'm sure Lord Stoneclough will be very impressed."

A wide grin spread across Henry's face as he skipped over to his horse. "Tis not Stoneclough I seek to impress." He bounced into the saddle and sat tall and proud. "Once

I rally Lady Blackmere's allies and liberate her castle, the beautiful lady will owe me a great boon. This will be the making of me."

Natalie frowned at the suggestion. If he expected more gold, he would be waiting a long time. There was little she could offer beyond gratitude.

Henry kicked his horse into a trot and rode off between the trees. The atmosphere around the cottage grew lighter without him nearby.

Genevieve took a deep breath, and grimaced.

"Good luck," Brandon chuckled.

"And to you, Bear." She bowed her head towards Natalie. "Barmaid." She clicked her tongue twice, urging her horse to walk on.

Every step the champions' horses took tightened a knot in Natalie's stomach. She grew all too aware of her breathing. Her throat grew thick and she was overcome with the need to swallow. They were alone.

Beside her, the large man shuffled his weight between his feet and cleared his throat. "I'm sure all will be well."

"Oh... yes...I'm sure of it." Natalie cringed at the uncertainty in her voice. "They'll be back in no time."

"They should've rested the horses though. Poor things."

Natalie made a small sound of agreement, her chest tight and breath as unsteady as though she had just climbed a mountain.

Brandon raised his hand to smooth his tousled hair. "I'm…" He looked around himself, peered around the side of the cottage and cleared his throat again. "I'm just going to… keep myself busy with something."

"Very good," Natalie smiled, desperate to get away. The warmth spreading across her chest reached her throat. "I'll go and check the… cottage."

She hitched up her skirts and turned towards the cottage door, fleeing into the gloomy dark. Once inside she buried her head in her hands and groaned.

"Ridiculous," she whispered to herself. "Ridiculous. You've been alone with men before. You've lived with a man before. This is nothing to panic over. He's just a man."

She wiped her forehead on the crook of her elbow and winced at the stench of smoke, stale alcohol, and horse. The sleeve of her dress was stained brown with blood; Robert's blood. Her heart hardened at the sight of it.

She turned back to the door to see if Brandon lingered, but the clearing surrounding the cottage was empty. With a deep sigh, she set to work clearing the fireplace. If nothing else, she could ensure they would be warm.

Over the years, she had become adept at lighting her own fires. Fewer people working in the castle meant fewer conversations and questions. Her chamberlain took care of what he could, but she could not bear to watch him bend his weary legs to light the fireplaces.

As she worked, she thought of Jenny, and prayed she would be safe. Jenny was much stronger than she – accustomed to handling rough drunks in the tavern, and defending her staff as well as herself – but that wasn't the same as facing down bandits who were baying for blood. The sooner they could rally a force to take back Blackmere, the better.

By the time Natalie finished cleaning, her hands and arms were black with soot. The air tickled her nose and stung the back of her throat, but the hearth was clean and ready for a fire. They just needed wood. She sneezed into her elbow, and wiped her face on the apron, grimacing as the dusty air assaulted her sinuses. Vision blurred, she stood, and called out. "Brandon?"

The only sound was that of the birds, and the rush of the water outside. She squinted through the grimy windows, but could not see the Bear.

"Where are you?" she whispered. An unease at being left alone in the middle of the woods crept across her mind, but she shook it off. He was close by, she was certain.

Wiping her hands on her skirts, she wandered outside into the clean, fresh air and stretched her aching back. Once she felt pliable and rested, she searched the forest floor, picking up dry sticks and branches to burn. She filled the pockets of the apron with pine needles for kindling. With her arms full, she returned to the cottage, and piled the wood in the fireplace. After a few more trips she had enough wood to keep them warm for a few hours, and barely enough energy to stand. She reminded herself to ask Brandon to bring more.

She found a tinderbox on the mantle, and with a few

practiced strikes of flint and steel, produced a shower of sparks, which got the pine needles smoldering. In no time, a bright blaze crackled in the hearth, filling the room with the sweet aroma of pine smoke. If nothing else, at least the years of solitude in Blackmere had taught her to build her own fires.

The heat made her weary, and her eyes felt raw after a long, sleepless night. She longed to stretch out before the fire and sleep, but the need to bathe was far more urgent. Bloodied and filthy, reeking of soot and smoke, the sound of rushing water called to her.

Natalie checked outside one more time, ensuring she would not be seen. The forest was still, but for the flitting of birds and squirrels. Satisfied by her privacy, and desperate to feel clean, she tugged open the laces of the woolen dress, and headed towards the waterfall.

CHAPTER EIGHT

Natalie was accustomed to cold water.

Blackmere castle was named for the vast lake at the heart of the surrounding land, and she often swam in the solitude of its dark waters. The landscape was both bleak and beautiful, surrounded by rolling green hills, and ancient forests. As she stared into the clear waters of the pool by the cottage, her heart ached.

The taupe wool overdress hung over an oak tree branch, softly swaying in a gentle breeze. She had managed to scrub out the worst of the stains, though she expected it would take a long time for the dress to dry out.

She pulled the white smock over her head, dropped it onto the rocks beside the pool, and taking a deep breath, plunged naked into the water. The cold turned the air in her lungs solid. She clenched every muscle she could, gritting her teeth until she grew accustomed to the frigid temperature. When she was able to, she forced her breaths, until her lungs were assured that there was oxygen to breathe. The initial shock waned, and she treaded water in the pool, skimming her hands across the surface.

In the stillness, her guilt clawed at her. The image of Ironclaw, life slipping from his eyes in an instant, haunted her. She closed her eyes and prayed to the Goddess that Jenny would be kept safe. It might take days for Genevieve and Henry to come back with word from the Lord of Stone-clough, days of worry and guilt.

She had no choice but to hold on to hope. After all, she had three champions, three of the strongest champions, helping her. With the aid of her allies, all would be well. She did not know Lord Stoneclough well, but she was certain no nobleman would want bandits as his neighbors.

She dipped her head below the surface and rinsed the blood and soot from her skin and hair. Compared to the waters of Blackmere, the little pool was almost comfortable. She swam around, keeping a close eye on the trees.

The forest was still, and there was no sign of human life. Satisfied she was alone, she pulled the soiled white smock into the water with her, and rubbed the stained parts against the rocks. Grime billowed from the fibers, clouding the water around her.

A song ran through her mind, one which she would often hear drifting up to the keep from the tavern. Ringing out the water from the smock and leaving it on the rocks to dry, she kept her voice barely louder than a whisper as she sang;

"Brandon the Bear, strong and brave and fair.

Taller than two men and twice as strong.

Blessed is his blade, beware you wicked knaves,

He's bigger than two men and twice as lo—"

"My lady?"

Natalie's heart leapt into her throat at the sound of Brandon's voice. She wrapped her arms around her chest, and searched the trees.

The sound of his heavy footsteps reached her before she spotted him. He strode towards the cottage, his arms laden with the spoils of his hunt; rabbits, pigeons, and small green wild onions. The champion paused before he reached the door, transferred his burden to one arm, tugged at the tight fabric of his tunic with his free hand and smoothed back his hair.

A drum pounded in Natalie's throat. She ducked down until her eyes and nose were all that remained out of the water and waited for him to go. Every agonizing second was measured by the frantic rhythm of her heart.

After an eternity, he stooped beneath the doorway and disappeared inside the cottage. Natalie took a deep breath, steeled her nerve, and hoisted herself out of the pool. She snatched the sodden smock and hurried for the cover of the trees. Her limbs were a lead weight as she clambered across the forest floor.

"My lady?" Brandon's call sounded from within the

cottage. His voice was strained with urgency, and his heavy footsteps pounded against the floorboards.

She had little time to act. Darting behind a thick old tree, she wrestled with the wet fabric, tugging the clinging undergarment over her soaking skin. She pulled the smock over her hips as he appeared in the doorway.

"Nat?" Brandon's voice was rough with desperation and fear.

"Here," she gasped, frantically lowering the skirt. She stepped out from behind the tree, raking her fingers through her soaking hair. "I'm here."

"Where did… oh. Forgive me." His eyes dropped to his feet. "I worried something had happened to you."

A treacherous blush crept across her jaw as she crossed her arms over her chest. "I thought you would be gone longer."

"I hurried back. I thought you might be hungry. I can go back out if you'd like me to?"

"No, it's quite alright. Stay, please."

The worry faded from his face, and for a moment, his eyes lifted. They followed the shape of her figure, trailing over the swooping curves of her generous hips. His gaze left searing heat where it lingered on her body. For a moment, he seemed bewitched by her figure, covered only by the thin, translucent layer of her smock. An ache rolled through her, and her head grew light.

Breaking the spell, Brandon cleared his throat and moistened his lip with the tip of his tongue. "I'll be inside." His voice was thick and dark, like storm clouds swelling above mountains, as he regained his composure. "I'll get the stove going and try to warm up the cottage a bit more."

She opened her mouth to speak, but all that escaped her lips was a strained, shuddering breath. Fire blazed across her cheeks as she followed him.

CHAPTER NINE

THE COTTAGE flooded with a delicious aroma as Brandon prepared the meal, roasting the meat and onions in the iron stove. He hurried back and forth, his brow etched with concern and frustration.

"I can help," Natalie insisted. "Just tell me what to do."

"Stay by the fire, my lady," he muttered as he searched through the cottage for plates and utensils. "You'll catch your death."

"I'm fine. I swim in colder waters than those back home."

"Perhaps, but I'm sure back home you have dry clothes to change into afterwards."

She sighed and threw the last of the branches into the fire. Despite her protests she welcomed the heat. Closing her eyes, she pulled her knees up to her chest and felt her body grow lighter.

"Here," Brandon said softly beside her, snapping her back to earth. He held out a steaming plate of food.

"Already?" she muttered. "That was fast."

He chuckled. "You were asleep for some time, my lady."

She rubbed the sleep from her eyes and turned to face him. A wave of heat washed over her as she realized he was bare from the hips up. She tried not to focus on the dark patch of hair on his broad chest, or his thick biceps as he held the plate towards her. It took all her strength to drag her eyes over her shoulder towards the windows. The sky had grown dark, and silver raindrops raced down the glass.

"Oh no," she whispered. "It's raining."

"I brought your dress inside," he assured her. He gestured beside her, towards the staircase where her dress hung over the bannister. His clothing hung beside it. "You'll have to forgive me, I had to wash my tunic too. I couldn't bear to be covered in—"

"That's quite alright." In fact, Natalie did not mind one bit. With the initial shock subsided, she turned back to face the fire, chancing another glance at him. The nickname "Bear" was well-deserved. His broad chest and stomach were covered in a layer of dark hair.

Her fingers flexed with the desire to run her hands across his chest, to explore every curve, every swell and valley. His lips quirked as he nudged the plate towards her.

"Here. You must be starving by now."

With a grateful smile she took the plate. He groaned as he lowered himself to sit on the ground beside her. The firelight danced across him.

Warmth spread throughout her body as they chewed in silence. In the midst of panic and exhaustion, Natalie had not realized how hungry she was until she began devouring the hearty meal. "Thank you."

Brandon forced a swallow and beamed. "My pleasure."

"You cook well."

"Aye, sadly a little too well." He patted the soft, hairy mound of his stomach and chuckled. "Robert always—"

Natalie's stomach dropped at the sound of the man's name.

Brandon pressed his lips together, and his jaw twitched. "Forgive me."

Her heart ached for him. She placed her plate on the floor beside her, and briefly touched her hand to his knee. "You cared for him."

"Aye. We lived together for ten years. He became family, you know? We spend most of our lives at the Guild." A gentle laugh shook his shoulders. "He was such a cock-sure little ass when we first met. He made it his one goal in life to unseat me from the top of the victors' board. It took a few years, but he managed it."

"But you remained friends?"

"Aye, he was an ass, but he was a good man—funny, good company. He was… he was like a brother. I loved the little sod."

The way Brandon's eyes gleamed like crystal as he spoke of Robert twisted a knot inside Natalie's gut. Her throat tightened as she held back tears. She longed to reach out to him, to offer him comfort. It occurred to her she had known Brandon for most of her adult life, and yet she had only just met him.

"I'm so sorry for what happened." Natalie's voice wavered as she spoke.

Brandon rested his forearms on his knees and his expression hardened. "I'm angry… heartbroken. How can Lady Blackmere be in charge of so many lives, yet care so little for them?"

His words struck her like an avalanche. "I… she cares."

"Does she?" He turned to her, his dark eyes searching her face for answers. "I keep running over it in my mind. Was it just carelessness that made her send the guards away? Was it malicious?"

Natalie longed for the ground to swallow her. Her vision blurred as tears glazed her eyes. "The guards were sent out to deal with the bandits on the road. We couldn't have known they would storm the town and take the castle."

"Hmm." Brandon took a deep breath and tightened his jaw. He shrugged a shoulder and pushed his food around his plate.

"I expect that doesn't make your loss any easier to bear." She took a deep breath. He had every right to be angry. She pressed her hand to his arm, and let it linger, hoping he took solace from the gesture. "I only knew Robert for a little while, but I imagine if he saw us now, he would have laughed himself to tears."

Brandon gave a sharp chuckle. "Aye. He would've had the time of his life, laughing, teasing me."

"That's exactly what he was doing, when…" Her throat clenched, and she found herself unable to speak of his end. "Back in the tavern, when you stood to investigate the smell of the smoke, he said you were just trying to impress me."

"What an ass."

The fire crackled, and sap on the branches popped. The air in the cottage grew lighter as they lifted the darkness with laughter.

"You said you have no family in Blackmere," Brandon asked. "Where are they?"

"Caer Austwick," Natalie smiled.

"The castle?"

Her heart jolted at his quizzical expression. "Oh, aye. Yes. My mother is a kitchen maid, and my father's a guard."

He cocked an eyebrow and smirked. "I imagine that caused something of a scandal."

Natalie laughed and bit into a piece of rabbit meat. Her guard was slipping, and if she was not careful, her ruse would unravel and he would know who she really was. He would despise her.

"I wonder if news of what happened at Blackmere will reach that far." He cleared his throat and pushed his food around his plate. "I expect they'd be afraid for your life, if it did."

"I doubt my mother knows," Natalie shrugged. "If she did, the bandits would already be withering under her ire."

Brandon laughed. "She has a temper?"

"No, not a temper. She's always fully in control, cold, calm, like an icicle ready to drop down and impale someone below."

Brandon raised his eyebrows and puffed out a breath. "She sounds…"

"Terrifying?"

"Aye."

"She is, somewhat," Natalie chuckled. "And the complete opposite of my father. I think I take after him. He's the soft one."

"You're not soft," Brandon frowned. "Far from it."

The corners of Natalie's lips tugged upwards into a smile as she turned her attention to the food in front of her. "And what of you? Where do you come from?"

He sat back a little, scratching at his eyebrow. "For the past twenty odd years, all over. But Marshdown originally, though it's been many years since I was back there."

"Marshdown?" She smiled. It was far from Blackmere, a wet and craggy land, where the wind howled through the rocks, and the people were burly enough to withstand the year-round chill. It suited him well. It was a place known for its brewing—and its consumption of said brews. "Is that where your family lives?"

"Aye. My father's a butcher, and my mother works out in the peat bogs." His gaze fell to the floorboards. "Or rather, she did, before her back became too sore. I send her money for the healer."

Natalie smiled at his kindness. The flames danced and flickered up the chimney. She imagined him back in his homeland, younger and untroubled, his deep laugh rolling through his chest and his cheeks ruddy from the bite of the wind, and the spirits in his cup. Her pulse quickened as she noticed him in her periphery. He was watching her.

There was something about him, the quiet intensity, the sheer size and strength he exuded, which set her heart alight.

He cleared his throat and turned his gaze to the glowing red embers in the hearth. "You said you have no family in Blackmere. So, no spouse? Children?"

Natalie's breath snagged. She had anticipated the question was coming, but the answer was barbed and caught between her ribs. The rain and wind pelted against the glass behind them, as the silent, agonizing seconds passed by. A small sound of discomfort escaped her lips. "I... I did have a husband, ten… no, twelve years ago. He was a childhood friend. We'd only been married a month before sickness took him. We had no children."

"Oh, by the Goddess, forgive me for being so brash. I'm so sorry for your loss."

"It was years ago. And there's nothing to forgive. He was my friend for many years before we agreed to marriage. When he died, I grieved for him more as a friend."

"My lady—"

She turned to meet his gaze. "Why do you call me that?"

He shifted his weight, and turned towards the fire so that she could not see his face fully. His frown deepened before he spoke. "It shouldn't matter if a woman is born with titles or no. She deserves respect just the same, be she queen or commoner."

Silently, she cursed him. She added "silver tongued" to his growing list of attributes and picked up her plate. "You address every woman as a lady?" She took a bite of her meal and chewed as she watched him.

"Aye. Well, except Genevieve, but only because she made it quite clear that if I ever did, she'd knock me onto my arse."

With her mouth full, Natalie's laugh forced its way through her nose instead. She snorted, and reddened as she buried her face in her hands. Brandon's deep laughter solidified her shame.

"I apologize," she cried, her voice muffled against her hands. "That keeps happening."

His hands grazed around hers as he coaxed them away from her face. They were rough, calloused, the hands of a fighter, yet his touch was so gentle. A voice in the back of her mind questioned how they would feel against the tender, soft skin of her thighs.

She was grateful for the scarlet glow of the fading embers which cast red light across their faces and concealed her embarrassment.

"Don't apologize," he smiled, running his thumb across her knuckles and sending a shiver across her flesh. "It lifts my spirit no end to see you smile. Does it bother you?"

"To have you call me your lady?"

"Aye? I'll stop if it does."

"It doesn't," she smiled. "But you may call me Nat, if you wish to."

Brandon smiled and released her hand, whispering "Nat," as though trying it out on his tongue. He cleared his throat and returned to his meal, staring into the dwindling fire.

As they finished their food, Natalie's eyes grew weary and raw. The patter of the rain on the roof slates was comforting, and she longed to lay down.

"The fire's dying. Where did you put the spare wood?" Brandon mused as he chewed.

"I used all the wood I brought in. Didn't you get any?"

The charred remains of the wood in the fireplace crackled, scarlet and black, and a blast of cool air howled down the chimney.

Brandon wiped the corner of his lips with his thumb and sighed.

Natalie stared into the darkening hearth. "Oh."

CHAPTER TEN

"My lady, forgive me. I should've planned better."

Natalie brought her knees up to her chest and shivered beside the dark hearth, rubbing warmth into her toes "There is nothing to forgive. It was I who fell asleep without telling you we needed more wood."

The wind whistled through the roof slates, and battered the sides of the cottage. The wooden beams running across the ceiling groaned beneath the barrage.

Natalie raised her eyes to the ceiling. "At least Henry is probably having a terrible time."

Brandon chuckled. "Aye. Poor Viv. She'll be at her wits' end by now."

"I thought she and Henry were friends," Natalie frowned. "She was with him upstairs at the tavern."

Brandon shrugged. The cold did not seem to bother him as it did her. He reclined against the table leg, bathed in the dappled blue moonlight breaking through the clouds. Natalie's eyes skimmed over his body, following the dark line of hair which ran from the top of his curved stomach, and disappeared beneath the waistband of his breeches. She lowered her gaze and focused on rubbing her hands together.

"Viv's amicable with everyone, but her face often gives away what her lips work hard to withhold," he grinned. "Both in the arena, and the tavern."

"She was watching us over the balcony all night."

"Watching us? No. She was looking for someone. There was another barmaid in the tavern earlier in the day she seemed pretty keen on. She was dressed similarly to you."

The gnawing guilt in the pit of her stomach rose as she thought of what could have been between Jenny and Genevieve. The list of her wrongdoings was ever growing.

Brandon yawned in the darkness. "Perhaps after we stop those bandits, she'll find her again."

Or perhaps, Natalie thought, when Genevieve realizes that the Lady of Blackmere is actually a tavern landlady, they would know Natalie as a liar. A liar with blood on her hands.

"I hope so," Natalie said, forcing the cheer into her voice.

She wrapped her arms around her chest and lowered

her head. Total darkness crept into the cottage as the storm swelled above them, and the moon was lost entirely behind the clouds.

"Did you ever look in the chest upstairs?" Brandon's voice rumbled through the darkness.

She had quite forgotten the chest. "No."

"I'll look. It could have blankets." He groaned as he stood, and the sounds of him running his hands around the edge of the table, and stumbling across the cottage floor filled the air. There was a crash, and a hissed curse, before the slow, methodical pounding of his feet on the stairs. The floorboards on the top floor creaked beneath him as he explored the darkness.

"It's a little warmer up here," he called down. "Can you find the tinderbox? I think there's a candle."

Natalie rubbed some warmth into her feet and stood. She ran her stiff fingers along the mantel, until they closed around the small, round box. Clutching it to her chest, she edged around the table towards the stairs. Her fingers found the cold, soggy woolen garments hanging over the bannister, and she grimaced at their touch. As she climbed, she breathed warmer air.

"Here," he whispered. "Take my hand."

She reached out, fearful of blundering into a wall or of plummeting down the edge. After flailing in the dark, she found his hand, and he laced his fingers with hers as he led her across the room.

"The candle's here." He guided her hand until she found the smooth wax cylinder, no more than two inches long. Her hands trembled as she struck sparks, once, twice, three times, before muttering a curse and flexing her fingers. On the fourth try the wick took light.

The room brightened, and the two of them found themselves bathed in the amber glow of a small candle stub by the bedside. Shimmering clouds of breath burst from their lips, as they chuckled.

"That's a bit better," Brandon smiled.

Natalie nodded and placed her hand over her nose in an effort to keep it warm. "What's in the chest then?"

"Let's hope something to keep us warm." He grunted as he tried to open the lid. "Of course, it's locked."

"Perhaps there's a key here somewhere?" Natalie raised the candle stub, pinching the base of it between her fingertips. Shadows elongated and danced around the room as she searched. The bed was rickety, and the mattress old and dusty, and she did not relish the thought of spending the night on it. Holding on to the hope that the chest contained cleaner blankets, she crouched and peered below the bed. "Where would you keep a key if—"

An ear-splitting cracking sound cut her off, the sound of wood splintering, clattering metal, and leather tearing. Natalie darted upright and her eyes widened. Brandon stood with the trunk's lid in his hands, and a broad grin across his face. The hinges flapped back and forth as he shrugged his shoulders.

"I don't need a key," he smirked.

"Well now you're clearly just trying to impress me."

"Did it work?"

"Absolutely."

The boldness in Natalie's voice drew another smile from the champion. He placed the lid on the floor and sighed. "There's a decent axe for chopping wood. Not that it'll do us much good tonight. No blankets though."

Natalie's spirits dropped as she sidled around the bed to see what else the chest contained. Brandon crouched before it, and her eyes lingered on his muscular, broad back. An urge to trail her hands across the curves of his shoulders overwhelmed her. She longed to rake her nails across his skin, to hear that deep, growling voice reduced to moans.

She stopped and took a deep breath. "What is it?"

"Were you serious about wanting to fight?"

Her determination bristled. All her life, she craved the life of a champion. The stories of their victories, the adrenaline, the camaraderie, were all she clung to as a child, beating her fellows with sticks. She memorized their songs, bellowed them at the top of her lungs, even when many of the words went over her head.

As an adult, dreams of joining their ranks were sometimes all she clung to.

But the thought of battle, real battle, was terrifying. It was confusion, fear, undignified deaths. She had seen enough of it already, but she could not stand idly by.

She peered over Brandon's shoulder and saw steel gleaming in the chest. The sight quickened her blood, and tied knots in her throat. Brandon lifted a long knife from the chest, and held it upright.

"These are good blades. Four of them." He smiled as the candlelight reflected off the metal and sent amber beams dancing across his face. "Good size for you too. If you're serious about it, and you want to stand up to the people who took your home, then I'll teach you what I can."

She nodded, unable to summon words as he passed the dirk back to her. She took hold of the leather-wrapped grip and held the dagger to the light. The blade was as long as her forearm. Vicious sharp steel gleamed in the candlelight, as though newly forged.

As her eyes traced the length of the blade, she became aware he was watching her, his eyes as sharp as any steel. She lowered the knife and looked back into his gaze. "I would like that."

"Hmm?" He blinked rapidly.

"For you to teach me."

"Oh. Yes, my lady. As you wish."

"Nat. Please."

Pressing her lips together to suppress a smile, she placed the blade gently in the chest. "Just Nat."

If she achieved nothing else in her life, having Brandon

the Bear teach her to wield a blade would be all she had ever dreamed.

Cold wind whipped through the cottage, sending shivers across her flesh. Her gaze fell to the bare bed. The realization there was only one somewhat comfortable place to sleep dawned on her. The looming awkward conversation slithered in her gut. She very much doubted Brandon would take the bed, leaving her to sleep elsewhere, but she did not feel comfortable forcing him to sleep on the floor.

Brandon stood and ran his hands across his stomach as he grimaced at the bed. "It's no good."

"What is?"

"The bed." His eyes creased as he winced at the state of it. "It's not exactly clean or comfortable looking."

"I'm sure you've slept on worse," Natalie smirked. A blush rose to her cheeks as she realized the implications behind her words; the beds he must have shared, and the people he shared them with. "On the road, I mean."

"Aye, but I bet you haven't. It's no good for a lady."

Her heart warmed at his concern, but her skin prickled with the cold. "I'm sure it'll be fine." She wrapped her arms tight around her body and tightened her jaw to disguise her chattering teeth. "There is of course, the rather awkward matter of there only being one bed."

"Aye." A deep line of sympathy appeared between Brandon's eyebrows. "You look uncomfortable."

"I can't stand this cold."

He took a deep breath and bowed his head. "Then I must make the decision for us, or we'll be dancing around all night and you'll freeze to death."

Her pulse raced as he climbed onto the bed. She was bound to the spot, as he patted the mattress beside him. The rushing sound of her heartbeat pounded in her ears and her mouth turned dry and useless.

"My lady," he whispered. "You have my word that there will be no impropriety. We will be warmer if we lay together."

"Together?" The freckled skin of her arms rose into goosebumps as the cold crept through her flesh. She could not fight it any longer.

The rise and fall of his chest became fast and shallow, and above the dark shadow of his beard, his cheeks shone pink. "I swear to you, my lady, nothing untoward will happen. It's just to stay warm."

She nodded slowly, summoning all her courage. Hitching her smock at her thighs, she lifted one knee onto the bed, then the other, and shuffled beside him.

The air between them pulsed, and an inferno tore through her veins. It fanned across her face, drew sweat from her palms. She could barely breathe as she snuffed the candle and lay back, her mind a tangled maelstrom of need and fears.

The bed frame groaned as he rolled onto his side, pressing his back against her arm. "This should be warmer than sleeping alone," he said softly.

She swallowed and pushed out a shuddering breath.

The mattress's musty odor filled her nostrils, as she lay staring at the darkness above. The rain slowed to soft spatters, rattling on the slates, and Brandon's breathing grew deep and languid.

Natalie closed her eyes and begged the Goddess for sleep. She shivered as her heart cantered against her sternum. With the soft skin of his back against her arm, the hardness of his muscles beneath, a desire in the pit of her stomach tormented her. The ache intensified at the top of her thighs as she closed her eyes and tried not to think of him.

The night dragged, the darkness and silence were endless. A thousand thoughts clamored for her attention; fear for Jenny and the people of Blackmere, horror at the memory of death. She worried they might not succeed, worried what would happen if Brandon discovered she was responsible for what happened. Either they would fail, and more people would die, or they would win and her identity would be known. Her betrayal. Her heart skipped at the thought that Brandon would hate her. They might all despise her.

Drawing a deep breath, she tried to ignore her thoughts. The chill spread into her bones, and trickled down her cheeks, riding the tears of her despair. She rubbed her frozen, aching toes together.

"My lady?"

"Forgive me, I didn't mean to wake you," she whispered. The moisture from her breath was cold on her lips as she spoke. "My feet are cold."

"You're still cold?"

"I'm freezing."

"Do you want to sleep closer?"

"Please."

He grunted and shifted beside her, sending bolts of lightning through her heart. The scent of his body flooded her senses; salt and warm earthy musk. She clung to the mattress as it slumped and undulated beneath his weight. In the darkness she felt the flutter of his breath against her cheek. She barely had time to think as he slid his arm beneath her shoulders and rolled her onto her side, pinning her against him.

The ache spread through her again, more intense than ever, pulsing and pleading as she lay with her cheek against his chest. The soft curve of his stomach pressed against her, his body a furnace burning through the thin linen of her smock. He rubbed her back with his broad, strong palms and a chuckle rumbled in his chest.

"By the Goddess, you're made of ice." His throat twitched as he rolled his hips away from her and a breath billowed her hair. "Try to get some sleep," he whispered. "Tomorrow will be better. We'll find dry wood, and build the biggest fire Aldland has ever seen. I'll keep you warm."

She smiled against his chest, already feeling much

warmer and secure. "That would be grand."

In truth, she would be quite content to spend every night in his arms instead.

CHAPTER ELEVEN

SHRILL, RELENTLESS birdsong roused Natalie from her dreams. She groaned, and rolled over, burying her face in the fusty mattress. She lay with her eyes closed, listening to the birds. At any moment her chamberlain would burst in and tell her she was late for an audience with some farmer with a dispute over his farm's borders.

Awareness crept upon her, and her eyelids fluttered open. She was surrounded by crude stone walls, strung with thick, grey dusty cobwebs, lying on a rough straw mattress.

She was not in Blackmere Castle.

Eyes wide, she bolted upright. "Oh, sweet merciful Goddess!"

The events of the previous two days clattered around her. She rubbed her palm across her face and tried to put them all in order. Pressing her hand to the mattress she found the bed beside her was cool and empty. She was alone.

"Brandon?"

She strained her ears, listening for his voice, or the thump of his boots, but the only sound in the cottage was her own hurried breath, rasping from her tightened chest. Her eyes widened as she realized her smock had bunched around her thighs. Tugging down the pale linen, she climbed from the bed and edged towards the stairs on tender, tingling feet.

"Brandon?"

Part of her wondered if it had all been a dream, a way of coping, conjured by her desperate, panicking mind. But she was in the cottage, that much was real. The rickety bed where he had cradled her to sleep lay empty and rumpled behind her.

A bold, meaty scent wafted from the stove, whetting her appetite. She followed the aroma, and edged her way down the stairs, digging her fingertips into the wood of the bannister rail as she looked around the cottage.

Where the rickety table once stood, there was now an empty space. Damp branches sat in a pile beside the fireplace, left to dry out in the shelter of the cottage. As she reached the bottom of the stairs, she realized her woolen dress, and Brandon's tunic were gone from the bannister rail. Instinctively, she folded her arms across her chest.

Mercifully, her boots were waiting for her by the door. She slipped her feet inside the butter soft leather; a little too fine to pass as the shoes of a barmaid, and stepped outside into the bright morning.

The forest was dazzling. Dappled white light steamed through the golden leaves, making shades of green dance across the forest floor. The little pool was full to bursting after the night's heavy rain.

She filled her lungs with the cool and clear air. The ground underfoot was still a little damp as she peered around the side of the cottage. There she found their clothes, bathed in sunlight as they swung from a branch. The kitchen table stood against the wall of the cottage.

"Ah!"

The sharp gasp spun her around and her eyes searched through the trees. "Hello?"

Birdsong came back to her, undaunted by the strange sound.

"Mmh."

Natalie frowned and strained her ears. The sounds were most definitely human, and by their depth and coarseness, she was certain they came from Brandon. She took a tentative step forward, listening closely.

"Ah! Ahh!"

They were sounds of pain. Her heart quickened as she sped up, tiptoeing through the trees, following the grunts and gasps. As she rounded a thick, gnarled sycamore tree, her heart skipped.

Brandon stood beside a pile of freshly chopped logs.

His biceps strained as he raised his arms above his head, lifting a large, thick log. With a deep growl, he lowered the wood to his chest, and then pressed it back up into the air.

Natalie's parched lips parted as his muscles quivered and strained under the effort. His chest and stomach flushed pink. The arch beneath his ribcage deepened, and his stomach tensed as he raised the trunk again. His deep groan sent a thrill through Natalie's body as her eyes raked across his stretched, straining torso.

Sweet merciful Goddess.

He widened his stance, and lowered his head, lowering his arms until he rested the log against the tops of his sturdy shoulders. With a deep exhale he squatted down, thighs straining beneath their burden.

Natalie sunk her teeth into her lower lip as waves of need crashed inside her, swelling and rolling between her thighs. She drew in a sharp breath and her heart stopped for a moment as he raised his eyes to look at her.

"Oh! *Ah!*" He smiled as he lifted the log from the back of his neck. "Good morning. *Ah!*" He pressed it up over his head. "Did you sleep well, my lady?"

He lowered the log and let it thud onto the forest floor, wiping his shining brow on the back of his arm.

Natalie tried to keep her eyes away from the rapid swell of his chest. "Yes. I think so."

"I'm glad." A wide smile spread across his face as he smoothed down his beard. "You're the deepest sleeper I've ever known."

She chuckled, heat rising in her chest as she tried to keep her eyes level with his. "So I've been told. I see you've been busy this morning; you should have woken me, I would've helped."

"There was no waking you. I made so much noise I'm sure half the bandits in Blackmere know exactly where we are." His expression softened. "Besides, I didn't want to disturb your dreams. I thought you might need them, if they were pleasant, after so many horrors."

Her blush deepened. "But this is the second time I've slept through whilst you've done all the work. Please wake me next time and let me help."

He swept his hand back through his hair and smiled. "It was no hardship at all, my lady. Though if you don't mind, I could use your help, stacking the wood." He gave a breathless chuckle and raised his eyebrows. "I'm not as fit as I once was, and if I carry all this back myself, I'm liable to fall asleep after."

"I don't believe that for one moment."

He chuckled and tapped the discarded log with the toe of his boot. "It's true. I was planning to nap here in the woods after my morning exercise, until you came along, that is."

"Oh stop," she chuckled.

He flashed her a broad grin as they set to work. They loaded their arms with as much wood as they could carry and set off to walk the short distance back to the cottage. Once they reached their humble dwelling, they stacked the wood inside where it would remain dry. Panting, they stepped back outside.

"I wonder how far Viv and Henry got last night," Brandon looked off into the woods as they made their way back to fetch more wood. "As much as I enjoy the idea of Henry being wet and miserable, I do hope they found shelter."

Natalie gave him a reassuring smile, though as she loaded up her arms again, her muscles were already aching. She stood, ready to head back to the cottage, and attempted to keep her breath steady to conceal her fatigue. "You care for him, despite it all?"

"I do." Brandon's defeated smile creased his eyes. "He's a sniveling little sod, but he's the closest thing to family, you know? Sort of like an annoying nephew. champions aren't permitted to have families by blood."

The forest floor crunched beneath their boots as they carried the firewood.

"You aren't?"

He shook his head. "It's hard to have a spouse or children anyway when we're never in the same place for long. We live by the rules of the Champion's Guild, and they say relationships would be too distracting. Our job is to fight, to entertain. We're forbidden from falling in love, having children, that sort of thing. As far as children go, even if we wanted to, we can't."

Natalie thought on his words as they entered the cottage and began to stack the wood. The champions' conquests were legendary, especially those of the mighty Bear. The bards told tales of his prowess.

She watched him as he arranged the logs to his satisfaction, his brow knitted in concentration. In the daylight she could make out silvery scars across his skin.

"There," he sat back on his heels, satisfied with the neat pile of firewood. "We'll be comfortable tonight."

"Thank you." Natalie smiled as he stood, though her gratitude was tinged with more than a little sorrow. She rather enjoyed lying in his arms, pressed against his burly, battle-hewn body. She sucked her lower lip between her teeth and lowered her gaze as he headed towards the stove. The iron door squawked as he opened it a crack to check inside.

"Breakfast should be ready shortly," he beamed as he shoved the door closed. "Then we can get started with your training."

Natalie returned his smile. "You're too good. Let me cook tonight. I can't promise it'll be edible, but I feel I should at least try after all you've done."

"Very well." He pressed his fists to his hips and raised his eyebrows. "I promise I'll eat anything you put in front of me. Now, my lady, it cannot have escaped your notice that I'm in desperate need of a bath."

"Oh," she chuckled. "Not at all."

He looked down at his chest, still gleaming, and covered with streaks of mud and debris from the forest. "You are too polite, my lady. I'm in no fit state to be standing before you."

"I think you look very fine—" She snapped her jaw shut and her eyes darted towards the window. "I mean…"

The sound of his soft inhale made her stomach flutter, and her legs weakened beneath her. Her eyes drifted back towards him, to the blush blooming on his chest.

He cleared his throat and took a step to the door, his brow dropping low. "I should wash up. Excuse me."

As his footsteps faded, Natalie closed her eyes and silently cursed herself. In the darkness behind her eyelids she saw him, his bare chest, straining biceps and thighs. She saw her hands skating across the curves of his body, feeling the rough bristling hair beneath her palms as she caressed his chest. It would take so little effort for him to lift her, to hitch her thigh against his hip…

Her breath shuddered between her lips as she buried her head in her hands and tried to shake away the images.

"Stop this," she whispered, barely loud enough even for her own ears. "Once he knows who you are, he won't even want to speak to you again."

She took a deep breath and tried to occupy herself with something other than thoughts of him. With a labored breath she dropped to her knees and began to sweep out the fireplace. In the distance she heard a faint splash, and Brandon's sharp gasp as he plunged into the frigid water.

Pulling herself to her feet, face burning, she hurried up the steps, away from the hoarse gasps coming from the pool.

Her eyes were drawn towards the broken fragments of the chest, and the shining contents within. She sat on the edge of the bed and ran her fingers across the handles of the knives. There were four in total, each simple and sturdy in design. A small pile of brown leather belts and sheaths were tangled beside them. She pulled one of the belts from the pile and wrapped it around her waist.

Checking over her shoulder at the empty cottage, a playful smile tugged the corner of her lips. She snatched one of the blades from the chest and stood tall, pinning back her shoulders as she lifted her chin.

"Ladies and gentlemen," she whispered watching her shadow pose on the dusty walls. "Please welcome to the arena, on the day of her debut, Natalie, the Lioness of Blackmere."

She held the dirk aloft and lifted a cupped palm to her imaginary audience, signaling their applause. "The Lioness of Blackmere promises to be a strong contender in the melee, wielding not one, but two razor sharp blades." She lifted a second knife from the chest and widened her feet into what she assumed was an excellent fighting stance. "Please, boo with all your might, as we reluctantly welcome her first victim; The Dragon."

"Boooo!"

The sound clenched around Natalie's heart like a fist.

She whirred around, daggers poised, eyes wide with fear.

"Easy," Brandon chuckled from the bottom of the stairs. He held out his palms "Forgive me, my lady. I did not mean to startle you."

The skin on her back flashed hot and cold and shame scorched her cheeks. The knives clattered into the chest and she fumbled with the leather belt.

She chanced a look at him. He was still bare from the waist up, his broad and hairy body scrubbed clean and flushed pink. Crystalline droplets of water fell from his hair onto his broad shoulders, and slid down his chest.

"You must think me so foolish." She tore her eyes up towards the deep creases around his eyes, and the tight line of his lips as he suppressed a laugh. His effort only added fuel to the fire of her embarrassment.

"Not at all." He chuckled. "I'd be lying if I said I hadn't done it myself."

His admission drew a smile from the corners of her lips. "Truly?"

"Oh, aye. I used to get in trouble all the time at the Guild. When I was a squire, I had to empty the entire Guild's chamber pots for a month after stabbing my pillows. There were feathers everywhere."

"You were a squire?" She rolled her eyes. "So you were a child. Children are expected to play make believe."

"Who said I stopped? Ask Viv when she gets back. I

pierced a sack of grain just last week and we got thrown out of Finchburrow's tavern."

Natalie laughed and shook her head. She placed the blades back in the chest and made her way down the steps towards him, taking his offered hand.

His beaming smile calmed her nerves. "Please, don't be embarrassed."

Her breath caught as his rough hands enveloped hers. "I'll stop being embarrassed if you forget what you saw."

"I will try," he grinned. "My Lioness of Blackmere."

She bit her tongue as he let go of her hand and strode towards the stove. As he passed, she caught scent of his body, waves of heat and salt and musky strength.

He was dangerous, she decided. He knew how to set her at ease, and how to pull the floor out from beneath her and send her heart skittering. In the past, whenever she had imagined Brandon the Bear, she'd imagined a god, chiseled and honed of marble, skin taut over bulging muscles, silent and stoic.

As he fussed over the stove, she decided she rather liked the reality more than the fantasy.

"Are you hungry?" he grinned as he pulled out a tray of roasted wood pigeon.

"Desperately."

CHAPTER TWELVE

"PLEASE REMEMBER, the fights you see in the Tourney aren't real." Brandon leaned against the table, resting the backs of his thighs on the edge. "I mean, the blades are sharp, and we do get hurt, but it's like a dance. We practice, memorize the moves and how we can counter them. All that spinning and jumping is for show. We don't know the order the moves are coming in, but once we learn the tells, it's easier to defend against them." He gave a brief one-shouldered shrug. "In theory."

Natalie stood before him; arms folded across her chest. A cool breeze wafted between them, ruffling the thin material of her smock. Her heart thundered as she hung on his every word, desperate to hold on to the information.

He took a slow breath and his eyes grew distant. "Fighting for real isn't like that. You can practice fancy moves all you like, but most of the time, strength and boldness win over style." The muscle in his cheek danced as he gave a brief shake of his head. "My lady, are you sure you want to do this?"

His eyes, sharpened with worry, danced over her. The rise and fall of his broad chest ground to a halt as he awaited her decision.

"I do." She longed to smooth the crease between his eyebrows, to brush her thumb between them and sooth his concerns.

The crease only deepened. "But we don't have any armor, and only days to train. my lady, if you get hurt—"

"Blackmere is my home, not yours. It is I who should worry after you." Her words sent a surging storm through her veins. "None of you; neither you, nor the other champions, nor Stoneclough are under any obligation to fight."

"We have all lost something because of those bandits." He sighed and mirrored her stance, folding his arms over his chest. "We lost many more champions than Rob, and many squires; young men and women who died fighting, defending the castle of some daft noblewoman who never even took the time to come and speak to them."

Natalie's heart hollowed at his words. Cold sweat pricked her upper lip.

"Do you know her well?" he frowned. The twitching muscle in his cheek became even more persistent as he clenched his jaw. "I can't figure her out. For years she wrote to us, begging us to come to Blackmere. Every year her letter came, as certain as the seasons."

Natalie felt herself redden as she prayed Brandon had never had the opportunity to read them himself. There had been many letters over the years, but she remembered them all with mortifying clarity. She had mentioned him by name several times; spoken of his valor and her deep desire to meet the man in person.

"Finally, the Guild caved. I think they pitied her, to be honest. But she wasn't even there when I fought, and when she did arrive, they say she sat on the walls, so high I doubt she could even see anything."

"That wasn't by choice," Natalie's voice rasped in her arid throat, and the way his eyes snapped towards her sent her legs trembling. "If she'd been allowed, she would've been there, right at the front."

"You really think so?"

"I know it."

"I meet lords and ladies all the time," he frowned. "They swan around with little care for the common people, taking whatever they please because someone once ordained that it belongs to them by right." Thunder brewed behind his eyes. "Anyway, I'm not fighting for Lady Blackmere. I'm fighting because common folk's lives are in danger. I couldn't care less about the castle, or whose neck is on the chopping block. A life is a life, no matter their status."

Natalie pressed her lips together as the storm surged behind her ribs. Some reckless part of her longed to be rid of the burden of her secret. Holding on to it would make it fester like an untreated sickness. She would rather tell him and have done with it.

He inhaled and straightened to his full height, looming above her. "Let's get on with it," he muttered.

She bit her tongue as her courage faded.

He rubbed the back of his neck and scowled at the collection of blades beside him on the table. "I don't want to practice with these. Not today, anyway. If they go dull or break, they'll be of little use. Besides, I don't know if I could live with myself if I cut you." With a smile he pushed himself from the table and found two fallen branches, the length and thickness of a chair leg. He offered one towards her. "We'll train with sticks."

Natalie locked her burden away at the back of her mind and smiled. She closed her grip around the rough bark of the branch, testing the hefty weight of the wood. "They're a little larger than sticks."

"Alright, big sticks. We'll just practice with one, for now." He paused, and his lips flickered upwards. "Though I know the Lioness of Blackmere fights with two."

His gentle teasing soothed her worries, and she could not help but return his smile as the heat returned to her cheeks.

"Now, the most important thing to remember is to keep your opponent in sight." He widened his stance, placing his left leg slightly ahead, and rocked his weight onto the balls of his feet.

Natalie mirrored his position, keeping her eyes on his.

"Like this?"

"That's it. Now, let's work on blocking."

* * *

A deep burn settled into Natalie's arms, and no matter how she moved she could not shake it. Her shoulder screamed as she raised the branch to meet his blow again, and again. Her breath came in ragged puffs as she worked, hair sticking to the back of her neck.

"Again," Brandon ordered.

She took a deep breath, raised her arms, and grunted as he stuck from above.

"Again."

His next attack forced the breath from her lungs as he stuck low. She blocked the blow by her hip and pushed him away. There was no doubt in her mind he was holding back, using only a fraction of his strength, but every hit felt like being run down by a mason's cart.

His brow creased. "Is this too hard?"

"Not… at… all," she said through labored breaths.

He jabbed straight ahead, towards her stomach. There was a loud *clunk* as their sticks collided. She swept his arm up and away. The effort sent a spike of pain coursing through her bicep. She grimaced through the pain.

"My lady? I hurt you." His eyes widened as he lowered

his makeshift weapon.

"No, I'm fine." She gritted her teeth and circled around him. "Come at me again."

His next blow was slow, soft, and hesitant. He announced his intentions with an upwards flicker of his eyes before he struck from above. It took little effort to stop him. Natalie's frustration grew, simmering on the back of her tongue.

"We should take a break," Brandon announced, wiping his brow on the back of his forearm. He raked his fingers back through his hair and smiled. "You're doing well."

She wiped her sweaty forehead on the back of her arm and pressed her fists into her hips. "Because you're being gentle. The bandits aren't going to be so thoughtful."

"I told you, there's only so much we can do." Brandon walked towards the pool and scooped handfuls of water towards his face, washing away the sweat.

Natalie lifted her long hair from the back of her neck, relishing the cooling breeze against her skin. Her body ached, and the reserves of her energy were all but depleted, leaving her feeling hollow and empty. "It feels hopeless."

"You're doing well." Brandon repeated as water rained from his beard. "I've had recruits who would've quit by now."

"Truly?"

"Aye."

Pinning her hair back in both hands, she closed her eyes and took a deep, calming breath. "I can do this. I have to."

When she opened her eyes, he was watching her, lips parted. The lingering look tightened her chest, and left her feeling dizzy as blood rushed to her head. Then, as though nothing had passed between them, Brandon turned back to the pool, and scooped another handful of the icy water over his face.

"Right," he grunted, squeezing the water from her beard and smoothing his hand over his eyes. "We've covered the basics of blocking, and that'll get easier with practice." He strode towards her, flipping the stick over in his hands. "Let's go over a few basic attacks."

She nodded, her throat too tight and dry to speak. Part of her wondered if one of his techniques for battle was to confound her so completely, she could not fight back.

He crooked an eyebrow at her and leaned into a fighting stance. "I want you to strike me, as hard as you can, however you want."

Her chest hollowed. "I can't."

"Hit me, push me. Try to beat me."

"I don't want to hurt you."

He smiled and reached out his arm, until he cradled her shoulder in his hand. "I'll try not to let you." With a grin, he released her and took a step back, lowering himself ready to block. "Ready."

Natalie steadied herself, and forced her breath to slow. The heat from his touch lingered on her shoulder as she struck, aiming first for the stick in his hands.

The sound of the wooden clunk as he easily blocked her creased his eyes. "Now who's being soft?"

She bit down on her worry and stuck again, aiming high. His eyes widened as he moved to block her.

"That's it," he grunted, pushing her back. "Harder."

She drew back her weapon until it disappeared from her periphery, and feigned for his ribs. At the last moment she swept it down towards his thigh.

Brandon flinched and blocked her strike. "Good!"

His approval widened her smile. Breathless, she lunged again, aiming high, then low, then across his body, making him work to defend himself. His body shone from the effort, flushed pink by the cold air and exercise.

She inched towards him, forcing him backwards. The sound of him, his exhausted grunts and gasps, sent shivers across her flesh.

"If you back me into the water," he panted. "I'm taking you with me."

Tumbling into the pool with him would not be the worst thing in the world. She smirked and struck him overhead. With a groan he lifted his arms, and met her blow, stepping towards her to limit the range of her movement.

They were close, so close the hairs on his chest brushed

against the top of her breasts as they faced each other, catching their breath.

Natalie's heart raced as his chest heaved against hers.

He looked down into her eyes, and his head bowed a little, bringing his lips achingly close.

The forest stood still and silent around them for an eternity.

"Very good." His breath was no more than a whisper, a deep rumbling growl which began in the depths of his broad and powerful chest.

Natalie's head spun as his eyes darted across her features.

"Did I hurt you?" she breathed.

"Not at all." He stepped away and turned his back to her.

She relaxed her arms, and took a deep breath, feeling every hair's breadth of their distance as her body cooled. He raised his head and closed his lips. His expression turned to cool iron.

"Again," he growled, sending a thrill along her spine. "As hard as you can."

She lunged, striking low, *clunk*, high, *clunk*, low again.

"Harder," he growled. *"Harder!"*

His demands dried her throat and tightened her chest. Goddess, she wanted him. Desire clouded her mind, thickening the air as she fought for breath. She swung towards his ribs putting all of her weight behind the blow, her shoulder jarring with the force as the thick, heavy branch connected with flesh. Brandon cried out in pain.

Dropping the branch, the blood drained from her face. "Oh, by the Goddess, Brandon!"

He screwed his eyes tight, breathing in strained, agonized hisses. His face reddened as he dropped to a knee.

Natalie's heart broke into a gallop as she crouched beside him, placing her hand over the already scarlet patch on his side. The area was swollen, fiercely red, and grazed. "Oh, Goddess. Forgive me, Brandon. Please forgive me."

He flinched away from her touch, sucking in his breath through clenched teeth. "Don't—"

"Brandon?"

Tears pooled in Natalie's eyes as he stood and with a sharp inhale, trudged back to the cottage. She watched him, helpless, as the forest floor soaked her skirt, and the cold wind whispered against her.

CHAPTER THIRTEEN

THE TABLE creaked as she perched on the splintered wood, her skin chilled and bristling in the autumn breeze. Her jaw ached from clenching, and her fingernails left red crescents in the palms of her hands. Hot flashes of shame fanned across her cheeks as she tormented herself, running over the incident again and again.

She had always been too boisterous, had always gotten carried away, and now she had hurt Brandon. Digging her elbows into the soft flesh of her thighs, she leaned forward and buried her face in her hands. She rubbed her fingers against her eyelids until she saw stars.

"Fool," she muttered.

She had to do something. Sitting out there in the cold was no good. Facing his hate was better than waiting for it to descend on her.

The woolen dress fluttered beside her, dried by the breeze and the warm air. She slid from the table, and took one of the knives to it, tearing a strip from the bottom of the skirt. Carefully, she folded it and tiptoed over to the waterfall, glancing over her shoulder towards the darkness within the cottage.

She soaked the woolen bundle beneath the icy waters and took a deep breath, summoning the courage to walk into his den.

Treading lightly on the balls of her feet, she crept into the gloom, her breath shuddering as it left her trembling lips. "Brandon?"

"Up here." A soft moan sounded from the bed.

She tiptoed across the floor and slowly climbed the staircase. He came into view inch by inch, staring at the ceiling.

The sight which greeted her shattered Natalie's heart. The flesh on his side was mottled pink, a near-perfect impression of the stick emblazoned across his ribcage. Elsewhere his flesh was pale, and gleaming with sweat. The rise and fall of his chest staggered, as she approached.

"Brandon," she stepped towards the bed, and lowered herself to sit beside him. Her throat tightened and her voice wavered. "I'm so sorry." The pulse in her throat pounded so hard she wondered if he could see it leaping. She pressed the cold, wet wool against his reddened skin.

His eyes closed as he flinched at her touch. Beneath the brush of his beard, his jaw twitched. His chest swelled and shuddered down. "There is nothing to forgive, my lady. You only did what I asked of you. I'm sorry you have to see me this way."

"Is anything broken?" she whispered.

"Just bruised, I think. My pride suffered the worst. I fell from my horse a few years back during the joust, and those ribs never felt fully healed."

"It's my fault. I got carried away."

"I asked you to. I wanted you to." He pressed his lips together as his eyes grew glassy. An exasperated growl rumbled in his chest. "Oh, this is ridiculous. I used to be the best. I was Brandon the Bear, the legend of the Grand Tourney." He flinched and screwed up his eyes as a bitter laugh erupted from his chest. "Now look at me."

Natalie's heart ached. "You're still that man."

"I can't even win a fight against an untrained barmaid," he glowered. "Henry's right. I'm not fit to be a champion. I'm a mess. I was given all that strength and beauty, and I wasted it. I drank and ate too much, telling myself I'd always be young and handsome. I spent my days with women instead of training. Then the women didn't want me anymore and the training got too hard."

A muscle tightened in Natalie's jaw, and a surge of heat told her she was glowing red again.

Careful not to press any harder on his bruise, she bunched her knees up until the bed held her entire weight. She steadied her breath and moistened her lips with the tip of her tongue. "You know, when I was younger, I dreamt of meeting you."

His eyes rolled across the ceiling towards her, and his lips hardened as his gaze met hers.

She pressed her teeth into her lower lip for a moment, and smiled before continuing. "When I heard you were coming to Blackmere, I practiced what I'd say to you, but I never found the right words. I loved the song, *Brandon the Bear, strong and brave and fair.*"

A soft, half-hearted chuckle shook his chest. "Well, I'm sorry you met me now, when I'm Brandon the Boar, old and fat and sore," he sighed. "That's Henry's favorite song."

"Henry's a prick."

"You'll get no argument from me on that." The corner of his moustache twitched above a faint smile. "As much as I care for the little sod, I hate him, because he's the man I used to be; handsome, skilled, as cock-sure as an alley cat, the darling of the Guild."

Natalie ran her hand across his forearm, surprised by her own courage. The cords of his muscles flexed beneath her touch. "You are handsome, and you are skilled, and I'm so glad I met you now and not then."

He drew a soft breath, his gaze falling to where her hand lingered on his forearm. "Do you mean that?"

"I wouldn't say it otherwise." The well of her bravery was rapidly depleting, so before she could freeze, she stood, feeling his eyes trail after her. She turned towards the staircase, and bit into her lip. His breath hitched behind her, sending a thrill across her flesh. Closing her eyes, she conjured the final, fading sparks of her boldness. "The songs don't do you justice. You're stronger, braver and even more handsome than I ever imagined."

As she descended the staircase her heart pounded in her ears, louder and more rapturous than the crowd at the Tourney. "Get some rest. You'll feel better for it."

"Thank you, my lady."

When she reached the bottom, she rushed out of the cottage into the cool air, and leaned back against the wall, pressing the back of her head against the cold stones.

An excited squeal built up behind her lips. Trapping it behind a wide smile, she buried her face in her palms. "Natalie, you lovesick fool."

She wished more than anything that Jenny could be there. Jenny would tease her, but embolden her. She would make her giggle as though they were still maidens, flirting with the stable hands.

But she was not a maiden.

She was Lady Natalie Blackmere, the noblewoman of a castle, the woman who—although he did not know it—Brandon despised. For all she knew, Jenny hated her too. She had every right to. They both did.

Her heart turned to flint as she lowered her eyes and the heat slipped from her face.

She was a liar.

If he cared for her at all, he cared for this version of her, the barmaid, not the noble responsible for the deaths of his companions. The deaths of his friends.

Darkness hung above her as she washed away the scent of their training—the scent of sweat and heat and him—in the icy, cleansing waters of the pool. She kept her eyes on the doorway, simultaneously hoping and dreading he would appear.

Though the smock was comfortable and freeing, Natalie was grateful for the warmth as she squeezed into Jenny's dress. A faint tang of smoke lingered in the fibers, but it was better than spending the afternoon freezing. She searched the forest for more fallen twigs and dry pine needles, and brought them inside, along with the knives and Brandon's tunic. They had more than enough firewood to get them through the night.

She stood before the dark fireplace, listening for Brandon's breath. His soft snores brought her comfort. If there was one thing her stout father had taught her, it was that rest and a good meal could cure almost any ailment of the heart and the body. Glancing out of the dusty window, she guessed she had a couple of hours of daylight remaining. Hopefully enough time to find something to eat.

Carefully, and quietly she built a fire, and strapped one of the blades around her waist. She tiptoed out of the cottage and pulled the door closed as the birds began their dusk songs.

CHAPTER FOURTEEN

Natalie crept through the woods, her fingers brushing against the cold steel of the dagger's pommel. Tiny birds flitted between the treetops, and grey squirrels bounded and crashed through the leaves, scurrying away when she got too near. Her stomach growled.

"How does Brandon do this?" she muttered.

Light was fading fast, and she had nothing to show for her expedition other than a pocketful of questionable looking mushrooms, and a churning stomach.

She followed the stream, sticking close to the banks so she did not get lost. The fish were too small and quick, the deer spotted her before she even knew they were there. Besides, she had no arrows to bring them down. The sun dipped below the horizon, and copper ribbons of light danced across the surface of the river. Darkness pressed in around her, and the forest turned murky indigo.

119

In her heart she knew it was futile; she had even less chance of catching anything to eat at night. She muttered a curse beneath her breath, frustration building in her chest.

The orange glow of fire caught her attention. It was faint and distant, somewhere between the tangled branches of ancient trees, but as moments passed and darkness grew deeper, the glow intensified. The scent of cooking meat drifted from a camp.

Steeling her nerve, Natalie crept forward. The dried leaves beneath her feet crackled beneath her step, and every small sound echoed through her ears, tensing the muscles in her body.

Turn back, her skittering heart begged her, but still she edged towards the light.

The harsh voices of men rang out between the trees, their boisterous laughter drawing beads of cold sweat along her spine. As she inched closer, she could see two men sitting beside the fire wearing cobbled together pieces of her guards' armor.

Breath trembling, weak legs aching, she hid behind a tree trunk and peered into their camp.

A brace of rabbits was strung by the fire, already prepared to eat. Bulging supply packs slumped by the men's feet, and the remnants of apples, bread crusts and chicken legs lay strewn by the fireside.

Natalie's stomach growled. There had to be enough food to feed her and Brandon a couple of days, long enough for his bruised ribs to heal. Perhaps even long enough for her to learn how to hunt. She had little chance of winning a fight against the two men, but she could sneak into their camp once they fell asleep.

One of the men yawned. "Part of me hopes they find us."

His companion chuckled as he picked his teeth with his thumbnail. His head was covered with a dark hood. "I've been itching for a fight since we left the Eastwoods; I'm not waiting around in Blackmere for something to happen."

Natalie's heart hollowed as she strained to listen to the conversation above the frantic pounding of her own heart.

"Aye. It was alright when we took the castle, but it was over before it started." The man reclined on the ground, stretching his gangly body. His red hair gleamed in the light of the fire. "Why doesn't Walden just kill the lady and be done with it?"

"He's waiting for someone to pay the ransom."

"Aye. Well he'll probably be waiting a long time."

"End of the month he says."

Her throat dried out, and the shrill, relentless ringing in her ears drowned out their words. The month would be over in two weeks.

The thunder in Natalie's chest pulsed through her veins, giving strength to the muscles in her legs. She tightened her grip around the hilt of the dagger until her knuckles shone white in the light of the full moon.

"Well," one of the men groaned as he stretched. "Whatever he does, he's doing it without us. I ain't waiting around in a dusty old castle waiting for some lord to—" The distant crunch of leaves rendered the bandit silent. Natalie's chest ached as she held her breath. The bandit leapt to his feet. "I think someone's out there."

"Get 'em!"

Natalie's heart sprung like a rabbit released from a trap. Her breaths became short and ragged as the bandits crashed towards her. She pressed her back into the rough bark of the tree and unsheathed the dagger.

The musty scent of their clothing wafted over her as the men thundered by. Their footsteps faded as they charged into the woods. In the distance she made out the silhouette of a deer, bounding between the trees.

Gasping, Natalie clutched her chest. There was no time to panic. She had to work fast. When the bandits realized the nature of their prey, they would return to the camp.

Hunger rose in her throat, acidic and bitter. She glanced over at the packs by the fire, and the plump rabbits ready for eating. The bandits had stolen her home from her. She would take the food from them.

With her heart in her throat, she darted forward. Every footstep was unnaturally loud in her ears, every breath a roaring hurricane as she dropped to one knee. She heaved one of the packs onto her shoulder and unhooked the rabbits from their spit. The pack was heavy. She eyed the other, sorry to leave it behind.

Go.

She bolted back into the darkness and returned to the cover behind the broad tree trunk. The bony, warm rabbits pressed against her hip as she waited, holding her breath. Footsteps rustled through the trees as the bandits returned.

"Oi! Where's my stuff?" The gangly man's voice was shrill with outrage.

His companion laughed and sheathed his blade. "Mine's still here. I don't give a rat's arse about yours."

Natalie grinned through strained breaths as the men began arguing. A rush of excitement coursed through her veins, making her lightheaded, and giving her the strength to run. She reined in her excitement and reminded herself that she still had to be cautious.

Taking a deep breath, she left the sanctuary of the tree and took a tentative step. She teetered as the pack on her back threw her off balance.

A sly smirk curled her lips as she imagined what Brandon might say when he saw her spoils. The heavy pack must have been stuffed with food, and the rabbits alone would provide them with a good dinner as well as breakfast the next day.

As the firelight faded, and the darkness of the forest pressed in around her, she felt her shoulders relax.

The voice at her back sent ice trickling down her spine. "Where's a little thing like you going with all that food?"

Her breath solidified in her throat, and panic darkened her vision as a blade nipped the tender flesh of her throat.

CHAPTER FIFTEEN

Nᴀᴛᴀʟɪᴇ ᴡᴀs born an Austwick, and as her mother often reminded her, *"Austwicks do not cry. We do not show fear and we do not show them that they are hurting us."*

Bound to a tree stump, her arms bent backwards and the bindings biting into her wrists, Natalie struggled to remember her mother's lessons. Tears stung, collecting on the rims of her eyes, dangerously close to tumbling over the precipice. She drew in steady breaths through her nose, locking her lips together so that they would not tremble. The scrawny redheaded man crouched before her, twirling her dagger between his bony fingers. His thin smile carved his bone-white face in two. He made her guts slither.

With a sneer, he pointed the tip of the blade towards her. "I don't like thieves."

"Neither do I." The hardness in her voice surprised her.

Her mother would have been proud.

The redhead scoffed and turned to his friend, pressing the tip of his tongue to his back teeth. "Whaddya think?"

The second bandit stood close by, his warm brown face highlighted bronze in the light of their campfire. He rolled his eyes, jerked one shoulder upwards. "Don't care. Kill her."

Natalie's muscles screamed at her, straining against the bindings as every instinct of self-preservation kicked in. Her mind raced as she searched for a way out. The dagger was agonizingly close, but the bindings around her wrists were immovable. Her mother would have been furious at her for allowing herself to be bound in the first place.

The redhead smirked as he balanced the very tip of the blade between his thumb and the second knuckle of his finger. "Nah, not yet. Too quick."

His friend shook his head and folded his arms across his chest. He jutted his chin at Natalie. "Where're you from anyway?"

She clenched her jaw and stared ahead.

A satisfied grin spread across the redhead's face. "You know what I think? I think she came from Blackmere. Nowhere else for miles."

She exhaled slowly, keeping her eyes forward and her mind busy. She would not give them the satisfaction of fear. She thought of the songs of the champions, the tales of their feats and victories.

"Aye," the second bandit chuckled, stepping away from the fire and into the darkness. "I bet you're right. Pretty plump thing like her. Probably a baker or a butcher's wife."

The redhead snickered and wiped the corners of his mouth with his thumb. "D'you know the Lady of Blackmere then?"

Natalie distracted herself with song; *Brandon the Bear, strong and brave and fair.*

She flinched as he thrust the dagger towards her, stopping less than an inch from her stomach.

The redhead's eyes were wide and animalistic. "Answer me, or I'll gut you."

Her breath shook as she nodded.

"That a yes?"

"Yes." She despised the tremble in her voice, despised how the bandit relished it.

"Good. Well our boss, sorry, *former* boss, has her prisoner."

Taller than two men and twice as strong.

He slapped her, the force twisting her head to the right, leaving a burning, stinging patch on her cheek. The tears spilled over the dams of her eyelids and rolled down her cheeks. Her mouth flooded with the coppery tang of blood.

"You know what he's going to do?" The bandit snarled. He leaned forward and placed the knife to the side of her neck. With his other hand he tugged a clump of her hair over her shoulder and sliced through it, letting it fall to her lap. "He's going to kill her, unless one of her noble friends gives him money."

Natalie winced as he pulled more of her hair towards the knife. Behind him the leaves rustled as his friend moved around.

"An awful lot of money...."

He waved a lock of her coppery hair in front of her face, grinning at her. His breath against her cheek reeked of sour meat and stale liquor.

"...since the lad who hired us didn't pay."

Blessed is his blade, beware you wicked knaves.

"And if no one pays for her, then Walden's going to kill her, in front of everyone. Then he'll be the Lord of Blackmere, and no one will dare challenge him."

The bandit's eyes widened. Before he could make a sound, he was pulled back into the dark. Natalie's heart raced as muffled grunts, gasps, and the rustle of leaves filled the black forest around her. Her breath shuddered in the heavy silence which followed.

Panic froze her in place. She stared into the abyssal dark, waiting for her attacker, too afraid to make a sound, too afraid to move. Each pounding heartbeat counted down the moments before she would be pulled into the dark too.

"My lady?"

The sound of Brandon's voice drew a whimper from her lips as relief washed over her like a cool wave.

"Brandon—"

He knelt before her, and cupped her face between his hands. His eyes flitted around her face, frantic with desperation and fear, scouring her features for signs of injury. "What in the Goddess' name happened to you?"

She opened her mouth to speak, but the words could not find their way past her tongue.

"Nat, what happened?" His voice was little more than a growl. There was pain behind his eyes. Natalie leaned into his touch as he brushed his thumb across her cheek, which still ached from the bandit's slap. "Are you hurt?"

"No."

"Why are you out here?"

"I came to find food, to help you."

His lips parted, and the inner edges of his eyebrows pushed together, forming that crease she longed to smooth. He bowed his head and his shoulders slumped. "You could've been killed."

Her words and tears fell freely as she strained against her bonds. "I wanted there to be food when you woke up. I didn't want you to feel as though you had to hunt and find our supper, but I didn't know how to do it. I found them camping here and they had food."

He released a heavy breath and shook his head. "Keep

still," he whispered as he slipped the dagger between the rope and the tree stump.

"They're going to kill her, Brandon. They're going to kill Lady Blackmere."

"I heard."

Her arms sprang free from their bindings, and a dull pain coursed through her shoulders as she brought her arms in front of her. She rubbed the red marks around her wrists and stood, brushing the leaves and debris from her skirt. Her eyes fell to the black-clad bodies lying on the forest floor behind Brandon.

"Thank you." She tore her eyes away from them and looked down at the man kneeling before her. "Thank you for coming for me."

With a groan, Brandon stood, clutching his bruised side. His tunic was bloodstained again. He looked around the camp, pointedly avoiding Natalie's eyes.

"We may as well take their food, since you almost died for it." His tone was sharp, almost bristling.

The tendons in his neck were taut and the muscles in his cheek twitched as he clenched his jaw. He strode towards the fire to pick up one of the packs, heaving it across his broad back with a grunt. The fire hissed as he kicked dirt over the flames, plunging the forest into darkness.

Natalie followed him. "What should we do about Lady Blackmere?"

In the dark she made out his shadowed, hulking figure, storming around the camp. "What *can* we do? There's only two of us."

"I don't know. Something."

"Well, if you figure out what *something* entails, let me know."

She released a sigh and bit back the desire to retort. It would solve nothing, and he had every right to be annoyed at her. She had endangered both their lives.

As her eyes adjusted to the dark, she searched the area close by. The pack she had tried to escape with, and the brace of rabbits rested by the stump. She wrapped the strap of the pack around her knuckles and heaved it from the ground.

"Leave that," Brandon muttered. "I'll carry it." His boots crunched through the leaves as he came toward her and took the pack from her, lifting it as though it weighed nothing. Swinging it over the opposite shoulder, he held both straps with one hand at his chest. He snatched up the rabbits and turned his back on the camp. "Come on."

Natalie's frustration swelled "Let me carry something."

"I've got it."

"Brandon. Please."

Deflated, he sighed and turned to her. The moonlight bathed them both in feeble steel light. "Let's get back to the cottage, we can talk there."

He turned, and began his march back towards the river. Natalie's chest hollowed as she trailed after him.

The full moon followed them, leering through the trees. In two weeks, the month would be over, and unless they did something, Jenny would die...publicly.

She scoured her mind for shreds of a plan, but Brandon was right, it was hopeless without aid. The bandits had mentioned a ransom, but not the price they asked. Natalie's blood chilled at the thought of the demand reaching Caer Austwick. Her mother and father would be sick with worry.

As for highborn friends who might pay for her life, the list was short; disturbingly so, and anyone on that list was there because of her family. She cursed herself for not listening to her father. He had nagged her to attend parties, to flatter the nobility and win them over. It was expected of a highborn lady, especially the daughter of Lord and Lady Austwick.

Natalie's heart grew heavier with every passing moment. She and Brandon followed the gurgling waters of the stream, until the cottage's golden windows came into view. Her mood lifted a little at the sight of it, and at the smell of the smoke from the chimney.

Brandon's labored breath erupted in plumes of steam as he pushed open the door and trudged inside. He unburdened himself of the packs and raked back his hair, his fingertips brushing against the silver streaks at his temples.

Natalie rubbed at the fading marks from the ropes on

her wrists and waited for him to speak. He lumbered over to the fireplace and threw on more wood. The loud clatter and hiss rang through the heavy air.

"Are you angry with me?" After so much silence, her voice came as a shock.

"Why would I be angry?"

"Because I endangered our lives," she said, her voice shaking.

"It's not that."

"I'm reckless."

"Aye," he sighed. "A little. But I'm not angry."

"Then what is it? I know something is troubling you."

He turned towards her, and his eyes fell to her feet before he dragged his gaze up to meet hers. The stony expression remained, hardening his features. "My lady, men died by my hand just now. I have their blood beneath my fingernails."

Natalie's breath hitched as Brandon held up his shaking hands. Beneath each nail, a thick crescent of black blood served as a reminder of what he had done to save her. The creases on his knuckles, the fine lines of his fingerprints, his newly washed tunic, were all stained with their blood.

He raised his eyes and threw back his head, exhaling a shuddering breath. "I know...I know they were bad men, and they deserved to die. If I hadn't done it, then they would have hurt you. But they were still people. They were someone's sons, maybe fathers, husbands, friends. They were people. They had lives, and I took them."

An urge welled at the back of Natalie's throat; the urge to speak comfort, to wrap her arms around him. But she froze to the spot, watching as he paced three steps left, three steps right, over and over, with the ferocity of a caged beast.

"The first one I... I killed." He raised his palms and held them out before him. "He looked at me, and he was afraid. I was no better to him than sickness, or injury. I was nothing more than the blade in my hand. He might've been someone's best friend, someone's *Robert*."

"Brandon..." Her voice was little more than a whisper as she stepped towards him.

He stopped pacing and pressed his palm to his forehead. "They were cruel men. Weren't they? It was the right thing to do."

As Natalie approached, he turned to her, as though shocked to see her. His eyes darted around her face. There was desperation in them, but what she did not expect was the loneliness.

Though Brandon appeared to have limitless strength, the night had shattered him. He brought a shaking hand to her hair and ran it between his fingers.

His gentle touch struck her like a lightning bolt, all but forcing the air from her lungs. Her knees grew weak.

When he spoke, his voice was distant thunder. "I'm not the man I was, my lady. I'm not a great fighter, I'm not beloved by everyone, I'm not the best, but I've tried to be a good man."

"You are." Her words barely formed a sound. She took his hand in hers, and ran her fingers across his knuckles. The skin at the base of his fingers was scarred and smooth, worn by years of fighting. She longed to press her lips to each one in turn, but more than anything, she wished to see him smile again. "Wait here."

"My lady?" The fear in his voice returned as she stepped away from him.

"I'll be but a moment." She picked up a wooden pail from beside the stone washbasin, and hurried towards the door.

CHAPTER SIXTEEN

WHEN SHE returned to the cottage, breathless even from such a short walk with the pail of water, her heart squeezed at the sight that greeted her. Brandon was perched on the steps; his forearms braced on his thighs as he stared at his bloodied hands.

There was pain behind his eyes, grief for the lives he had taken. For *her*, she reminded herself. He had done it for her.

Setting the pail before the fire, she summoned her courage, crossed the room and reached out to him, taking one of his hands in hers. "Brandon?" Her throat clamped shut as his grip tightened around her fingers, seeking reassurance.

She met his eyes, finding herself lost in their gentle warmth. "Let me help."

He did not resist as she led him to the pail and slowly

lowered herself to her knees before him. The thrumming of her pulse made her dizzy as he towered above her, silent and solemn.

She patted the floor beside her, as the firelight danced across his face. "Sit with me."

Brandon's movements were slow and labored as he winced and sunk down to the ground, sore, tired, and worn. His lids hung heavy over his eyes.

"Tell me about the Tourney," Natalie whispered as she lifted one of his hands in both of hers. She rested the heel of his hand on the edge of the bucket, and dipped his fingers into the water, easing the dirt and blood away with slow, circular motions of her thumb.

"The Tourney? What do you want to know?"

She smiled as she took a strip she had torn from her dress and began to clean his fingernails. His voice was a soothing balm after such painful silence. "Everything. How did you start?"

"As a squire. We all begin as squires." He watched the movements of her fingers with an intensity which made her nervous. "I was ten years old. I squired for a champion named Elisa. Elisa Beldorna."

"The Falcon." A grin spread across Natalie's lips. "I've heard of her. I had no idea you were her squire."

"Aye." Brandon's mood lifted a little as his lips mirrored her smile. The creases at the corners of his eyes, trails left by decades of laughter, deepened. "I think the best she did was fourth in the joust."

"Fifth."

Natalie held her breath as Brandon frowned in concentration. "Aye. I think you're right. You know your stuff."

Natalie beamed with pride as she took his hand out of the water, and dried it with the other end of the woolen strip. She held his hand up for inspection. "Your first victory?"

His nails were pink and clean once more, though some of the dirt on his skin was ingrained, deeper than she could get to in one night. The backs of each finger were hatched with white scars from blades, and the inside of his palm and fingers bore rough, hard calluses. She ran her fingers across the lines on his palm, her heart pounding at the overfamiliarity. She barely knew him, but being close to him felt as natural as breathing.

A sigh passed his lips. "You have to remember I was young and cocky. At first it was overwhelming, the cheering, the rush of adrenaline, the prizes. It was more than a butcher's lad could dream of. Then it became something I expected. The first time my name wasn't called as a victor, I was furious to have it taken from me."

She released his hand and gestured for the other. "What's life like for you?"

"What do you imagine it is?" He smiled as he held his hand out towards her.

"Like a never-ending party. Lots of celebration, drink,

women."

She slid her fingers along the back of his hand, and laced them between his. In the water he reached for her, attempting to hook his fingertips upon hers.

"There were celebrations," he whispered. His voice was soft and deep, an outwardly dormant mountain whose heart was filled with fire. "Especially when I was a younger man, when I was on top. There was a lot of drink. And yes, women. A fair few, but they tend to come and go with rankings."

She hoped he did not notice the staggering in her breath as she watched their hands locking together beneath the water. "Do you have children somewhere?"

"No. I can't have them," he shrugged and pressed his lips into a thin line. "Part of becoming a champion is giving up the ability to have children. The men are cut." He grimaced a little as he gestured to his thigh. "Inside, I mean. The women take a tonic. The Guild doesn't want champions breeding, doesn't want rankings to be fixed by families designed to be bigger and stronger than everyone else. Plus, it makes life a lot less complicated when—you know?"

"You don't have to worry about women left to struggle with an unplanned Bear cub." She smiled, though her cheeks blazed.

"Exactly. Sex is given to champions as a prize. It's just to be enjoyed, no complications. We visit the healers before and after each contest to make sure we're healthy."

Natalie pulled his hand from the water and wrapped

the dry wool around it, resting his wrist on her knee. His fingers hovered an inch above her thigh, sending pulses of heat across her flesh.

She sunk her front teeth into her lower lip to keep her smile from spreading. "It sounds like an exciting life."

"It is, while you're winning." He took a deep breath and drew back, taking his hands from hers and holding them up to inspect. "Thank you, my lady."

"You still never call me by my name."

"I suppose I don't, do I?" He gave a slight chuckle. "Thank you, Nat. Forgive me for bringing it up, but your hair…"

"Oh!" Natalie brought her fingers up to the severed chunks of her hair. They flicked out close to her ears, mangled by the blade. "Does it look awful?"

He looked at her and narrowed his eyes, parting his lips as if to speak. Silence descended on them as the fire popped.

"I take it that means yes?" Natalie sighed.

"It's… noticeable."

She scrunched her nose and let her hands fall to her lap. "It'll grow back. It's fine. I consider myself lucky that bad hair is all I suffered."

"I'm sure we can make it a little less obvious." His brow creased in contemplation, and he rocked up to rest on his knees. "May I?"

"Of course." A thrill filled Natalie's chest as he shuffled towards her, and his fingers threaded through her hair.

The sensation of his touch was as soothing as it was torture; soft and firm, skilled yet tentative. There was a slight tug as he began braiding, his dexterous fingers dancing through the strands of copper. His big, rough hands, so accustomed to the harshness of battles, relished the opportunity for gentleness. She glanced up at him through her eyelashes as he worked, his lips pressed into a tight line and his eyes focused on nothing but her hair.

His concentration faltered a little as he met her gaze, and the creases around his eyes deepened as he smiled. "It won't take long," he said, much to her disappointment.

She closed her eyes, enjoying the sensation of his touch, and the warmth of the fire. For a few moments she allowed herself to believe there was no danger, no looming threat behind the walls of Blackmere. There was only her and the man she admired, warm and safe, hidden from the rest of the world.

Finally, he wrapped the end of the braid in a woolen thread pulled from his tattered tunic and leaned back to admire his work.

Lifting her fingers to investigate, she found the braids were smooth and intricate, disguising the severed ends of her hair. They ran down the sides of her head, meeting at the top of her neck before continuing into the cascade of her locks.

"Thank you," she beamed.

"It was my pleasure." He turned from her and dragged one of the bandits' packs towards them. "Let's see what we have."

She could not help but smile as she brushed the side of her head with her fingertips once more. Brandon opened the pack and raised his eyebrows.

Natalie watched his expression for clues. "Please tell me it was worth our while."

"Bread," he said, pulling out a large round loaf marked on top with a cross.

"Just bread?"

His smile brightened with every passing moment. "Cheese, meat, apples. We have a feast. And..." His eyes widened as he took a brown glass bottle from the bottom of the bag and pulled out the cork. The scent of strong honeyed wine flooded the cottage. "Shall we?"

CHAPTER SEVENTEEN

T HE BANDITS' wine was far stronger than any Natalie had ever drank in Blackmere. Combined with the warmth of the fire and the delight of Brandon's company, by the time they finished the first bottle, she was a little more than giddy. Brandon seemed to fare no better.

Sat before the fireplace, he groaned and stretched out his legs, placing his hands behind him. "Goddess, if I sit on this floor any longer my arse will never fully recover."

She snorted, opening the second bottle and taking a deep swig. "We don't want that."

He chuckled, taking the bottle when she offered it. "We'd be more comfortable if we went upstairs to bed." He paused, his eyes widening. "I mean, so we don't have to sit on the floor."

Heat fanned over Natalie's face as she suppressed a

smile. Her cheeks burned brighter than embers. "Oh, but then we'd lose the warmth of the fire."

He passed the bottle back and climbed to his feet, a smile spreading across his lips. "I have an idea." He offered her his hand, helping her up from the floor. She held fast to him as she found her footing, swaying a little as the world tilted around them.

"What's your idea?"

"I'm going to bring the bed down to us." The mischievous glint in his eye stole her breath. "Come with me. You'll be safe up there."

Her heart had never beat so hard as he kept hold of her hand and led her up the stairs to the loft. His palm was coarse and strong around her hand. She found it impossible not to imagine how those hands would feel against the soft insides of her thighs, holding her legs open. By the time he released her hand and left her at the side of the bed, she was burning up.

Brandon awaited her verdict on the opposite side of the bed, his bare chest heaving. "What do you think?"

She clung to a low hanging beam, steadying herself from swaying. The fire blazed bright below, at the bottom of the sheer drop. "Now that we're up here, I can think of perhaps a dozen reasons why this is ill-advised."

Brandon placed his hands on his hips, his unfocused gaze drifting on the bed. "I just want you to be warm and comfortable, my lady. It'll be nice, sleeping by the fire."

Emboldened by the wine, she let her eyes drift across his torso. Her throat dried with the longing to touch the hair on his chest, to feel the swell of his soft, rounded stomach pressed on top of her. The bruise on his ribs had shrunk, but a pale pink blossom shone where she had struck him. She imagined soothing it with kisses.

"What do you think?" he asked again. His cheeks were rosy above the shadowy darkness of his beard. "Should we?"

She tightened her grip around the bottleneck. "Do you think you're strong enough?"

"I know I am."

She bit her lip at the dark sound of his voice; just a hint of that legendary cockiness. He left her breathless. "What should I do? Can I help?"

"No need. Just stand back, my lady."

She did so as he bent over, biceps flexing as he hooked his hands beneath the mattress. With a heave he lifted it onto its end. Dust and cobwebs swirled around in the draft caused by the disturbance.

With a roar Brandon hurled the mattress over the edge of the platform, sending it crashing to the ground floor. Natalie shielded her eyes from the debris with her arm and hurried to the ledge.

Brandon hissed a curse as he ran down the steps after it. The mattress leaned against the fireplace, and was already smoldering by the time he got there. He pushed back against it and threw it flat onto the floor. An empty bottle of wine by the fireplace rattled across the floorboards as he shifted the mattress a safe distance from the flames.

"Ladies and Gentlemen, Brandon the Bear!" Natalie laughed from the now bare top level of the cottage. She took a victorious swig from the bottle, resting a hand on the rafters to keep herself steady.

"Are you going to jump?" Brandon grinned. He stood on the mattress staring up at her. "I'll catch you."

"I would break your back," Natalie snickered. She hitched up her skirts and carefully descended the staircase. "I'm heavier than I look."

"My lady?" Brandon smiled, offering his hand.

"I told you, call me Nat."

"My Nat?" he grinned, in the same smooth tone.

Heat rolled across her cheeks again as she took his hand and stepped down the last two steps and onto the floorboards. She cast a glance around the cottage. "At least you didn't burn the cottage down."

"A victory if ever there was one." Brandon picked up his tunic and grimaced at the fresh bloodstains. "Do you mind if I don't put this back on?"

She had half a mind to throw the tunic in the fire so he could never wear it again.

He smirked at her as though he could hear her thoughts. Her nerve faltered as a blush spread across her chest. Her breast ached, longing to be pressed against him, to feel his lips, his tongue, his teeth. She craved the touch of his hands, those rough hands which had pulled men from horses, swung swords, and carried lances, but which held her with such tenderness.

She cleared her throat and adopted the same practiced haughty tone she used when meeting with dignitaries.

"Sir, I'm starting to believe you rather enjoy parading around in naught but your breeches."

"Aye, of course I do," he chuckled, mirroring her tone. "What man would not be proud of this?" He ran his hand along the curve of his stomach and chuckled as he settled on the mattress.

Natalie hid her smile behind the neck of the bottle as she took another swig.

Brandon was staring into the flames when she turned her attention back to him. The fire's glow flickered across his skin; dancing amber waves of light kissing his shoulders, his neck. She longed to follow them, trace each line and curve with her lips.

"Are you alright?" The honey wine blurred the corners of her vision, made her head feel heavy, and her legs light. She dropped to her knees on the mattress beside him, and offered the bottle.

"Aye. It just... feels strange to be happy. People are in danger, people have died, and yet..." He touched the rim of the bottle to his lower lip and hesitated before he took a deep swig. When he was done, he exhaled loudly, and ran his hand over his mouth and beard. "Nat?"

She smiled at the sound of her name. She was never "Nat" to anyone. Her parents had insisted on Natalie, full and formal, a song on anyone's lips, no matter the context.

"Yes?"

"You said something earlier, and I've been thinking about it."

"I did?"

"Aye." He took another swig and handed the bottle back to her. She waited as her mind raced, watching the internal battle going on behind his eyes. "Back when, you know, you almost killed me…"

"Which time?" she smirked. "When I hit you with a stick, or led you to the bandits?"

"The stick. When you brutally assaulted me…"

"Oh, come now—"

"Just before you left me for dead…"

"You fiend, I did nothing of the sort." She gently slapped his thigh, earning her a hearty laugh.

They turned to face each other, smiles creasing the corners of their eyes. She adored how small she felt beside him, and yet how significant he made her feel. It was not the grandiose, forced importance of a high-born lady. Rather, the importance of a person whose time was utterly worthwhile and whose company was craved beyond any other pleasures. It was a feeling entirely reciprocated.

She swallowed a lump in her throat and asked, "What did I say?"

For a moment, his dark eyes flickered to her mouth, and his lips parted. "You said the songs about me don't do me justice."

Her chest hollowed. "Oh."

"Did you mean it?" He moistened his lips with the tip of his tongue and smoothed his beard with a stroke of his hand. "I know it's probably vain of me to ask, but it's been a long time since…" he turned back to the fire and snapped his mouth shut. "No, I drank too much wine. Forget I asked."

Natalie took a swig from the bottle, filling her with bravery as she lifted herself onto her knees.

"Brandon the Bear, strong and brave and fair. Taller than two men and twice as strong." She smiled and bit into her lower lip as his blush deepened. "Now, you're obviously strong and brave. Taller than two men? Not quite."

She edged closer, a little clumsy from the drink. Her mind begged her to be bold, to push through the plush softness of his beard and kiss his lips as they parted to meet hers. Sitting close, she could see the luxurious length of his black eyelashes, as his eyes turned to greet her. He looked at her like a man half-starved, desperate to satisfy his appetite.

"My lady." The words escaped his lips on a sigh as he slid his hands around her waist.

The frantic thump of her heartbeat made her dizzy. "The *fair* part isn't enough."

His throat twitched as he swallowed, and repositioned his knees so that she knelt between his thighs. The look in his eyes was that of a man dragged into the center of a ballroom, who once knew the steps to every dance, but had long since forgotten them. "What would you use instead?"

Natalie brought up a hand, brushing the side of his face with her knuckles. "I don't think there is a word strong enough."

She leaned down, until the end of his beard brushed against the tender skin of her breasts, and his lips were so close she could taste the wine on his breath. He made a small, shuddering noise of surprise.

Fire ignited between her thighs as she pressed her body against his. He was a mountain of muscle and soft, scarred flesh.

"My lady," he whispered.

"Nat. Call me Nat, please." She leaned in closer, brushing her cupid's bow against his full, soft lower lip.

"Wait. Nat." There was an urgency in his voice that startled her. "Don't."

She drew a sharp breath as she recoiled. She sat upright, her chest tightening. Her cheeks blazed hot enough to forge iron. "Oh. No. Forgive me—"

"I want this. By the Goddess, I've wanted this since I

first saw you, but not while we're drunk."

Shame weighed heavy on her shoulders as she brought her hands up to cover her eyes. He was a good man, an honorable man, and she was brushing herself against him like a feral cat in heat. "I'm such a fool. Forgive me."

"There is nothing to forgive my lady." He lowered her hands from her face, and brushed back her hair with a soft stroke of his fingers. "Believe me, I wanted you from the moment I saw you, and asking you to wait pains me more than anything I've ever felt. But I want to. I want to wait, and I don't want wine to make me forget a single moment, or for it to cloud our judgement."

Her breath hitched in her throat. Her body yearned for him, but in her heart, she knew he was right. She sat back on her heels and looked into his eyes.

He reached out and took her hand, pressing her knuckles to his lips. "I've always made sure never to leave a woman unsatisfied, and I'll be damned if I break my streak with you." His words send a twinge of pleasure between her thighs. "We can try tomorrow, if you still want to."

She shivered at the touch, yearning for more. "I will."

"I'll ensure you don't regret the wait." The intensity burned off from his stare and his eyes creased into a smile.

Natalie could not help but chuckle. He flashed her a grin as he lay back, basking in the warmth of the fire. Her eyes drifted across his figure again. She was an addict, devouring the sight of him whenever she got the chance to. The fabric of his breeches was tight around his thick, muscular thighs, the mound of his stomach stretched and softened as he re-clined. She chanced a look at his face and found he was looking at her with the same starved expression.

Smiles cracked their intense facades. They turned away from each other and laughed.

"Lie down with me?" He gave a breath of laughter, pat-ting the mattress beside him as he propped himself up on an elbow and rested his cheek on his hand.

The air was heavy, hot, and thick with the scent of wood smoke, wine, and their bodies. Slowly, she raised her fin-gers to her chest and tugged loose the knot holding together the laces on the front of the dress. Brandon's soft groan sent shivers across her flesh, and ignited the ache at the pit of her stomach. Her breath barely reached her lungs as she pulled the dress off, and sat before him in the chemise.

"You're so lovely," he whispered. She could hear the dryness in his throat, the shallowness of his breath. His eyes fell to her breasts, to the hard peaks of her nipples, pressing against the thin fabric. She held back her shoulders just a little, just enough to pull the fabric tight. Her display was rewarded with a soft, desperate growl.

Smirking, she shuffled along until she lay next to him, pressing her body against his as he rolled over to meet her. Her cheeks were glowing. The heat from their bodies, and from the crackling fire at her back left her light headed.

"I still feel so guilty about this." She traced her finger-tips around the bruise on his ribs, a feathery touch which made him jolt. Her face cracked into a smile. "You're ticklish?"

"No." He clenched his jaw and screwed his eyes as she tested her theory, brushing the tips of her fingernails along the side of his stomach. He twitched and wriggled, before snatching her wrists and pinning them to the mattress above her head.

"That's cruel," he growled.

She bit into her lower lip as he pinned her, her breasts brushing against his chest. "I've found your weakness."

His lips hovered mere inches from hers. "I will have revenge."

She lifted her head and hissed, "Do your worst."

She regretted her taunt immediately, as he tickled her underarms. His fingers were quick and strong, exploring her sensitive skin to find the areas which drew the greatest reaction. She writhed beneath him, shrieking and laughing until he saw fit to show her mercy.

"Do you yield?" He growled.

"Yes, yes," she giggled. "I yield."

A soft smile cracked his tough veneer, and though he only held her gently, his grip on her wrists lingered. She relaxed beneath him, secured by the weight of his arm across her chest.

"How did you get this?" she whispered, freeing a hand to trace a jagged scar across his left shoulder. The pale line of puckered skin was tough yet silken beneath her fingertip.

"The joust. I took a lance to the shoulder and it shattered. There was a shard lodged in there longer than my arm."

"That must've stung."

He chuckled and his chest rumbled, pressed against her side. "Aye, just a bit."

"Does it hurt now?"

"It gets stiff in the cold." He brought his left hand up to touch the old wound, and his eyes grew distant. "It can make blocking difficult when we travel further north."

She had placed a gentle kiss on the scarred skin, watching for his reaction. Beneath the dark shadow of his moustache, his lips quirked up into a smile.

Her eyes dropped lower, to a silvery scar on the side of his chest. "And that one?"

"Ah. That was Robert," he sighed. "The little sod. That was the first time he beat me."

She traced the line with her fingers, and her heart ached for his loss.

"I feel like I've known you all my life," he whispered. His eyes followed the features of her face, as though searching for her in his memories. "I can't believe we've only had a few days together."

The wind howled outside the cottage, whispering against the rooftop. Guilt stirred inside her, fluttering against her ribs; he did not know her at all.

She could not let him to know her.

He pulled her closer to him, and she felt herself melting against him, warmed by the fire and the heat of his body pressed against her. "How can we feel so connected in so short a time?"

"I don't know."

"When all of this is done, when Blackmere is safe, me, Henry and Viv must return to the Guild. There will be recruits to train, contests to prepare for." He released a pained sigh. "But I don't know that I can leave you."

The gnawing guilt clawed the back of Natalie's mind. Her throat tightened and the ringing in her ears returned. The wine dulled her reason, taunting her with the notion that she could simply give up Blackmere, forgo her name and title, and go with him. The thought of returning to the monotony of a noblewoman's life, the accounts, the balances and checks soured in her gut.

She released a sigh, which fluttered the dark hairs at the bottom of his beard. "The Guild wouldn't allow it, would they?"

"Sod the Guild."

"Brandon, you can't give up a life for someone you met only days ago."

"That depends on the someone." He brought her hand to his lips and kissed her knuckle. Her breath staggered at the sensation, the softness and heat of his lips. "But you're right. It's too soon to decide." Brandon released his hold on her and ran his fingers through her hair. "Whatever happens, we're here now, together."

CHAPTER EIGHTEEN

THE MORNING light struck Natalie like a fist to the back of the head. She grimaced as she shielded her eyes from the brightness. Her tongue was fuzzy and the astringent taste of sour wine lingered at the back of her throat. The bitter stench of cold ash clouded the cold morning air.

She ground the heel of her hand against her aching eyes and rolled onto her side, nestling against the warm body beside her. Brandon let out a long breath as she buried her cold nose against his bicep. Her senses flooded with the sensation of him; the soft, musky earth scent of his skin, the warmth pulsing from his body.

"Is it morning already?" His voice rumbled against her ear.

"No," she whispered, muffled against his arm. "Go back to sleep."

"Well then the moon is very bright." His body swelled against her as he took a deep breath in and pressed his nose to the top of her head. "Do you still want to train today?"

Natalie's heart picked up speed as the reality of their situation set in. Soon they would face the bandits, and they would have to fight. She might not make it. Brandon might not make it. The thought left a hollow feeling in her chest. "Yes. Though I promise not to maim you today."

"Ah." He rolled away from her and faced the ceiling. "So, you admit it."

"Don't make me tickle you again."

"You wouldn't dare." A cool breeze wafted across Natalie's skin as Brandon sat up and pulled himself to his feet. She watched him stretch, watched the muscles in his back flex and swell.

Without his body heat, she shivered, and the cold forced her to follow him. She stood, woozy and thirsty, rubbing warmth into her stiffened fingers.

They ate rabbit and the remaining chunk of the bread for breakfast, chewing in comfortable silence, as they perched on the table at the side of the cottage. When they were finished eating, they gathered wood for the fire and cleared a patch on the forest floor where they could train.

The silvery autumn sun was already high in the sky when they began their training.

"Come at me." Brandon ordered.

"You're sure?"

"Aye."

"Very well, keep your guard up this time though." With a smirk, she struck, one, two, three. The *clack* of wood on wood rang out through the forest.

"Again."

One. Two. Three.

"Again."

Sweat beaded down the back of her smock. She was tired, hungover, and sore, but the thought of the bandits in Blackmere drove her on.

"That's it," Brandon panted as he blocked her strikes. He watched her carefully, focusing on the direction of her blows.

She pushed him back, until he bumped against a tree trunk, and gave a breathless laugh. "You're quite ferocious, Lioness."

She wiped her forehead on her sleeve and gasped for air. "I don't know how ferocious I'll be when they're fighting back."

He chuckled and leaned back against the tree, fighting to catch his breath. His skin glistened in the afternoon sun. "I don't think anything I can do can fully prepare you for a real fight."

"Then what hope do I have?"

He shrugged one shoulder and stared down his body. "That your instincts kick in. That your opponents are unprepared and clumsy, or hesitant. Your best chance is to be bold, and show them no mercy." His eyes lifted to meet hers. They were distant with worry. He was afraid. "But I wish you wouldn't fight."

She pressed her lips together and inhaled through her nose, settling her nerves. "I have to."

"I know. What I truly wish is that we could just go. Run away and ignore it all." He scoffed at his own admission. "That makes me wicked, doesn't it? Weak."

His words sent a longing through her body. If she was honest with herself, she wanted to run more than anything. At times she felt it would take so little effort to forget Blackmere, to cast it to the back of her mind and distract herself with the world and him.

"No, you're not wicked, nor weak. It isn't your home, their victims aren't your people, and you've already lost so much to them. But I have to fight. I can't let them take it all, and I can't let them hurt Jenny."

"Jenny?"

Natalie's head spun, as the precarious raft of her deception began to sink beneath her. She floundered as her chest tightened. "My friend, back in the town. She may still be alive and I can't leave her to them."

He turned his eyes to the branch in his hand. "Forgive me. It was but a moment's weakness."

A surge of relief coursed through her as he occupied himself with peeling the bark from his makeshift weapon.

"There is nothing to forgive." She widened her stance and leaned her weight forward. "Let me defend myself against you."

"My lady?"

"Give me everything you have."

"My lady, I can't." His eyes grew wide at the thought of it. "I'll break you."

"I'm not made of glass."

"I'm not gentle with you because I doubt your strength, my lady, but because I know the full extent of mine." He reached out and pushed a loose strand of hair back from her face, tucking it away behind her ear. With the lightest touch he skimmed her jawline, until he crooked his finger and tilted her chin towards him.

His words were heavy with a promise which sent a thrill through Natalie's body. She looked into his eyes, silently begging him to break loose from the restraint he put upon himself. The leaves rustled, picked up by the cold northerly breeze.

"Show me." Her breath shuddered as his hand brushed along the curve of her hip. She rocked onto her tiptoes, and leaned against his chest as he stooped to meet her. As she caressed the soft bristle of his beard with her fingertips, his lips curled into a smile.

"May I kiss you?" His whispered request was barely audible over the pounding of her heart in her ears.

"Please…"

"*Hello?*" A voice echoed from between the trees.

Panic spiked through Natalie's veins. Brandon darted back, gripping the branch in his bloodless fist, in preparation to fight. The steady clatter of horses' hooves rustled in the leaves.

"Brandon?" Henry called as he and Genevieve drew closer. "Thank the Goddess, I thought we would never find our way back."

The young champion dismounted his horse, pulling off his gloves one finger at a time. A new dark blue travelling cape fluttered behind him as he walked towards them.

Natalie's heart battered against her ribs.

Genevieve gave her a subtle nod and dismounted her own steed groaning with the relief of being free from the saddle.

"You're back so soon," Brandon said, his jaw clenched tight. He held out a hand to greet Big Lad, who nuzzled against his palm and gave a contented nicker.

"Yes well," Henry sniffed as he stamped towards the cottage door. "Rejection doesn't take long."

Natalie's breath failed her as Henry disappeared inside.

CHAPTER NINETEEN

"WELL, ISN'T this cozy?" Henry smirked as he nudged the mattress with his foot. He raised his eyes to the ceiling, lips parted and brows furrowed as he looked around at the cobwebs. "It's even more ghastly than I remember."

"What happened with Lord Stoneclough?" Natalie's fingers trembled as she curled them against her palms, coiling her fists.

Brandon strode into the cottage, with his arms crossed over his bare chest. He stared at Henry with a calculated coolness.

Beside him, Genevieve cleared her throat. She shrugged and raised her eyebrows. "He said no."

"He just refused to help?" Natalie frowned. Indignation burned at her temples. "Did he give a reason?"

Henry chuckled and scuffed his boots along the floorboards. "No, but he didn't need to. He's an old man, well past his glory days and the fire in his belly has been quenched by ale. You should've gone in my stead Brandon. You have a lot in common."

Brandon did not acknowledge the insult, or at least, he gave no outward sign that it affected him. His eyes were glazed, his lips fixed in a soft, neutral line.

Dissatisfied by the lack of reaction, Henry tutted and grimaced at Brandon's bare torso. "Please put your shirt on man. That's the last thing I want to see after a long ride."

Brandon's eyes were flint as he stared, unaffected, into the empty hearth.

Genevieve made a small grunt of discomfort as she trudged towards the staircase, and bent her stiff legs until she could sit. "We need a new plan."

Henry tutted. "At least Stoneclough was kind enough to give me a cape. This dismal part of the land is as cold as it is ugly. What a waste of bloody time."

"Worried you'll never get your boon?" Genevieve rolled her eyes as she leaned back on the stairs. "All I heard from him all the way was boon, reward, marriage, fortune."

"Marriage?" Natalie's voice was loud and shrill as Henry cast a disdainful eye across her.

"Perhaps, when I meet Lady Blackmere, I may fall in love with her," Henry shrugged.

"You'll love her money." Genevieve spat.

Natalie's chest tightened as she weighed her limited options. Brandon remained stoic, fixing his eyes on Henry, on the floor, the fireplace, or anywhere where Natalie was not. The hazy passion they shared seemed but a dream, a fantasy.

"What do we do?" Genevieve sighed.

"Well," Henry groaned as he sat on the mattress and tugged off his boots. "If this was some commoner, I'd say we're out of options, but we must think of something. The first thing I'm going to do is sleep. We've been riding for two nights." He eyed the empty bottles of wine by the fireside and raised an eyebrow. "Unlike some, who've been lounging in comfort."

Genevieve scowled and rubbed her eyes. "I should rest too." Her dark eyes passed over Natalie, and flickered towards Brandon. "We will talk soon."

* * *

The cottage door creaked closed behind Natalie and she squinted in the bright afternoon light. Brandon had secured the horses by the brook, where they could eat, drink and rest. He buried his face in his hands, before running his palms along the length of Big Lad's dappled grey neck. "Goddess, forgive me," he muttered, raising his eyes to the treetops. He took a few lumbering steps towards the pool, before turning back towards Natalie, his eyes ringed with tears.

She held her breath and took a tentative step forward, as though stepping out on a frozen lake. A lump formed in her throat and tightened as she closed the gap between her and Brandon. He pinned her to him, one broad hand pressed against the back of her head, the other wrapped around her waist. His breath shook as he held her.

"What's going to happen?" His words blew hot against the top of her head.

"I don't know," she said softly, nestled against his heart. She tilted her face towards him and searched his eyes for answers. He was drawn, exhausted, and staring off into the woods. "Is something the matter?"

The weight of her question gathered in his brow, and his throat twitched as he worked up to the answer.

"Guilt." He shrugged and released her from his embrace. "People are suffering. Lady Blackmere is in danger. Who knows what's happening to her people? They're waiting for someone to help them. And while they wait, I'm here, with you, and I know it makes me a terrible man, but...Goddess forgive me." He drew a deep breath. The pain in his eyes spread to her heart as he fought to retain his composure. "The only thing that truly matters to me is you." He stepped back away from her and shook his head. "I need to think, my lady. I need some time alone to think."

Natalie held her head high as he marched off through the trees. Only when his heavy footsteps faded and were drowned out by the birdsong did she allow her tears to fall.

* * *

Gleaming patches of pink and orange sky peered through the branches as Natalie sat by the pool, scrubbing the bloodstains from Brandon's tunic. He had not asked her to do it, but the work gave her something to focus on; something honest.

She stared into the water as she polluted it with clouds of brown blood. Jenny would die at the end of the month, and it was all her fault.

A single hot tear rolled down her cheek before she could catch it, burning against her chilled skin as the sun dipped towards the horizon. Guilt surged over her like a wave over a sinking ship. Her stomach churned.

"You'll scrub a hole." The sound of Genevieve's voice sent a shock through Natalie's heart.

The Thorn approached from behind, the sound of her footsteps masked by the tumbling waterfall. The handles of the axes at her hips clacked together as she drew closer.

Natalie greeted her with a slow bow of her head. "I thought you were going to sleep?"

"Henry snores." Genevieve gave her a faint, exhausted smile. "And I'm tired of being near him."

"I can't blame you for that."

The champion twisted around to look behind her. "Where did the Bear go?"

"I don't know," Natalie sighed. "He wandered off."

"Hm."

Genevieve groaned as she lowered herself onto the ground, clearly stiff from days in the saddle. She pulled off her boots and dipped her feet in the pool, hissing as the cold bit at her toes. "Mother of the Mountains, that's cold," she grimaced.

Natalie gave a half-hearted laugh and tossed a pebble into the dark water of the pool. The warrior took a deep breath, and forced her feet below the surface pushing out a shuddering breath.

Natalie chuckled, ringing the tunic between her raw pink hands. "It's funny."

"What?"

"Before this week, the thought of even being in the same town as the champions made my head spin. And now..."

Genevieve shrugged and kicked her legs back and forth. "I feel the same way about barmaids."

Natalie laughed, the sound of it far too loud, but a much-needed release. Tears stung at her eyes and a tremble in her lower lip threatened to broadcast her anguish. She pulled herself to her feet and turned away to hide her face, draping Brandon's tunic over a branch. The soft grinding sound of the horses grazing nearby filled the air. The muscles in the mounts' flanks twitched as they listened to the rustling of squirrels and chirping birds.

Natalie turned back to Genevieve and swallowed the knot in her throat. "I want to thank you. You didn't have to ride all the way to Stoneclough, but you did."

The Thorn's eyebrows flitted upwards as she picked her back teeth with her tongue. "The lady and her people need our help. I had to."

Guilt clawed at Natalie's back, tormenting her like a specter. "I wish I had your strength and the skill to face them."

The Thorn sighed, watching the ripples spread across the pool. Natalie's vision blurred as her mind drifted back to thoughts of Brandon. His silence was so sudden, so blunt. She was at risk of losing him, she could feel it in the gnawing dread in her gut, but her heart was so unimportant compared to what was happening in Blackmere, what was happening to Jenny.

Genevieve was looking at her, her hard eyes scrutinizing her. "Did you and the Bear train to fight?"

"Yes."

"Are those your blades?" Genevieve jutted her chin towards the gleaming dirks on the table.

"They were going to be," Natalie muttered. She wrapped her arms around her chest and tucked her frigid hands beneath her underarms. Her stomach fluttered as she caught Brandon's scent wafting from the fibers of her smock.

Genevieve cocked her eyebrow. "Why aren't they yours now?"

"Because we can't fight. We can't win."

"Who says so?" The champion pulled her feet from the water and stood. She stamped warmth into her legs and gripped Natalie by the shoulders, her strong fingers pinching tender flesh. Her dark brown eyes narrowed. "Do you want to fight?"

The muscles in Natalie's jaw clenched as she steeled her nerve. "Yes."

"Why?"

"I want to help my friends. I want my home back."

"Good. Hold on to that. Let's fight."

Natalie could only watch, astonished as Genevieve pulled on her boots and stormed over to the table. She picked up one of the blades and inspected it. "You didn't use these to train?"

"Oh, no. We used sticks," Natalie stammered. "Branches. Brandon said he didn't want the blades to grow dull."

The Thorn pressed her lips together as though suppressing her thoughts. When she came to peace with the battle raging behind her eyes, she shoved one of the blades towards Natalie. "Here. Get dressed," Genevieve ordered. "As soon as you're ready we'll head out."

"Head out?" Natalie breathed, her teeth chattered from cold and fear. "Where?"

Genevieve turned to her. The indomitable look in the warrior's eyes sent a chill through Natalie's veins. "We're taking back Blackmere."

CHAPTER TWENTY

T HE AIR barely reached her lungs as Natalie watched Genevieve tack the horses. It was madness. The warrior's eyes grew glossy throughout her frantic preparations. She secured the buckle on the belt around the horse's belly, and rested her forehead against the leather saddle. A strained shuddering breath broke through the stronghold of her lips.

"I can't do this," Natalie whispered. "I'm not good enough to fight them yet."

"Well you have to. The lord won't help. Henry and Brandon are scared. She's going to die."

Natalie's jaw clenched as she stepped forward. "Genevieve, if we charge in there like this, we'll die too."

Genevieve lifted her face and gave a breathy laugh. She shook her head and closed her eyes. "I was supposed to meet someone that night. She didn't come."

"What do you—?"

"A woman from the tavern. She was supposed to meet me, but she said she had to see Lady Blackmere first."

Hot waves of guilt rolled over Natalie as she closed her eyes, unable to watch as Genevieve's stony demeanor crumbled.

"I searched for her. I didn't find her. I don't know if she got out, or if she still lives. I searched for her after the fight." The strength in her voice faltered, as footsteps rustled in the forest behind them. She lowered her head as the footsteps drew closer. "I have to know she is safe."

"We'll find her. I promise." Natalie inwardly cringed at her deception. "I'm sure she's safe." Desperate, she turned to the forest in search of Brandon. Surely, he could convince Genevieve to wait instead of charging straight into the bandits' stronghold.

Her breath stopped as shadows prowled between the trees.

The dark figures charged towards them, the pale blue glimmer of fading winter sunlight shining on their blades. Genevieve's bloodcurdling war cry rang out. Steel clashed.

In the chaos, Natalie's instinct kicked in. Fire flashed through her veins. She ducked as a man charged towards her, heard the whoosh of his blade over the top of her head. Gripping the blade tight she thrust forwards with all her strength, sinking her blade into the closest assailant. A warm splash across her face jolted her like a slap, making the world clear and all too sharp.

"Nat!" Brandon's distant voice rang through the dusky woods. She searched for him among the trees as Genevieve fought back a bandit, swinging the small throwing axe with such ferocity as to cleave the man in half. Natalie turned away from the fight. "Brandon?"

Fingers tangled in her hair. The sharp pain in her scalp forced a scream. She hit the earth hard, fingernails digging into soil, boots scrabbling among leaves for a foothold. The knife was lost in the darkness.

A bandit snarled above her, his teeth yellow, his sharp sour breath hot against her cheek. He coiled back his fist and she raised her arms to block him. His knuckles pounded against her cheek, sending a blinding flash of pain through her jaw.

Summoning every ounce of her strength, she kicked him square between the legs, digging the heel of her boot into his groin as he screamed, red faced. She flailed her arms across the forest floor, until her fingers found the cold steel hidden among the leaves. Clenching the hilt in her fist, she thrust it into the bandit's shoulder. He screamed and clutched at the wound as she stood.

Her legs were a crumbling foundation. The world tilted and throbbed around her as she righted herself, swaying from the panic and the pain.

A hand clawed at her ankle as the bandit attempted to unbalance her. She lunged towards him, yanked the blade free, and raised it to strike again.

"Wait!" He held out a hand towards her, searched her face with wide, desperate eyes. His voice was strained, trembling with fear. "Don't kill me."

Genevieve dispatched the last of the bandit's companions and turned, wide eyed and furious towards Natalie.

Relief surged through Natalie as Brandon appeared between the trees. His gasping breaths told of his own battle with bandits, and his desperation to get to her. He clutched the woodcutter's axe in his hand, ready to strike the man at her feet.

A gash beneath his eye dripped crimson, igniting a protective instinct deep within her. "You're hurt."

"I'm fine." He fixed his eyes on Natalie, a look of pure fear spread across his bloodied, mud-caked face as she stood panting above the whimpering wretch.

"You need help?" Genevieve wiped her brow on the back of her hand, still clutching her axe. "Kill him, quickly."

"I'll do it if you want," Brandon said in a low growl as he came closer.

The bandit's eyes widened. His shallow, fast breaths stole the air from Natalie's lungs. "Don't kill me; please, please they made me come here."

Genevieve chuckled and stepped over to the sobbing man pressing the sharpened steel of her axe against his throat. "Die with dignity."

The bandit's lip trembled as he scrunched his eyes shut. "Please. Don't."

"You came from Blackmere?" Natalie's voice sounded strange to her ears. To the bandit, her voice was flint; hard and sharp. But inside, she knew the truth, she was cracking glass; the slightest breeze might reduce her to dust. She steeled her nerve and fixed the bandit with a cold stare, pointing the tip of her blade against his throat.

The bandit turned to her. "We were told to find out where the smoke was coming from."

"And what do you plan to tell them you found here?"

"N-nothing."

"Nothing doesn't make smoke."

His lips quivered as the whites of his eyes glistened silver. "Hunters."

"Alright." Natalie relaxed her grip on the dagger. She felt Genevieve's eyes burning into her back. Leaves crunched behind her as Brandon took a step forward. "You've got about two minutes to buy your life."

The bandit's eyes widened and his mouth opened and closed like a landed trout. "Miss?"

"What can you tell us? What's going on at Blackmere?"

His breath trembled as his eyes darted across the ground where the bodies of his companions lay motionless. "Uh…

well... our boss, Walden is—*says* he is—forgive me—the Lord of Blackmere now, on account of there is no lady."

Cold fear dripped from Natalie's temples, and her breath froze in her lungs. "What do you mean? He killed her?"

"N-no, she was never there. The woman he thought was the lady, wasn't the lady at all. He's still going to kill her though, make an event of it so everyone respects him."

She dared not even glance at Brandon.

His voice boomed behind her. "How many bandits are in the castle?"

The bandit frowned and squinted. "Um... forty? Maybe? People keep leaving."

Natalie frowned "They're leaving?"

"Yeh. There's nothing in Blackmere 'cept dust."

Genevieve scoffed in disgust. "Can I just kill him now? Then there are only thirty-nine."

The bandit's lip trembled. "Blackmere's worthless. No gold, no treasure. Just a load of sheep, and the woman."

"And she's still alive? You're certain?"

"Yes."

Natalie's eyes drifted across to Brandon. The blood below his eye was black in the fading light. He tilted his head slightly towards the woods, signaling her to let the bandit go.

"I'll tell you anything you want to know," the wretch pleaded through desperate, glassy eyes. "Just let me have my life. We were paid to do this. Paid to take the castle, but the boss realized the castle was worth more than our client was willing to pay."

"And who was the client?"

"I don't know."

Her heart lurched as Genevieve raised her axe to strike the man's skull.

"I don't know!" He cried. "Walden didn't tell us his name. I just take orders. Please."

"Go then." Natalie stood, unable to look at the bandit as he whimpered and scrambled to his feet.

Genevieve glared at her as his footsteps faded. "He didn't deserve mercy."

"Maybe not," Natalie muttered as she stared down at the bloodstained blade.

"Are you hurt?" Brandon's voice beside her sent a pulse of shock through her body. "Is that your blood?"

"No." She turned to him and wound her arms around his neck, pulling him into a tight embrace.

"So, their prisoner isn't Lady Blackmere?"

"No." Though she tried to stop them, her tears spilled, rolling onto his chest. "No, it appears not. But we still have to save her."

"Of course. I told you, it doesn't matter who she is, we have to help."

"Thank you." Natalie wiped her tears on her sleeve and sniffed. "We need a plan."

When she broke free from his arms, Genevieve was pacing. "If the woman in the castle isn't Lady Blackmere, who is she?"

The cottage door creaked. Henry stood on the doorstep, faintly illuminated by the firelight within. He stuck his fingers in his ruffled hair and stared, wide-eyed at the bodies. "What in the Goddess' name happened here?"

"Did you enjoy your nap?" Genevieve spat as she pulled an axe from the back of a bandit. "We were attacked."

"Aye," Brandon growled. "And if they sent one group who doesn't return, more are bound to follow. Nat's right, we need a plan, and we need it now."

His arm pressed against Natalie's shoulders as he guided her inside.

CHAPTER TWENTY-ONE

NATALIE'S MIND raced as Brandon paced back and forth before the fire. She watched his every movement, her heart and body aching for him. It was selfish, so selfish, to want him, but she did. She wanted him completely, but the chance he was even remotely hers was fading. She was a liar, and he was on the precipice of discovery.

Henry's eyes followed Brandon, like a cat taunted with a feather. Genevieve leaned against the wall close to the door, as though she might bolt at any moment.

After what seemed an age Brandon stopped pacing. He threw a log onto the fire, and rested his hands on the mantle. "An innocent woman will die unless we do something."

"Something?" Henry inhaled deeply and released a chuckle. "Well you've surpassed yourself with that plan."

"Oh, by the Goddess, shut up Henry!" The outburst

plunged the room into silence. Brandon's face reddened as he collected himself.

Despite her nerves, Natalie had to force down a smile as the young champion's expression grew stony.

Brandon cleared his throat. "Nat, you've the best knowledge of this area. Are there any other nobles nearby who might help?"

She shook her head slowly as dread knotted her stomach. "No. Lady Blackmere isn't particularly cared for among the nobles."

"Why?" Henry frowned.

"She's not the most social person."

A deep sigh sunk Henry's chest. "So, she's not particularly well loved, and she's no good at her job. No wonder the bandits targeted her castle. By the Goddess, I hope at least her looks are worthwhile."

Tears pricked in Natalie's eyes as she pressed her tongue against the back of her teeth. Frustration, fear and guilt swelled inside her.

"Just stop!" she snapped.

Her lip quivered as the champions turned to look at her, their questioning stares burning against her, flushing her face red.

She took a deep breath and tried to steady her voice. "Stop, please."

"Nat?" Brandon's eyes were heavy with worry.

Natalie's ears burned as the world crumbled around her. She felt distant, detached from her body as though she was watching herself from the rafters. Heat pulsed at her temples, along her jawline and throat. "I need to tell you something." Her eyes flickered to Brandon, just long enough to see the concern etched in the line between his eyebrows. "Especially you."

"Nat?"

She sucked on her lower lip and wrung her hands together. "I should have told you in the beginning."

She took a deep breath and braced herself, as though preparing to dive into Blackmere's ice cold waters. "The woman in the castle, the prisoner, isn't Lady Blackmere. I am."

Brandon's breath left him in a strained huff. Genevieve stared blankly, and Henry chuckled to himself as he pressed his fist to his forehead and turned away.

Tears welled in Natalie's eyes. "I know. I should have told you right away, but I was afraid."

"Why?" Genevieve mumbled.

"Because it's my fault the castle was taken. I sent away the guards that night. I was told there were bandits on the roads, and I thought it best the issue be resolved quickly. I sent every guard I had to deal with them."

"Foolish," the woman spat.

Natalie's tongue felt dry and thick in her mouth as she nodded slowly and tried not to cry. She felt as she had done so many times as a child, owning up to broken windows, torn pages, crying friends. She stared straight ahead, avoiding the eyes of her jury.

"Wait," Brandon rubbed his forehead as though he could ease the information into his mind. "But you said you were a barmaid even before the bandits attacked."

"I wanted to meet you as a person, not a title."

He lowered his head and his brow grew heavy. "But you kept up the charade."

"I was afraid you would know I left the castle defenseless. And then, when you decided you would try to save Lady Blackmere, I did not want to tell you the truth and risk you leaving her behind."

"I would never." The horror on Brandon's face wounded her.

"So, who is their prisoner?" Henry asked.

"Jenny. She's my friend, she worked at the tavern." She battled with the lump in her throat. "Please help her."

Genevieve scoffed and turned her back as she ran her hands over her face.

Natalie searched Brandon's face, desperate for something, anything. It was as if he was carved from stone, emotionless, numb, eyes distant and weary. It was only the twitch of his throat which betrayed his stillness.

"Somebody… please say *something*," Natalie begged.

"What is there to say?" Henry sunk to sit on the staircase, and rested his chin on his fist. "It was all for nothing."

Brandon's expression darkened. He turned away, staring into the blackness beyond the windows. "This doesn't change anything."

"It changes *everything*," Henry snapped.

The door creaked as Genevieve stormed outside, and an icy blast of the air wound its way through Natalie's veins.

Brandon shook his head. "We're still saving the woman in the castle, regardless of whether their prisoner is noble or not, or I'll see your titles stripped."

"My titles?" Henry scoffed. "You wouldn't dare."

"I've done worse for far less."

"You still think you hold any influence in the Guild?"

"Are you willing to risk it?"

The young champion huffed and ran his hand through his hair.

"Now, if you please, Henry," Brandon muttered. He jutted his chin towards the door. "I need to speak to Nat, alone. See that Viv's alright."

Henry gave a sigh and pulled himself to his feet. "Fine." He fixed his sword and scabbard to his hip and fastened the clasp of his cape at his throat. "Don't leave us out there all night. It's bloody cold."

The moments following the click of the door dragged forever. The stillness in the cottage made her muscles twitch and her breath snag on her ribs as she searched for the right words to say. Brandon was unreadable, still and stoic, watching the flames in the hearth as they licked at the air.

"Brandon?" His name escaped her lips, a strained plea, a desperate sigh. "Please look at me."

He did, turning his deep and sorrowful gaze to her. "What do I call you?" He thought on it a moment before forcing a bitter laugh. "I suppose it is my lady after all."

"Call me Nat. I'm still the same person I ever was."

She waited for his reply, like waiting for rain after a drought. The cut beneath his eye had stopped bleeding, but the skin around it was red and sore. His shoulders were bloodstained, and covered in mud and bits of leaves.

She stepped towards him and picked a brown shred of dried leaf from his hair. "Please forgive me."

His eyes raked across her face. "It's less than a week since we met, and there are so many things we don't yet know about each other."

"We can learn them."

He held out his hand towards her, palm upwards and inviting. "Brandon," he greeted her. "No family name. Nothing so grand."

Her fingers trembled as she placed her fingers across his. "Lady Natalie Blackmere. Nat, please."

He raised her hand to his lips, and placed a gentle kiss on her knuckle. "I'm glad to finally meet you, though I wouldn't say it's a pleasure."

Tears welled in her eyes, and her throat clenched. "Everything is falling apart."

"You made a mistake, Nat. The Goddess knows I've made many of my own throughout the years. But you are not one of them."

"You're being too kind. I... I've ruined everything. I've made so many mistakes."

"Then let's work to fix them."

Her heart lifted as he once more took her hand and pressed her knuckles to his lips, letting his kiss linger a little longer than a simple greeting. Warm breath tickled against her skin.

"I'll admit, I was confused when Lady Blackmere didn't come to speak with us after the Tourney," he smiled. "She... *you*... sent letters for years and then, nothing."

"I was afraid if you met me as a noble you would be formal and guarded. I should've told you sooner, but you were so angry at Lady Blackmere. At me."

He lowered his head and tightened his grip on her hand, "And for that, I'm truly sorry. I needed someone to blame for what happened. I needed to be angry. It was easier than admitting I felt helpless."

She wrapped her arms around his shoulders and buried

her face against his chest. "I'm sorry. I lacked the courage to tell you. I should have trusted you."

He rested against her, slumping forward onto her as though the admission had sapped away some of his strength. Deep within his cavernous chest, his breath shuddered.

She staggered a little beneath his weight, but held tightly to him. "We can do this, Brandon. We'll help Jenny, and we'll make them pay for what they took from you."

"But what can we do?"

"I don't know. I don't care about the castle, let them have it, but I have to help Jenny. If it weren't for me, she wouldn't be in this mess. None of you would be."

Brandon took a deep breath and straightened his back. "Nat, getting pulled into this mess with you is the best thing that's happened to me in a long time."

"Oh," she gave a breathless chuckle against his shoulder. "That's actually tragic."

He returned her laugh and tightened his hold around her. "In the few days we've been together, I've been happier than I have been in a long time."

Nestling her face against his neck she felt safe. He shielded her against all that was wrong with the world. His hand skimmed her back, simultaneously soothing her and spurring the urge to feel his hands on her bare skin.

He turned slightly, breath hitching as he pressed his cheek to hers. "May I kiss you now?" he whispered.

A wave of excitement surged inside Natalie as she gazed into his eyes.

She inched her face towards him, until their lips were agonizingly close. The air between them pulsed with heat and need. His breath shook as their noses grazed, and they savored the tension, the desire.

Natalie made a soft desperate moan as he leaned closer, pressing her chest to his. He lifted her chin with a crooked finger and grazed his lips against hers, a soft, tender kiss, which deepened until she felt her heart would explode.

Kissing him was like cartwheeling down a mountain-side. Once she began there was no way to stop. She felt herself spinning, turning, tumbling down, giddy with the thrill of it; there was only him, his lips, and the rest of the world was insignificant. He was unbreakable strength and unfathomable softness; a man molded of iron and wool.

The room continued to spin even after their lips parted. He held her tight, one arm around her, the other, cradling her cheek as she leaned into his touch.

"That was…" she whispered as she looked into his eyes. Her words disappeared beneath the thrum of her heart.

"Aye," he breathed. His throat bobbed as he swallowed hard. "But we left our friends outside, and we still have a plan to make."

She sighed as reality crashed around them, tearing them apart and allowing cool air to flow between them. Brandon stood and strode over to the door, casting a longing glance over to her as the cold night air blasted into the cottage.

The two champions trudged in, blowing warm air onto their fingers and casting accusatory glances at Natalie. Her heart sunk as Henry raked his pale blue eyes across her, his lip curled into a snarl. She met his stare, and hoped she looked unperturbed.

"So," Henry flung Brandon's soggy tunic towards him and turned to warm his hands by the fire. "What's the verdict? I take it you've forgiven her on behalf of us all?"

"There's nothing to forgive." Brandon hung his tunic on the bannister and placed his hand on Natalie's shoulder. A shiver coursed through her as he stroked the back of her neck with his thumb. Despite it all, her heart fluttered at the touch. "She was afraid, understandably so. She didn't know us, and she didn't know if she could trust us."

"But we don't know her." Genevieve frowned. "She lied to us. Why should we trust her now?"

"I'm still me." Natalie stood and was grateful for the billowing skirt which hid the tremble in her knees. "I just have a different job. I'm not a barmaid. I still need your help, and I'm still willing to fight beside you."

Henry sighed and ran his hand across the coarse stubble on his chiseled jaw. Her muscles clenched as his eyes trailed across her body. "And what will you give us in exchange for the risk? Hmm?"

"I'm not going to fight for a reward," Genevieve said firmly. "I'm fighting to save an innocent woman's life."

"Aye," Brandon said. His hand trailed down Natalie's back, resting on the curve at the base of her spine. "Henry, the odds are stacked against us, but without you we've next to no chance."

"Ah, is that you admitting I'm better than you?"

Brandon took a deep, slow breath and bowed his head. "Aye."

"How delightful." Henry chuckled and shook his head. "I shall remember this day forever. But their prisoner is no one. What is she? A barmaid? A serving girl? We're tourney champions. We're the most celebrated warriors in all of Aldland. Why should we risk our lives and everything we've worked for the sake of some tavern wench?" Natalie's throat tightened as Henry looked at her. "What are you willing to pay?"

Her heart trembled beneath Henry's cold stare. Her mother would scold her if she was there; pathetic, irresponsible, and admitting to weakness. "I have no money."

Henry raised his face to the rafters and sighed. "Goddess preserve me."

"Perhaps I could find some? Or I could find a way to give you land? A title? I could speak to my parents and—"

Her jaw snapped shut as Henry held up a hand. "A title will do."

Brandon shifted his weight in the corner of her eye. Her mind raced. Henry was the best fighter among them. Despite his misgivings, she could not deny his was necessary to their success. "Yes. I could see you knighted?"

He shook his head and stepped towards her. "Not a knighthood. A title."

What choice did she have? "Very well. What title do you wish?"

He fixed her with a piercing glare, one which burned through her nerve and turned her lungs to husks. "Lord Blackmere."

His words snatched the breath from her lungs. Brandon stepped towards the young champion. "Come on now, Henry. You can't help her take back her home and then take it away from her. That's cold, even for you."

"You think so poorly of me," Henry lamented. A smile slithered across his face. "I'm not taking her home from her. She'd be living there too, as my wife."

CHAPTER TWENTY-TWO

NATALIE'S THROAT tightened around a breathless laugh as Henry's eyes burned into her. "You can't be serious?"

His teeth bared for a moment before he spoke. "Believe me, it will be a marriage of convenience and nothing more. I cannot produce an heir, so securing a lineage is of no interest to me.

"But—"

"If you wish, you can keep a lover." His gaze fell to Brandon as he pressed his tongue against the side of his cheek to stifle a chuckle. "I intend to keep many."

His words rang through her mind, molding together into a whining drone.

Her vision tilted and blurred as she watched Brandon. Part of her expected him to lash out, to become the version of himself which had once dominated the arena; brutal, and indomitable. But he merely stood, eyes downcast and lips pressed together.

It was not his decision to make, nor was it Genevieve's, who stood with her hands buried in her hair, with a twisted look of disgust and disbelief on her face.

The decision was Natalie's.

The fate of Blackmere hinged on her answer.

Lives could be lost if she refused.

She sat on the stairs, resting her elbows on her thighs as she stared ahead into an unfocused haze. The fire crackled behind Henry, casting a dark orange outline around his figure. For the first time since the Tourney, his alias, The Dragon, suited him.

"Your answer?" he pressed.

"Give her a moment." Brandon's voice was a beacon in the chaos of her thoughts.

"You'll be out of the Guild if you marry," Genevieve snapped.

"Personally, I think it best to retire at the top of my game," Henry sneered, casting a glance over at Brandon. "Rather than allowing myself to grow old and losing my dignity altogether."

Natalie's eyes snapped to the Dragon, as though she could blast him out of the cottage with a look. Again, Brandon did not react to the insult. He carried the burden of it on his broad shoulders, but in his silence, there was defiance.

Henry scoffed and turned away, frustrated that his prey had not taken the bait.

Thoughts tumbled around Natalie's mind. She despised him, but if the marriage was merely one of convenience, it might not be entirely hateful. He would be her husband only in name and title, and her parents would not be dissatisfied by the match. Henry was handsome, and what he lacked in lineage he made up for in infamy. It was a small price to pay to save Blackmere, to save Jenny.

She would no longer have to run Blackmere alone.

But the thought of seeing him every day, of travelling with him, keeping up the charade of their marriage, and yet more lies, churned like sour milk in her throat.

"Nat," Brandon whispered as he came towards her. He knelt on the stairs below her, his kind eyes searching her face. His lips moved silently, as thoughts were born and died on his tongue.

She ached with the longing to be alone with him.

He wrapped his calloused fingers around her hand and brought her palm to his chest. The steady thump of his heart beat against her fingers. "Sleep on it."

She sniffed back the urge to cry, to flee. The ache turned to dread as she raised her eyes to meet Henry's. "May I give you my answer tomorrow?"

The Dragon exhaled through his nostrils. A muscle leapt in his cheek as he clenched his jaw. "If you must. But if I have no answer by noon, I'm leaving."

Genevieve made a small sound of disgust and scuffed her boot along the floorboards.

"Very well," Natalie whispered.

The air in the cottage remained tense, and Natalie could bear it no longer. She pulled herself to her feet and climbed the small wooden staircase. The slow, heavy thump of Brandon's footsteps at her back reassured her. As she reached the upper level, she turned to face him, longing to fall into his arms.

"Get some sleep," Brandon said.

He was still standing halfway up the stairs, pulling the damp woolen tunic over his head. The material clung to him, and Natalie could not help but let her eyes wander across his chest. He smiled and reached out to take Natalie's hand. His voice was just a whisper as he assured her, "All will be well."

No sound emerged from her throat, but her lips formed the word, "How?"

He lifted his hand, and reached out towards her face. She bowed to meet his caress, and his eyes traced her features as though committing every part of her to memory. "The sun will rise tomorrow. It always does. Sometimes you can't see it for the clouds, but it's always there."

A smile tugged the corners of her lips as she leaned into

his touch.

There was a soft rustling sound as Henry lay on the mattress below. He stared up at the ceiling, as a soft patter of rain began on the rooftop.

The wind blew the rain against the windows, and etched concern across Brandon's brow. "We've no shelter for the horses."

"They're fine," Henry snapped as he rested his hands on his stomach.

"You could sleep out there with them. See how fine they are?" Genevieve growled as she slid down the wall to sit on the floor.

Natalie's cheek grew cold as Brandon withdrew his hand and turned. "Does anyone object if I bring them inside?"

"It can't smell any worse in here," Henry sighed.

Natalie straightened her back and brushed off her skirt. The sudden movement left her lightheaded. "Do you need help?"

"No, stay inside. There's no point you getting cold and wet My la—Nat. My Nat."

The blush returned to her cheeks. Deep down, she was secretly grateful she did not have to go out. "Don't be long."

Turning her back to the stair, her heart leapt as he took her hand.

He brushed it with his lips. "I'll be back soon. I swear it."

As he pressed a lingering kiss to her knuckles, the heat of his breath fluttered against her skin, stoking the fire in her stomach. With a gentle smile he released her hand, turned and climbed down the stairs.

"Don't let the heat out!" Henry called.

Natalie watched after Brandon from the top of the stairs. He twisted his head as if to glance over his shoulder towards her, thought better of it, and opened the door to the bitter wind and rain.

As the door slammed shut, she turned to inspect the dusty floorboards. Splintered wooden shards were still dotted around the bare bed frame. She could not suppress her smile as she remembered Brandon tearing the lid from the chest.

She pressed her fingertips to the back of her hand as though she could somehow capture the sensation of his lips.

Whatever happened, she had him, and no one could take the moments they stole.

Finding a relatively clear spot, she lay down against the cold wooden boards and listened as the door creaked open. Hoofs clattered below, and Brandon's soft assurances to the horses drew a smile from her. With the weight of her deceit lifted from her shoulders, she felt a wall between them crumble. He knew her, and she knew him.

Brandon the Bear, strong and brave and fair.

The door clicked closed, and she waited to hear his footsteps on the stairs. Hooves clipped on the floorboards as the horses explored their new surroundings, accompanied by the bubbling whoosh of their breath.

There was no sound from Brandon.

She peered over the ledge.

Two horses stood by the fire twitching their ears, one of them Genevieve's, the other Henry's. Big Lad was still outside.

Settling back down and staring at the ceiling, she reasoned Brandon must have gone back out to bring in his own gargantuan mount.

The soft, crackling sound of the fire, and the gentle tap of rain on the roof lulled her. The air in the busy cottage grew warm with the heat of so many bodies, and Natalie's eyes grew heavy. She fought back sleep as best she could, but it was not long before she was defeated.

CHAPTER TWENTY-THREE

HENRY'S LAUGHTER jolted her awake. The realization she was alone on the floor plunged her into consciousness. She bolted upright. Dust clung to her clothing, and the imprint of her sleeping body lay dark on the floorboards. There was no sign Brandon had slept beside her.

She peered over the edge to see Henry sitting alone on the mattress, poking at the fireplace with the tip of his sword and chuckling to himself. Brandon, Genevieve and the horses were nowhere to be seen.

Sunlight shone through the windows, casting squares of yellow light on the floorboards below, and yet the cold air in the cottage raised the hairs on her arms and made her shiver.

At the sound of Natalie pulling herself to her feet, Henry twisted towards her. He smirked then shook his head as he returned his attention to the fire.

"Where are they?" Natalie asked as she descended the stairs. She held onto the rail as she stepped down, feeling the coarse grain of the wooden beam beneath her fingers.

"Depends who you mean by *they*?"

She curled her fingers into fists and breathed through her frustration. "Where's Brandon?"

"Gone."

The word rattled around the cottage, and struck against her chest like a battering ram. "Gone?"

"Yes." Henry spat as he pulled himself to his feet. "He's gone. He went outside to bring in the horses last night and then took off on his own. We haven't seen him since."

Icy fear pressed against the sides of Natalie's face as her vision tilted. He was lying, he had to be. "He's gone?"

"Oh, by the Goddess. Yes." He stood and sneered in her face. "Brandon gone. Brandon not here. Do you understand? No wonder Blackmere's so keen on its sheep, if their lady is this mutton-headed."

She flinched as his breath blew against her eyes, though she kept her head high and her expression neutral.

"Are. You. Com. Pre. Hen. Ding?" He tapped his finger against her forehead with each syllable.

Natalie clenched her jaw as she suppressed the urge to fight back. She was coming to understand Henry lived to provoke, but she would not give him the satisfaction.

"Clearly you weren't worth sticking around for." He turned his back on her, and strode back towards the fire, snatching his boots up from the floor.

Her heart leapt at the sound of clattering hooves. She hurried to the door, yanked it open and let the sunlight pour into the cottage.

Hope dwindled as Genevieve shook her head, approaching the cottage on horseback.

"No sign." She dismounted and shrugged her shoulders. "I looked for him, but nothing."

Natalie's mind clambered through ideas. "Perhaps he went to hunt?"

"No. He's been gone all night, his horse too."

"Maybe…" Natalie searched the forest floor, as though some clue would reveal itself to her. She shook her head in desperation. "He wouldn't just leave."

Henry's footsteps behind her, sent dread creeping through her stomach. "Oh, you know him, do you? After, what? Four days?" He pushed by her and stepped outside, his boots crunching in the dry leaves. "I know Brandon. I've travelled with him for years, we both have, haven't we Viv?"

Genevieve lowered her head and moistened her lips with her tongue. "Yes."

Henry placed his hands on his hips and gave a single

sharp nod. "Believe me Natalie, you are not the first woman he's run away from. I'd be shocked if you were in the first hundred."

"No." Natalie's protest choked her. She despised the weakness in her voice. "He was coming back."

Henry's face twisted into a mask of pity. "I've heard that before, too many times, by women far prettier than you. What did you expect from a man who has songs written about the size of his cock?"

Genevieve recoiled at his words and busied herself with some task involving her horse's saddle.

"Tell me I'm wrong?" Henry laughed.

Natalie looked to the other woman, silently pleading with her to vouch for Brandon's character. With every passing moment her stomach lurched, and her heart grew heavy.

After a slow breath the warrior shrugged her shoulders.

Tears pricked at Natalie's eyes as she scanned the forest, more to avoid Henry's smirk than with any hope of seeing Brandon.

The sun was shining, and warm rays dappled the forest floor. Birds sang in the yellow-leaved trees as though nothing in the world was out of place.

But it was. Brandon was gone.

It was all wrong.

"So," Henry snapped, bringing her focus back to him.

"You've had plenty of time to think on what should've been an easy decision. What say you?" He straightened his posture and chuckled. "Will you marry me, Lady Blackmere?"

"No." The word burst from her lips. She stood firm and tilted her chin, adopting the indomitable stature she had learned from her mother. Her answer hung in the air around the cottage as Henry's throat reddened.

Air hissed from his nostrils as he shook his head. He took a step towards her, clenching his teeth as he snarled. "You are a fool."

"She gave you her answer." Genevieve's voice was low and calm, but the hand on his shoulder was crowned with bloodless knuckles; four snow-capped peaks, capable of crushing the life from him.

Natalie held her breath as he seethed. Heat crept along her spine.

"Mark my words, there will be blood on your hands." His finger shook as he waved it in her face. With a scoff he turned on his heel and strode over to his horse.

"Where are you going?" Genevieve barked.

"Away," Henry groaned as he pulled himself up into the saddle. "There's nothing for me here. Enjoy destitution, Lady Blackmere. The life of a wench suits you far better than nobility." He dug his heels into his horse's flank and spurred it into a trot.

Natalie's breath escaped her in ragged, panicked gasps as he rode away and disappeared among the dense cover of the trees. She closed her eyes and inhaled until her lungs were filled to bursting. As she exhaled, she heard the creak and shuffle of Genevieve's saddle as she pulled herself onto her mount.

Natalie's eyes sprang open. "You're leaving too?"

Genevieve took up her horse's reins and cleared her throat. "I know where Brandon is. You do too."

Natalie frowned at her words. "He could be anywhere. A horse like Big Lad could travel miles and miles in a single night." But even as she dismissed Genevieve's statement, the answer came to her. "Wait. No. You think so?"

"I'm certain." Genevieve said firmly. "I've known the Bear for ten years. I know what kind of man he is. He went to Blackmere."

Natalie muttered a curse beneath her breath. She knew Genevieve was right, she had to be. Though the thought of him walking into the hands of their enemies, was somehow infinitely worse than the thought of him leaving. She had to help. "What do we do?"

"Well, I'm going to Blackmere. The big fool is probably in trouble."

"I'm coming with you."

Natalie darted inside the cottage and found the broken chest tucked beneath the stairs. Only two blades remained. She wrapped a belt around her waist and fumbled with the buckle with trembling fingers. Steadying her nerve, she secured the fastening and slid the blades into the sheaths at her hips.

Her feet pounded the floorboards as she hurried back out, half expecting to have been left behind.

Genevieve gave her a nod of approval as she turned the horse around. "Hurry. We have to share the horse. It will take a while."

Natalie swallowed as she tried to steady her pounding heart. She cast a glance back at the cottage, feeling like a fledgling about to leave their nest. Brandon was gone, and the cottage was no longer safe and warm.

With a deep breath she stepped out, and closed the door behind her.

CHAPTER TWENTY-FOUR

THE SUN climbed as they picked their way through the woods. Genevieve rode in silence, her eyes scanning the trees as they followed the path of the stream. Natalie's feet ached as she marched, but she forced herself through the pain, until they grew numb and walking came easier.

"I forgive you," Genevieve muttered. The words were so quiet Natalie half thought she had imagined them.

"Thank you."

"You did wrong, but you were afraid. We all were. I was angry at first, because I blamed you for putting her in danger."

"Jenny?"

Genevieve sighed. "We only spoke a few words after the tournament, but she said she would be in the tavern that night after she had spoken to you. I waited but she didn't come. At first, I thought she just didn't want to. Then, after the bandits came, I was afraid she didn't come because she couldn't."

"I think she would have." Natalie's chest tightened as guilt snaked around her. "She spoke of you."

"She did?"

"Aye, as we were swapping clothes, she said she wished she had the courage to talk to you."

Genevieve gave a soft laugh. "I wish I had that courage too."

Natalie glanced over the towering figure of the warrior. Like Brandon, she was a mountain of muscle and physical strength, built upon a soft and gentle heart. She resolved to make sure Jenny got her chance to meet Genevieve, the chance Natalie had taken from them. She would make it right.

"Jenny and Genevieve," Natalie chuckled. "Your names match so well."

"Well my friends call me Viv." Genevieve cleared her throat and sat up straight in her saddle. "Just call me Viv."

Despite her fears, a smile tugged the corners of her lips as she walked, but it soon dropped away. She tried not to think of what might have befallen Brandon, but the image of him suffering, alone, tormented her.

"Nat?"

"Viv?"

"Do you think about what the bandit said last night?"

"Which part?"

"That someone paid him. He said a man paid the bandits to take Blackmere."

Natalie shook her head. She had quite forgotten her interrogation of the bandit. Her confession, Brandon's disappearance, and Henry's proposal had overwhelmed everything else.

Genevieve turned to look at her. "Do you have enemies who might've paid them?"

"Enemies? No, Goddess, I barely know *anyone*. I keep to myself unless I have to."

The Thorn made a soft murmur of contemplation. "Then it's someone who wants your castle. Maybe even a friend."

Natalie frowned as she rifled through the short list of names of her acquaintants. The neighboring lands were far wealthier than Blackmere, and conquest would disrupt centuries of peace. It seemed unlikely.

Thundering hoofbeats roused her from her thoughts. A flash of grey appeared between the trees, and sent her heart leaping into her throat. "Is that Brandon's horse?"

Genevieve clicked her tongue, and spurred her own mount towards the mighty grey horse. As she rode, she called out to him, "Thunder! Thunder! Big Lad!"

The horse slowed and nickered at the sound of her voice. His breath gusted as he brushed his muzzle against that of Genevieve's mount.

For a moment, Natalie hoped Brandon would be close behind his horse, chasing after him after being thrown from the saddle. But her blood turned to ice as she drew closer.

The ground beneath her feet was uneven, covered in branches and twigs which wound around her feet and tried to trip her. She could not look down. She could not tear her eyes from the sight.

The horse's grey coat was streaked with blood.

Genevieve scowled and pulled a bloodied scroll of paper from the saddle. Her eyes scanned the words as Natalie held her breath. The horse was uninjured. The blood was not his.

"Do you read?" Genevieve asked. "They don't teach us at the Guild."

Natalie nodded. Her hands trembled as she took the scroll from Genevieve and unfurled it. She swallowed to clear her throat and read the scribbled words. "We have two prisoners: Lady Blackmere and Brandon, Champion of the Tourney. Both of them will be executed by the end of the week unless the sum of two thousand gold is delivered to Blackmere Castle." She crumpled the note between her hands and seethed as burning anger flowed through her veins.

"Bastards." Genevieve spat.

"Two thousand! My own parents wouldn't pay that for me."

"But they still think Jenny is the Lady?"

"No. The bandit last night said she wasn't. They know. They're just doing this to scare people. He said they were making a show of it." Her eyes traced the streaks of blood across the horse's flank. "Oh Goddess. Do you think they're still alive? What if the bandits are lying?"

Genevieve pressed her lips together and sniffed. The color had drained from her cheeks. "We have to hurry."

Natalie buried her fingers in the horse's black mane and silently prayed for Brandon and Jenny's safety. She released a shuddering breath and set her jaw. "Let's go."

"Take Big Lad." Genevieve urged her own mount on and headed back towards the stream.

Natalie climbed onto the mighty beast, unable to tear her eyes from the bloodstains. With every passing heartbeat her fear distilled, growing sharp and hateful. Gripping the reins with white-knuckled fists, she led Big Lad to the stream. Her heart thumped against her ribs like an iron fist.

They washed the blood from the horse's coat and raced downstream, riding as fast as the terrain would allow, until, as the sun began to descend, the trees grew sparse and the parapets of Blackmere Castle came into view.

Dread crept along Natalie's spine as the grey stone walls beckoned her.

A black flag fluttered from the top of the tower. As the wind rippled through it, she could barely make out a curved white shape in the center of the flag.

"The White Horns," Genevieve muttered as she pulled out her drinking skin. She took a long sip and passed the skin to Natalie. "They drink, they fight, they steal."

Fingers trembling, she tipped the bottle against her lips and savored the cool water. For all she knew, it was the last thing she would ever drink.

Genevieve's eyes burned into her as she wiped her mouth on the back of her hand and handed back the skin. "Are you ready?"

The knot in her stomach tightened at the question, and her hairs bristled in anticipation. She breathed steadily and ran her fingers across the horse's silver coat. Every detail of the world was brought into sharp focus by her fear; the tang of smoke in the air, the distant tap of the cartwright's hammer, the huff of horse's breath. Her pulse beat in her throat like a war drum. This, she imagined, was how it felt to step into the arena.

She steadied her nerves, pressed her lips together and gave Genevieve a determined nod. "Let's go."

CHAPTER TWENTY-FIVE

THEY CIRCLED the town, keeping a safe distance between themselves and the outer walls. There were a few lookouts on the ramparts, and just a couple of bored looking thugs guarding the gates. Natalie's gut recoiled as she realized they were armed with weapons taken from her guards, and clad in their armor.

The bandits sneered as people approached the gate, rifling through their belongings and taking anything which they deemed worth stealing.

Natalie's blood simmered as she weighed them up. She might be able to take one, if she surprised him. Genevieve could take the other without breaking a sweat. Then the bandits guarding the wall would join in the fray, or perhaps sound the alarm. They would be overwhelmed in moments.

"The bastards."

"We'll make them pay," Genevieve assured her, though her own voice wavered. "We need to think this through."

They wandered down to the lakeside, out of sight of the gate, to allow the horses to drink. Genevieve slid down from her saddle and beckoned Natalie do the same. She had quite forgotten how tall Big Lad was until it was time for her to dismount. Her feet dangled above the ground as she pointed her toes, feeling as though she dangled over an abyss. Finally, Genevieve steadied her beneath the under-arms and let her carefully onto the ground.

Black waters lapped the pebbled shore, reaching out towards Natalie's boots, as though they meant to drag her in.

Genevieve turned to her. "How much room do you have in your skirt?

"In my skirt?" Natalie frowned at the woman and flapped the fabric at her thighs. "Why?"

"They're letting people through the gate. There's no point picking a fight we can't win. Hide the weapons, and we'll pass through like everyone else."

Genevieve pulled the two throwing axes from her belt and held them out towards Natalie.

Hiding behind the horses, she sliced strips from her chemise and strapped the weapons to her thighs. She refastened her belt around her hips beneath the fabric, securing the daggers at her waist. Satisfied with their concealment, she stood and straightened out her skirt.

"It's going to be hard to get back on the horse. I'll

walk." Natalie took a tentative step forward. The axes' handles pressed against her, from her thighs, stopping just shy of her knees. Her gait was stiff, but the discomfort was manageable. She took the grey horse by the reins and walked beside him.

Genevieve chuckled behind her as she led her own horse. "You look like you're desperate for the privy."

"Aye, well hopefully it'll mean they'll let us go through faster." Natalie sucked on the insides of her cheeks to keep from laughing as she made her way towards the gate. Fear made her giddy as one of the bandits, nudged his companion, alerting him to the approaching woman.

"Ladies." The first man grinned, flashing his teeth. A long black braid hung over his shoulder. "Where're you off to then?"

Natalie's temples burned as his gaze raked across her. "Pub."

The second man's shoulders shook as he chuckled and fidgeted with the string of an empty, threadbare brown coin purse.

"That's a big horse," the first man smirked.

"Aye."

"We saw a big horse like that last night, didn't we?"

A slow trickle of icy dread crept down Natalie's spine. She silently cursed herself for not thinking they might recognize such a massive steed. "Oh… did you?"

"I did," the bandit sneered. "Exactly like that one."

Genevieve took a step forward, drawing the man's attention from Natalie. She patted her mount on the neck. "Good thing we found him then. He was running down the road in an awful state."

The bandit raised his eyebrows and pressed his tongue through a gap where his front teeth should have been.

"He's mine," the second bandit growled, stepping forward. "He must've gotten out of the stable last night."

The unabashed lie roiled Natalie. She clenched her jaw as she tightened her hold on Big Lad's rein.

"Well, we're glad we found his owner," Genevieve smiled, bowing her head. She glanced at Natalie from the corner of her eye as a muscle in her cheek leapt.

Natalie's arm felt as though it was forged of iron as she handed the reins over to the man. She released him, her mind uttering curses to the bandits, and promises of rescue to the horse.

The bandit's wide grin split his face as he tugged on the reins. "Come on."

As Big Lad's hooves clattered along the road towards the tavern stables, the first bandit smirked and spat on the ground. "Bet you thought you'd keep him for yourselves, didn't you?"

He chuckled as he swiped his arm across to slap Big Lad on his backside. The mighty horse kicked back, his hoof slamming into the bandit's ribs.

The bandit crumpled to the floor gasping and wheezing. "He's killed me! Your bastard horse has killed me!"

The remaining man staggered backwards with his arms spread wide to block Big Lad's attempts to escape as his companion retched onto the cobbles.

Natalie and Genevieve exchanged glances, before calmly walking through the gate.

The sight of her town in such disarray gutted her. Windows were boarded up, and once busy Market Street was lifeless. The gutters were blocked with debris, washed into piles by the rain. Broken toys, leaves, moldy food and tattered clothing littered the cobbles.

Natalie's eyes welled with tears as she took it all in, though she dared not speak, nor let her eyes linger. The guards on the walls had turned their attention to the commotion at the gate, and the way the injured man was screaming, it would not be long before they came down to investigate.

Genevieve's horse snorted and twisted her head towards Big Lad.

"This way," Natalie whispered, guiding Genevieve towards the stable. Without the horse they would be less conspicuous.

Her nose stung as they entered the stable, and the sharp stench of urine brought tears to her eyes. The long walkway, lined by stable doors, was empty. Somewhere deep inside the row of stalls, a shovel scraped against stone.

"Hello there?" Natalie called.

The shoveling stopped, and the soft shuffle of feet on straw drew closer. A figure shambled into view; bent over, frail and gasping for breath as they drew closer. Beneath the dirt and gloom it was hard to make out the person's features until they were at arm's length. Natalie realized with a start, the figure was an elderly man, one she knew all too well.

"Chamberlain?"

His grey eyes scoured her features, widening in surprise. "My lady? Lady Blackmere?"

Genevieve cringed and shushed the old man. "Don't let them hear you say that."

"Forgive me." His weary eyes turned glossy. He bowed his head as though it would make him harder to hear. "I thought you were dead."

Natalie's heart broke for the man as tears burned in her eyes. She took his hand in hers, and gently held his trembling fingers. His skin was like warm wax paper beneath her touch, and was littered with cuts and scratches.

"What are you doing here, Chamberlain? What's happening?"

The man's mouth opened and closed a few times, as though struggling to decide on where to begin. "My lady, the castle has been taken. They've taken some poor girl prisoner and are telling everyone she's Lady Blackmere."

"I know."

"They put me here to work. I've been trying to straighten it all out but there's just so much to do."

Natalie's chest ached as she wrapped her arms around him. "Oh, please forgive me."

His shuddered against her as his breath escaped him in a ragged gasp. "One of the champions came here last night. He fought bravely but there were too many of the wretches. They swarmed him. Even with so many of their number leaving, there are too many men, and they are well armed. Your guards never returned, and your people are too afraid to leave their homes." His words became choked as a sob broke him down. "We thought you dead."

Natalie's eyes became unfocussed as her mind tried to take everything in, to solve each problem. Her chest grew tight, burning as she unconsciously held her breath. The image of Brandon, swarmed like a baited bear, haunted her. She closed her eyes and prayed for his safety.

"We'll stop them." Genevieve's voice snapped her back to reality. She was not sure if the statement was meant for the chamberlain, for Genevieve's own benefit, or for herself.

Natalie released the man from her embrace and gave him a reassuring nod. "We need a meeting place. Do the bandits use the tavern?"

"Not since they dried it out." The chamberlain wiped his eyes on his filthy cuff and held out his hand to take the horse's reins from Genevieve.

Natalie stepped aside to let the horse pass. "Perfect. Get the word out to as many of the townspeople as you can. Get them to meet tonight in the tavern."

"And what will we do?" The chamberlain led the horse to a clean stall and loosened the buckle on his bridle with stiff, shaking fingers. "There are too many of them, my lady. Your townspeople aren't warriors."

"I know, and I'm sorry I must ask this of them. But this is our home. No one else is coming to save us, so we have to do it ourselves. All I ask, is that you fight the guards at the Northgate and on the walls. There were fifteen of them when we rode around the perimeter, plus two at each gate."

"Nineteen?" The chamberlain mused as he slipped the bridle off the horse's nose and opened a sack of grain. Soft munching sounds filled the stable. "Perhaps we can do it. I'll try to rally them all. What do we use for weapons?"

"Anything." Genevieve gripped his shoulder and stared into his eyes. "Anything you can swing, anything sharp. Use broken glass from the windows if you have to."

The chamberlain scratched his eyebrow with his bony finger. "And what of the bandits in the castle?"

"I'll deal with them from the inside," Natalie said. Her firm tone was at odds with the skittering rhythm of her heart.

"You?" Genevieve turned to her and chuckled. Her eyes raked across Natalie's face. "Have you lost your mind?"

The acrid air in the stable was too much. Natalie's head grew light and her chest ached from her reluctance to breathe in the foul stench. She turned and made her way towards the door, casting a look back at the chamberlain. "I don't ask that the people fight for me. I ask that they fight for their homes."

"Very good, my lady."

Natalie's feet skipped across the filthy cobblestones as she stepped outside. She turned her eyes to the sky and breathed the fresh air. Cold raindrops spattered her cheeks, and the wind fluttered the skirts around her ankles.

"What are you going to do?" Genevieve dug her fingers into Natalie's arm, as though she feared she would take flight.

"I'm going to give them what they want." Natalie smiled, though inside her heart was turning cartwheels. "I'm going to give them Lady Blackmere."

CHAPTER TWENTY-SIX

"THIS PLAN is ridiculous." Genevieve hooked the axe heads over her own belt as she cast her eyes around the tavern. The tables and chairs had been set upright since the last time they were there, but now crude ash drawings littered the walls, and empty bottles lay discarded on every available surface.

Natalie straightened her hair and nodded in agreement. "It's the best we have."

"How will we prove to the bandits who you are?"

A chuckle escaped her lips. "Who in their right mind would pretend?"

Genevieve conceded the point with an upwards flicker of her eyebrows.

Though Natalie put on a brave face, the sight of the mighty warrior, the Thorn of The Rose, so rattled sent her own panic cantering through her veins. It was a foolish plan, she knew, doomed and reckless. But she had to try. She had to. Jenny needed her. Brandon needed her.

Her people needed her.

A sharp spike of fear struck her heart as the image of Brandon, overwhelmed by bandits, haunted her. Her mind reached, imagining the source of the blood painted on his horse's coat. "Goddess, preserve him. I hope he's not suffering."

"You love him."

The statement caught her off guard. She turned, eyes wide, to see the warrior smiling. "I barely know him."

"Yet you're walking into a wolves' den to save him."

Her cheeks burned as she busied herself with the laces on her dress. Frustratingly, the lacing was already perfect, and the bow neatly tied. She tugged on it until it was skewed, then huffed and set to work retying it.

"People in love do ridiculous things, especially when the person they care for is in danger. That's why you're doing this stupid thing, and why he rode off to take back your castle like a knight in a fairytale. You may barely know each other, but you're both fools in love."

"It's too soon to say."

"The Guild won't be happy. If he's to remain a champion, you'll have to keep it from them."

"That's for Brandon to decide." Natalie's pulse quickened. "Will you tell them?"

Genevieve lowered her eyes. "No. The Bear is a good man, and I don't want to see him forced to choose between the Guild and you. He seems happy, and he deserves to be. Just please be careful."

"I will." The heat crept to Natalie's ears. The corner of her lips flickered into a smile, before fear gripped her once more. "How do I look?"

"Like a rat dragged backwards through a bush."

Natalie hitched her skirts and marched towards the door. "Flatterer."

* * *

The rain fell hard as they climbed the slope towards the castle. Natalie's heart galloped in her throat, and her breaths were shallow and unsatisfying. With every step she took towards the castle gate, the urge to flee for her life grew. Genevieve's shallow breaths shuddered beside her ear. The axe blade at her neck pressed against her tender flesh.

"Am I hurting you?" Genevieve whispered.

"It's fine. It needs to look real."

Doubt clawed at her heels, trying to drag her back down the hill, back to the safety of the woods. Still, they marched on.

She thought of the night she and Brandon drank honeyed wine, and held each other by the fire. She thought of the silvery scars running across his skin, of the stories he had yet to tell her, and the chapters they might write together. His lessons ran through her mind; boldness was her greatest weapon.

She stopped, planting her feet on the wet cobblestones and hissed, "Shove me."

"Hurry it along," Genevieve snapped, shoving against Natalie's back.

The axe bit into Natalie's throat, stinging as a thin trickle of blood slid down her neck.

A man stood huddled in the castle's gateway, sheltering from the rain. He lifted his head as they approached. Against the murky grey of the stones, the rain, and the clouds, his shock of orange hair stood out like a beacon.

"What do you want?" he called. "Walden hasn't told me anything about wenches."

"I need to speak with him." Genevieve called. "This is Lady Natalie Blackmere, and this is her castle. I'm here to bargain for the life of the woman your boss holds as his prisoner."

There was no going back.

The redhead's eyes widened as he stammered. "You're… what? What are you going on about?"

"Tell your boss I have brought him the true Lady Blackmere."

The redhead's eyes creased as he barked out a laugh. "We already have Lady Blackmere, you stupid cow."

The axe pressed harder against Natalie's throat, drawing a sharp gasp. Genevieve stiffened and shifted her weight. "We both know that's not true. Get your boss or I'll kill Lady Blackmere, and throw her body over the walls so he can see for himself."

Natalie winced as Genevieve's hold on her wrist tightened and the man scurried through the gate. Hot, ragged breaths blew against her ear.

"This'd better work," Genevieve whispered.

Raindrops streaked from the clouds, bouncing on the cobbles, and soaking the women to the bone as they waited. Cold air nipped at the skin exposed to the axe's edge.

"It will." Natalie's throat stung as she spoke. Her breaths shook as she stared at the gate. After an eternity, a heavy bolt shifted on the other side, and the redhead appeared. Behind him, another man sauntered into view. He was young, barely past his twentieth year, with deep brown eyes, cool olive skin, and curly black hair. The sword at his hip gleamed in the silvery afternoon light.

"What have you brought me?" He sighed as he raked his gaze across Natalie and Genevieve. His black leather jerkin creaked as he approached. "A pair of drowned dogs?"

The redhead cackled, though the uncertainty in his manner made the laugh unconvincing. He pointed to Genevieve. "She claims her prisoner is Lady Blackmere."

"Aye," Genevieve growled by Natalie's ear. "The *real* Lady Blackmere."

The young man's lips curled into a smile. "Interesting."

Natalie wracked her mind, searching for him in her memories, but he was a total stranger, not someone with a vendetta against her or her family. He took a step towards her and reached out, gripping her jaw in an iron grasp. He turned her head to the side and inspected her.

"Are you certain? She looks like a common serving wench to me."

A fire stoked in Natalie's stomach. "Unhand me," she growled, her words muffled by his grip. "Or I swear I will have your hide."

He stepped back, an amused look playing across his features. "Haughty little thing, aren't you?"

Her jaw ached as he released his hold. She raised her voice, and asserted, "I am Lady Natalie Blackmere, and this is *my* castle. You've no right to be here."

The men chuckled and shook their heads. "Hear that? We'd better go."

Holding onto her breath, she watched them as they mocked her, and prayed they believed her.

"Very well, friend," the young man smiled to Genevieve. "My name is Walden. Recently, Lord Walden Blackmere. This is my castle, and it's my pleasure to meet you. Let's talk business."

"I want the woman you have in there," Genevieve said without hesitation. "Release your prisoner to me and you can take Lady Blackmere."

"That's it?"

"That's it."

"Is she something to you?"

"Yes."

Walden smiled slowly and turned to the redhead. "Go get her."

"Yes boss." The redhead scurried away again, closing the gate behind him.

The air grew heavy with anticipation as Walden watched them. "How did you find her?"

"Hiding." Genevieve kept her tone level, though the axe at Natalie's throat shuddered. "She was hiding in the woods."

"Ah. A few of the guards on the walls saw smoke out there." He turned his dark gaze to Natalie. "Was that you then?"

Natalie stared straight ahead, her heart thrumming in her ears as she awaited the unlatching of the gate.

"She's gone all quiet now," he snickered.

"First time since I found her."

"Well she won't have a head tomorrow, so she won't be too chatty then either."

Natalie's legs weakened beneath her as his words rattled around her mind. Every instinct screamed at her to run. Every muscle in her body primed ready to defend herself. But the thought of Brandon, beaten, broken and alone held her fast.

The sound of the bolt on the gate sent a shock of panic through her heart. Through teary eyes she saw a flash of pale blue as Jenny was pushed out of the gateway. Genevieve steadied her stance, and tightened her grip around Natalie's wrist.

"Oh no, Natalie," Jenny whispered. Her voice was frail and shaking. "Oh, by the Goddess."

A knot formed in Natalie's throat at the sight of her friend. Her wan complexion, either from lack of food or sleep or both, was stark against the dark grey stones. Brown leather strips bound her wrists at her front.

The redhead dragged her forward and held her firmly in place by her bindings. Walden smiled and gestured to their prisoner. "This the girl you want?"

Genevieve's breath hitched. "Aye."

"She's all yours."

Natalie staggered forward as Genevieve shoved her. Jenny hurried over and cupped her still bound hands beneath Natalie's chin, lifting her face to meet her.

"Don't let them take you." Jenny whispered as she choked on her sobs. "Fight back."

"I can't." Natalie fixed her eyes on Jenny and hoped she somehow understood the meaning of the words. She stood on her tiptoes to press her cheek against Jenny's. "Go with her. It's all alright. It'll be alright."

Genevieve lunged forward and pulled Jenny towards her, backing away from the bandits. Natalie followed her gaze to the castle walls, where tightly drawn arrows followed their every move.

"I'm sorry." Natalie's voice cracked as she turned towards the gate and the muscles in her shoulders clenched.

Jenny's sobs faded as she was dragged down the road. Bows creaked as the archers' arms relaxed. A broken breath escaped Natalie's lips. Walden snickered and pulled open the gate.

The redhead charged forward, grabbing Natalie's arms in a completely unnecessary, but predictable show of force. He yanked her forward through the gate, muttering beneath his breath. "Oh, you just made a big mistake, love. A big mistake. We'll have your head on a spike."

CHAPTER TWENTY-SEVEN

N ATALIE WINCED as the bandit's fingers dug into the flesh of her upper arms. She slipped on the slick cobblestones as the lad yanked her towards the castle.

Walden strode ahead of them, triumphantly bounding across the courtyard. When they reached the heavy wooden castle door, he raised his fist and rapped his knuckles against the wood. "Let us in!"

A small metal panel slid across at eye level, and a pair of dark eyes peered through the gap. "Aye boss."

There was a clank as the bolt slid across, and the door creaked open. The sight of the tapestry-lined entrance hall simultaneously filled Natalie with dread and hope. She was home, and somewhere within the gloomy chambers, Brandon was waiting for her. Of course, there was a strong possibility that her death awaited her too.

She turned to face the man who had opened the door and stared at him in defiance. He was tall and gangly, with an Adam's apple so pronounced it looked like his neck had knuckles. Pale blue eyes passed over her, and her insides squirmed. She was already tired of their scrutiny.

"What've you got here?" His voice echoed around the hallway as he shouted over the crackling of the rain on the cobbles.

"It's Lady Blackmere. The real one."

The redhead's nose dripped as he rubbed his hands together for warmth. "How can you be sure?"

"Get back to your post," Walden snapped. "Make sure that big woman doesn't try anything."

The smile dropped from the redhead's lips as the gangly man laughed. "Aye, get back to your post. And don't rust in the rain."

The redhead huffed in frustration and turned back to the door. He hunched his shoulders and scurried out into the downpour.

Natalie turned her attention back to their leader and lifted her chin to look him in the eye. He did not speak, but merely held out his arm for her to follow. She pushed her soaked hair back from her face and proceeded down the corridor, as Walden followed at her heels.

She walked through the hallway, assessing the damage. A tapestry depicting her earliest ancestor's victories was torn, slashed by a blade. The antiquated weapons, which once hung proudly on the walls, protruded from the visors of suits of armor. Glittering shards of colored glass gleamed on the stairs, and the bitter wind howled through the castle, whistling down the hallways.

Walden ushered her into the dining hall. Long ago the heart of the castle had hosted grand feasts and dances, but under Natalie's watch it had become cold and bare. It was the place she ate alone, sat on the end of one of the long wooden tables.

Under Walden's rule, the dining hall was, apparently, once again the destination for parties. The same crude images painted on the walls of the tavern were carved into the fine wooden tables, and an enormous white pair of horns was daubed across the far wall. A large, high-backed wooden chair dragged from one of the seldom-used guest chambers sat at the head of the hall.

She smirked as her eyes explored the room. "You gave yourself a throne."

The bandit leader turned and slapped the side of her head. The heel of his hand pounded her left eye. Pain throbbed as she blinked, unsure for a moment whether or not she still had vision. Dark spots danced in the corners of the tilting room. She could not see Walden. The ringing in her ears set her off balance as she searched for her captor.

Fighting back the urge to retort, she cleared her throat and turned towards the wooden throne. Walden grinned at her from his perch as he sat back. "Lady Blackmere, the infamously anonymous." He bounced the side of his blade against the toe of his boot as he rested his right ankle on his left knee. "You know, we sent word of your capture to everyone. North to south, east to west. I sent riders everywhere. You know how many responded?"

Natalie released a shaking breath as she clenched her hands.

"One," Walden chuckled. "That's pathetic, isn't it? One man, in the whole of Aldland. I almost feel sorry for the sad sod who hired us. He was convinced that staging an attack which he could stop would win him favor. He thought he could make himself out to be a hero. Only he didn't account for the castle being worth more than he could pay us when we got inside."

"Who was it?" The question left her before she could stop it and hung in the air between them as Walden's grin split his face.

"Wouldn't you like to know?" He stood. She heard the sharp whisper of steel against leather as he sheathed his sword, but fear blurred her vision.

She held her breath in anticipation of pain as he stood and strode towards her.

"The man who came to save you is upstairs in your chamber. Since he's the only person in the country who cares enough to try to save you, I think it's only fitting that you spend the night with him." His breath burned hot against her neck. "And then tomorrow you can die together."

CHAPTER TWENTY-EIGHT

NATALIE STUMBLED as she was shoved through the door. Her breath was ragged from the climb up the spiraling staircase. She paused, hoping the bandit had not heard the clatter of the daggers beneath her skirt as she hit the stone floor. When the door closed behind her, she felt she could finally breathe.

She pulled herself to her feet, and looked around the room, searching for Brandon. An empty wooden bowl sat on the floor, and beside it, a small puddle of water where she had knocked over a cup. Candles melted down to stubs, flickered in the drafty room. The curtain around her bed was drawn and she noticed with a frown, that a strip had been torn from the side. Bloody fingerprints marked the white cotton drapes.

"Hello?" Her voice was small and shaking. A thought crossed her mind, that all of this was a trick, designed to torture her in her final moments. Dread cooled her veins as she stepped towards the bed, half expecting it to be empty. Slowly, she reached out towards the edge of the curtain.

A hand darted out and snatched her wrist, holding her in an unbreakable grip. Her heart leapt into her throat, and a scream swelled in her chest.

"Nat?"

The scream emerged as a cry of relief as Brandon threw back the curtain and pulled her towards him. She held his face in her trembling hands. "It's really you."

"Oh, by the Goddess. They got you too." He was breathless, placing kisses in her hair as she buried her face against his chest. He stopped and he gripped her by the shoulders, holding her out to look at her. Flinching, he drew back his left hand, and simply rested it on her arm. "Please tell me you didn't come here after me."

"Of course, I did."

His mouth fell open in a silent cry. "Nat! You weren't supposed to follow me."

"You disappeared without a word. What was I supposed to do?"

"I thought I could take them myself, reclaim your castle and be the champion you needed."

"You were already the champion I needed."

His smile was barely perceptible as he released his hold on her and sat back on the bed. The middle finger of his left hand was short, and roughly bandaged with a bloody strip of fabric. "I'm just a fool."

"What did they do to you?"

He sniffed and shook his head. "Let's not talk of it."

"Does it hurt?"

"I'll be fine."

Her heart ached as she looked at him. Bringing up a hand to caress the side of his face, she held back her tears. "Forgive me."

"I keep telling you, my lady, there's nothing to forgive. You still shouldn't have come here."

"I had to."

"But they're going to kill us tomorrow."

"We won't let them."

His eyes drifted from her feet up her face as he considered her words. Longing overcame her, drowning her worries as she looked back into his dark, kind eyes. She could think of nothing more than being with him.

Footsteps shuffled in the corridor, and the bandit's muffled conversation faded. Natalie held her breath, listening to the silence beyond the door.

She reached out, brushed her fingers against his silver temples. "All will be well."

He leaned into her touch, eyelashes fluttering against his cheeks as he took her hand and pressed her palm to his lips. The tender kiss lingered, and her heart quickened as his breath stuttered, passion tinged with fear.

She stepped into the space between his thighs and pushed through the plush of his beard to find his soft, eager lips. A soft groan sounded in his throat, stoking the fire in her. His hands wandered, starting at the sides of her knees, and brushing their way up the drenched wool of her skirt towards her hips. Surprise snatched his breath as he found the concealed knives against her thighs, and the corners of his mouth curled. "You brought us blades?"

"I did."

Smiling, he whispered against her lips. "You are lovely and brilliant, Lady Blackmere."

"I try."

"So, we have a plan?"

"Yes," she bit her lower lip as his fingers tugged the knot at the top of her dress. "And we have all night to go over it. For now, I have you in my bedchamber, as I've always dreamed."

A deep, breathless laugh rolled through his chest. "And what exactly did you dream we'd do here?"

She stepped back from him and slowly unthreaded the crisscrossing lace over her chest herself, relishing the wanton look of desire on Brandon's face. His lips parted as his shallow breaths left him.

Her throat was dry and tight as she let the lace fall to

the floor and shook off the dress. He was not the first man she had been with, but he would be the first to see her completely, the first to see all of her.

She took a deep breath and bunched her fingers in the fabric at her hips, pulling it upwards just an inch before he cut her off.

"Wait."

She paused.

"Allow me." He held out a hand, beckoning her to step back towards him.

She did, yearning for more of his touch as his hand brushed around her hip. His fingers glided down the back of her thigh, and gently he tugged the fabric up, exposing her legs, then her full thighs, the patch of golden hair, and the blades strapped to her generous hips. Her cheeks reddened as he revealed her soft stomach, and pressed a kiss to the tender skin beneath her navel. He traced a row of kisses from hip to hip, his teeth grazing her skin.

He bunched the fabric in his hands as he lifted the smock higher, trailing kisses across her sides, then inched upwards, to the undersides of her breasts. She held her head back and gasped as he teased the sensitive skin with his tongue. Her breasts ached with need as he pulled the dress up to her chest, rubbing his calloused thumbs over her puckered nipples.

"Lift your arms," he growled softly.

She did as he asked, goosebumps tingling as he lifted

the damp cotton over her head and arms, and let it drop to the floor.

He leaned back and sighed. "You're even lovelier than I imagined."

Her cheeks flushed and the corners of her lips pulled upwards. "You imagined me?"

"A lot." Reaching out, he wrapped the fingers of his right hand beneath the belt across her belly and pulled her towards him. "We'll leave the belt on, just in case they come in." He sunk his teeth into his lower lip. "And I rather like how it looks."

A thrill tingled along her skin at the thought of being caught. "Do you think you can be quiet?"

"Do you?" He leaned back on the bed, pulling her by the belt so she had to straddle his chest.

She stifled her laughter as she fought to regain her balance. The coarse wool of his tunic rubbed against her inner thighs as she shuffled her knees to his sides. She could not help but smile as he beamed up at her.

"This is madness," he whispered. "We may die tomorrow, but all I can think about is you." His eyes drifted down to her breasts.

She squirmed as he ran his fingertips along her sides, a soft, tickling touch which drew gasps from her. His fingers hooked around the belt at her hips, and he tugged it gently, urging her to shuffle forward. With a grin, she followed his lead, inching upwards until her breasts were positioned above his face.

A soft growl rumbled beneath her as he pulled her towards him, lowering her body until his lips brushed her nipple. A sharp wave of pleasure coursed down her body as he licked and sucked, worshipping her with his lips, tongue and teeth. She gasped as his fingers drifted down past the belt, following the curve of her backside. He let his fingers linger on the backs of her thighs, agonizingly close to where she needed him.

He moaned, and the vibrations resonated through her breasts. The sounds he made only stoked the fire in her blood; deep, desperate and primal. As he pulled away, he let his tongue flutter across her nipple, sending a wave of pleasure pulsing towards her core.

"I want to taste you," he whispered, desire turning his voice as dark as the waters of Blackmere. "I told you once, I never leave a woman unsatisfied."

Her stomach fluttered as he looked at her, hunger burning in his eyes. She wanted him, desperately. The thought of being caught only added to her excitement. She rocked back onto her knees and leaned to one side so she could lay back on the bed.

"Not like that." His lips were full and rosy with need. His cheeks and throat flushed pink.

"How?" she breathed.

He placed his hands at the sides of her hips and beckoned her forward with a gentle pull.

Her heart quickened as she understood his meaning. "You want me on top of you?"

"Aye." His lips quirked.

A single, strained "Oh," escaped her lips.

Her body quivered in anticipation as she shuffled up the bed, and hitched her knees over his shoulders. Nervous breaths snagged in her throat as she peered down, only able to make out the very top of his head beneath her. She sat as straight as she could. "I don't want to crush you."

He wrapped his arms around her thighs and tugged her down, until his breath and beard tickled against her sensitive skin. She steadied herself, placing her hands on the wooden headboard, and tried to steady her nervous breaths. A gasp escaped her lips as he ran the tip of his tongue against her, tortuously slow and gentle. "Bran—don!"

She threw her head back and whimpered as he continued the teasing, coaxing ragged breaths from her. Every lick was delicious torture, keeping her sensitive to his touch, tasting her wetness as her body begged for him. She shifted her hips, riding his tongue, guiding him towards her swollen clitoris. His gentle, muffled laughter maddened her.

"Please," she gasped.

Her back arched as he finally flickered his tongue against the sensitive bundle of nerves at her center, sending a wave of excruciating pleasure through her body. Her toes curled tight.

He did it again, and again, spurred by her gasps and

whimpers. With a growl, he moved one hand to the back of her thighs, before reaching though and sliding a finger along her slick folds.

She let out a sharp gasp as he slid his finger inside her. He pressed his lips to her clitoris, and almost sent her over the edge as he began to suck, still licking with the tip of his tongue.

She buried her face in the crook of her elbow as she gasped, afraid to make a sound. She bucked her hips as he hummed and groaned beneath her. Her muscles tightened as the pleasure grew, swelling like a dam about to burst.

"Brandon." His name escaped her lips again as she came, pleasure and release crashing over her. She clung to the headboard as her legs trembled, as her orgasm clawed through her body.

She gasped as he placed a kiss against her raw, over-stimulated flesh. Summoning life into her legs, she climbed off him and curled up by his side.

He smiled proudly and wrapped his arms around her. She breathed in the musky scent of his body as she kissed him, tasting the metallic sweetness of her own pleasure. Her tongue brushed against his, earning her another desperate groan, and his erection nudged her thigh as he pressed his body against hers.

"Take off your clothes," she whispered. "I want to see you."

He grinned, and pushed himself up off the bed. The frame groaned as he tugged his shirt over his head. He threw his shirt to the side and leaned back on his elbows.

Natalie lifted herself onto her hands and knees, and brushed her lips across the soft mound of his stomach. His breath hitched as he shifted beneath her, and as she looked up, she saw his eyebrows were bunched in concern.

"What is it?"

He lifted his hand and ran it across his belly. "I just wish I'd met you sooner, when this was muscle and I was a man to be proud of."

Her heart ached for him as she watched embarrassment take the light from his eyes. Lacing her fingers with his, careful not to hurt the injured finger on his left hand, she held his hands to the mattress.

"You're perfect," she smiled. She dipped her head, and pressed a lingering kiss just above his navel, letting her teeth graze against his skin. "I've never seen anything so beautiful as you."

He gave a breathy chuckle of relief as his body relaxed.

She grinned, tracing the curves of his body with her tongue, kissing his chest and stomach, coaxing gasps and groans from him. Had he wanted to, he could break free of her hold; he was by far stronger than her, but he let her hold him as she teased and worshipped his body.

The rise and fall of his chest became rapid and shallow as she trailed kisses down his torso, pausing beneath his navel. Releasing his hands, she tugged at the lace of his breeches, loosening the band around his hips. She inched down his trousers, revealing his dark patch of coarse curly hair. She sank her teeth into her lower lip as her curiosity beckoned her to inch lower.

"My lady," he sighed as his hips bucked beneath her. He placed his hand over his groin, preventing her from lowering his breeches further.

"Is something wrong?"

He pulled her towards him, and kissed her, tugging her bottom lip between his teeth, and brushing his fingers through her hair. When he released her, his face had reddened, and his throat twitched with anticipation.

Brandon cleared his throat. "You've heard the songs?"

A smile cracked her worried expression. "Yes."

A half-formed sound rattled at the back of his throat before he snapped his lips together. He shifted and brought his hands to the hem of his trousers, tugging them back to his hips. "I'm…" he let go of a shuddering sigh and pressed his head back against the mattress.

"What is it?" She caressed his cheek, brushed her fingertips against his brow, and stroked the line between his eyebrows. No amount of soothing could erase it.

"I don't want to disappoint you," he sighed at last. "Those songs, about me being twice as… as long as other men. They… A few women have expressed their disappointment in the past."

She placed a gentle kiss on his cheek and nuzzled her

nose against the soft hair of his beard. "I want you."

"I want you too," he whispered. "Goddess, I've never wanted anything more."

She inched her hands down to his thigh. "You won't disappoint me. You never have, and you never will."

She followed the solid curve of his muscular thigh, dipping her hands between his legs. Heat pulsed through the fabric of his breeches.

He inhaled slowly through his nose as the tension in his shoulders relaxed a little. Slowly, he pushed down his breeches lifting his hips from the mattress.

His hard cock bobbed free of its confinement. As it slanted up towards his belly, a clear bead of fluid slid down the darker pink flesh of his head. Natalie's breath caught in her throat. It was no different than any other she'd seen, and while not double the size as the songs claimed, she was secretly glad of it.

She wrapped her hand around his shaft, letting her hand drift up and down, in slow, teasing strokes. She kissed his lips as he moaned.

"You're perfect," she whispered against his mouth.

Pulling away from his lips, she worked her kisses along the length of his body, pausing to nibble the soft flesh of his stomach to draw a laugh from him. With a grin, she positioned herself between his knees.

"Oh, Nat." His strained whisper quickened her desire.

The size of his body, and strength he exuded thrilled her. She needed to pleasure him, to reduce the mountain of muscle and scarred skin to quivering rubble.

She leaned forward, moistened her lips with the tip of her tongue, and took him into her mouth. His body undulated as his breath sharpened. The salty-sweet taste of him flooded her mouth. Her lips stretched wide as she pressed him deep into her mouth, sliding her fingers down to grip his base.

He gasped as she cupped his balls, caressing the velvety, ridged skin with a gentle touch. She watched him as he gripped the bedsheets, his face reddening and eyes shut tight, lips parted to make way for his broken breaths. She committed to memory every movement of her tongue and lips which earned the biggest reaction, the sharpest breaths, the shattered moans, until his stomach twitched and his muscles tightened, and she knew he was close.

She slid her tongue up along his length, and leaned back on her knees. He gasped as she wrapped both hands around his shaft and began to massage and slide her hands along the slick swollen member. His chest heaved and his face reddened as he clenched his teeth and growled. It was a sound unlike any she had ever heard from a man; animalistic and raw, building to a crescendo as his seed splashed across her wrists.

He covered his eyes with his arm as his growls turned to sighs. Transfixed by the undulation of his throat, she wiped herself off on the sheets and rested her head on his chest as his breath slowed, listening to the heavy pounding of his heart. So many nights she had lain in that bed, dreaming of Brandon the Bear, ferocious, beautiful, and unlike any man in all the world.

"The tales about you still don't do you justice," she whispered.

He drew patterns on her back with feathery touches, sighing as she pressed kisses above his heart. "If this is our last night alive, I will die a happy man."

"It won't be." Natalie's heart leapt as men muttered in the corridors beyond their sanctuary. In the haze of passion, she had almost forgotten what was happening around her. "We have a plan, of sorts. Viv is in the town. She and my chamberlain will organize a group of the townspeople to attack the bandits out there."

"Viv's here?" Brandon sighed. "That is comforting. They'd be a fool to stand in her way."

"I don't doubt it."

His throat twitched. "And what of Henry? Did you give him an answer?"

Natalie's heart hardened at the sound of his name. "I did. I told him no, and he left."

"He left? The greedy little coward." He pressed a kiss to the top of her head and stroked her back with the palm of his hand. "I would have understood had you agreed to marry him, but I must confess I'm glad you didn't."

"I couldn't bring myself to spend the rest of my life in

his company." She shuddered at the thought.

Brandon chuckled. "I've spent years with the wretch, and I don't blame you." He brushed his fingertips against the pommel of one of the daggers strapped to her hip. "So, this plan of yours? I suppose you and I fight from within?"

"Aye. We'll take as many of them out as we can, get to the gate and let Viv in."

His chest rose sharply beneath her as he let out a grunt. "Easier said than done. It'll be dangerous."

Natalie lifted her head and smirked. "I wasn't expecting anything less."

She pulled herself up and sat on the edge of the bed. Her heart fluttered against her ribs as he ran his fingers through her hair, brushing it back from her face. The impending battle loomed ahead of them. She chewed on her nail as her vision became unfocused, obscured by tears she refused to let fall.

The bed shifted and creaked as Brandon sat and leaned over to her, covering her shoulders with tender kisses. "We must hold on to hope," he whispered, his breath warm against her ear.

She turned her head, and her eyes fell to his wounded hand. The make-shift bandage was bloodied and dark. "We need to dress that properly."

He sighed as he followed her gaze and flexed his fingers. "Aye. I'm sorry about your curtains."

She shrugged and took out one of the daggers, cutting into the curtain herself to tear out another strip. She grew lightheaded as he peeled back the bloody fabric, showing the true extent of his injury. His middle finger was severed in half and in desperate need of stitching. The worst of the bleeding had stopped, but she had to act fast to stem the flow with the new bandage.

Brandon winced as she tightened the knot.

"There's a physician in the town." She tightened her jaw as her body cringed at the sight. "She'll be able to help you."

He nodded slowly and forced a smile. "So, when do we attack?"

CHAPTER TWENTY-NINE

THE BREEZE lifted Natalie's hair from her shoulders as she stood in the window, watching the flickering lights in the town. She listened, straining her ears for sounds of battle, for cries to arms and the bite of steel on steel. The silence was agonizing.

"How many said they'd fight?"

Brandon's voice quickened her heart as he came up behind her. He wrapped his arm around her waist and sighed.

"I don't know." Her voice was harsh to her ears. She kept a fear locked away; the fear that no-one would fight for her, that the townspeople were as content to live under Walden's rule as they were under hers. After all, she had failed to protect them.

Her chest was tight beneath the restrictive bodice of her dress. At last, she was dressed in her own clothing; a dark blue gown with crimson sleeves, and embroidered leaves around the hem.

Brandon pressed a kiss to her temple and whispered, "All will be well."

She forced a smile and turned back to the window, running her fingertips across the cold, dimpled texture of the stone sill.

Fear of failure coiled her gut. She focused on maintaining her breath at a deep and steady pace. Closing her eyes, she found herself imagining what people would say if she failed. Her legacy would be one of defeat and humiliation, of dying in public to the sounds of cheers. Even more horrifying was the thought that the last thing she might witness would be Brandon's death.

"Nat?"

"Hm?" She sniffed and blotted the tears from her eyes.

"You're breathing so fast. Slow down." Brandon stepped to her side and wound his arm around her waist. "Listen, I know it's so soon, and we barely know each other, but I also know this might not go so well."

"Don't say that," she whispered, caressing his cheek with her trembling hand. His skin was hot beneath her touch. Sweat shone above the neckline of his tunic.

"It's just, I've come to care for you, a great deal, and I may not have many opportunities to tell you—"

"Don't." She rocked onto her tiptoes, tangling her fingers in the hair at the back of his head and pulling him down to meet her lips. When his body relaxed, she drew back, and smiled. "Don't say it now. Wait."

"But if we don't make it..."

"Well, now we have to."

The lines at the corners of his eyes deepened as he smiled. "Very well, my lady."

"Besides," she smirked as she nudged her hip against his thigh. "As lovely as our evenings together have been, I plan on there being many more."

He bowed his head and smiled as she stepped towards him, pressing her body against his. The lingering scent of their passion clung to his beard and tunic, and the fire sparked inside her again. Brushing her lips against his, she forgot about the impending battle for a moment. She would happily have him right there on the floor, or against the windowsill. Her hand caressed his bicep as she wondered if he was strong enough to lift her and hold her against the wall.

A distant cry pierced the air sending a chill through Natalie's heart and snapping her from her desires.

She pulled away from Brandon, gripped the hilt of her dagger and took a shaking breath.

"Look at me." Brandon turned her towards him as her vision blurred and ears rang. "Stay close to me, don't take risks. Remember, be bold. Strike hard and fast. You're the Lioness of Blackmere."

She nodded as she swallowed hard. "Boldness."

He stooped and kissed her, with his hands braced at either side of her head. For a moment she was lost, alone with him, and nothing else mattered.

When he broke away, she closed her eyes, committing the sensation to memory as her stomach fluttered with nerves and desire.

"Ready?"

She opened her eyes and squeezed his hand. "Ready."

Distant voices clamored outside, shrill screams, blood-lust roars, the clang of metal and wood. Her people were fighting. They were fighting for their home.

Natalie hurried towards the door, cleared her throat, took a deep breath and screamed. Her shrill cry echoed around the chamber as she beat her fists on the wooden door. "Help me! Help, please!"

With a heave, Brandon pushed over the bed. It landed behind her with a bone-jarring crash. He pulled down the bookshelves, hurling heavy tomes against the walls.

She screamed again, and again. "Help! Help me!"

A key rattled in the lock on the other side and Brandon hurried towards the door, pushing his back against the wall. Natalie tucked the knife behind her back and kept her eyes on him, as he panted, wide-eyed and flushed from the effort.

The door opened, just a crack.

"What's going on?" A man growled through the narrow gap. "What you screaming for?"

"He's escaped!" Natalie wailed. "He tried to kill me and then he jumped out of the window."

The bandit's eyes widened as he pushed the door wide open. "He what?"

In an instant, Brandon had him, his forearm straining against the bandit's neck. With a thrust of his arm, the bandit stiffened. His eyes bulged before his head flopped forward and his mouth hung slack.

Brandon recoiled from the dead man, and let him fall to the floor, tugging the dagger from the wretch's spine.

There was little time to process what had happened.

Natalie's eyes fell to the large iron key sticking out of the door's lock. She snatched it and wrenched it free, throwing it behind her so they could not be locked back inside.

Another man appeared in the doorway. He stood, brow skewed in confusion, then anger as he saw the man on the ground. His hand darted to his belt as he withdrew an axe, and raised his arms to strike.

Natalie thrust her blade into his side.

Warm blood flowed across her hand, as the bandit crumpled to the ground. The world shuddered and spun around her, snatching the breath from her lungs. Her eyes latched onto the body of the man she had killed. Fear and guilt swelled in her veins.

She had killed.

"My lady," Brandon whispered as he wiped his blade on the dead man's coat. "Are you hurt?"

His voice brought the spinning to a standstill, and all at once she could breathe again.

"No." She took a deep breath and suppressed her anxiety. "Two down."

"Aye, and we can only guess how many more to go." Brandon's eyes snapped up towards her as his throat twitched.

A cry at the door spun them round. Two men gawped, one of them clutching a wine bottle in his hand. The other man wielded a sword, topped with a carved ram skull, a blade taken from one of Blackmere's guards.

As the men stood, stunned, she and Brandon lunged. A blade to the gut, one to the throat, and two more bodies lay in her bedchamber.

Natalie's ragged breath scorched her throat as she picked up the blade and handed it to Brandon. "These are the swords my guards use. They're good blades. Can you make use of it?"

He took it from her and tested the weight, bouncing it against his palm. "Aye."

She gave Brandon a curt nod as they waited for the next bandits to storm into the room. Every moment stretched ahead, as blood thundered through her veins. She was honed to their task, her focus unbreakable as her eyes remained trained on the doorway.

Footsteps pounded toward them.

"Ready?" Brandon snarled.

She gave a sharp nod.

And then, silence descended on the castle.

Their heavy breaths echoed as they waited, nerves rising. Beads of sweat collected on the curve of Natalie's back.

"Do you see them?" she mouthed.

Brandon shook his head and craned his neck to peer down the corridor.

Crack.

A crossbow bolt struck the stonework beside his right eye.

"Get back," he panted as he barreled into Natalie, barging her behind the door.

Three more bolts pounded against the wood as he held her. He pressed his lips to the top of her head. "Stay here."

He charged.

"Brandon!"

Pure fear pushed her from her hiding place. She emerged in time to see him cut through the first of the archers. Two more charged, abandoning their crossbows in favor of knives. There was a flurry of arms and curses, grunts, screams and clashing steel. Brandon roared as a knife bit into his arm, slicing through the brown wool to reveal a crimson gash.

Seeing Brandon wounded, the desire for revenge pushed Natalie onward. She bolted towards them, striking the bandit across the back with the tip of her blade. He let out a pained gasp and turned to face her.

"You—" he spat, as blood dripped on the stones by his feet.

Before she had time to think, he pounced, pinning her arms against the wall in an iron grip. She buckled as he pounded his knee into her stomach, and a wave of nausea overcame her. His fingers dug into the bones of her wrist, sending searing, twisting pain through her arm. Her dagger clattered to the floor.

The bandit flashed a wide, bloodied grin and released his hold on her, drawing back his arm to strike her.

She thrust her knee into his groin, again and again until he fell to the floor, teeth bared in agony. Brandon pushed the ram-pommeled blade into the man's back, and his wailing stopped.

Natalie gasped as she rubbed her wrist, tears forming in her eyes.

"Are you hurt?" Brandon panted as he stood, and stepped over to her. He held her face gently between his shaking hands.

"Not badly." Her lip trembled as she spoke, and her eyes fell to the spreading blood patch on his tunic. "Oh, by the Goddess, Brandon. You're injured."

"I'm fine." He snatched up her hand and pulled her towards the doorway. "We need to get going."

She stooped and picked up her fallen dagger, wiping the blade on her skirt as she ran after him.

CHAPTER THIRTY

Peering into the empty corridor, Natalie's heart pounded in her ears. Brandon's chest rose and fell against hers as he shielded her body with his. His arm pressed against her back, comforting her before they ventured out into the unknown.

His breath was heavy and uneven as he assessed the danger. A tendon bounced in his neck, and his eyes darted back and forth across the corridor. The skin of his chest gleamed with sweat through the small valley in the neckline of his tunic.

"Brandon?" She kept her voice at a whisper against his shoulder. The scent of him flooded her senses.

"My lady?"

She pressed a kiss to the tender skin of his throat and held him close. He softened in her embrace, and let out a deep sigh.

"All will be well." She breathed in the scent of wool and leather, salt and warmth, and closed her eyes. It was just the two of them, back in the cottage, duty and bandits forgotten.

"Of course it will; I have you by my side." He stooped to kiss her forehead and took a deep breath, clutching the hilt of the sword. Candlelight danced on the dagger tucked into his belt. "Let's go."

They hurried through the corridor, hand-in-hand as their feet padded against the stones. The walls of the hallway were lined with narrow slits for archers, and the air was viciously cold as the wind whipped through them. Even through her boots, Natalie felt the biting cold of the stone floor, and the steam from breath shimmered ahead of her.

"Which way?" Brandon hissed as they reached the end of the hall.

"Down the stairs." She pulled him towards the narrow spiral stone staircase. The descent was steep, and the steps narrow even for her small feet. Brandon's footsteps pounded behind her, and mercifully he managed to stay upright.

As she rounded the bottom of the staircase, grazing her palm against the rough stone wall, her heart leapt into her throat.

Walden stood, waiting, his head cocked to the side in curious amusement.

"Where are you going?" he grinned. He unsheathed the

blade at his hip and shook his head in disapproval. "Did you really think you could just walk out the front door?"

Brandon took a step forward, edging his shoulder in front of her chest, blocking her from the bandit leader's blade.

"Back away," Brandon growled. "Get out of the castle, and no one else has to die."

Walden's face lit up with amusement. "You expect us to just leave? Has age muddled you, old man?"

"You are outnumbered," Natalie said firmly. "The people of Blackmere are fighting to reclaim what's ours. You haven't the men to stop them. I can order my people to stop fighting, if you leave now."

Brandon nodded. "We can end this without more bloodshed."

Walden's eye twitched as he grinned. He turned his attention to Brandon and pursed his lips. "You're a champion, are you not?"

"Aye."

The young man clicked his tongue. "If anything, this past week has taught me not to trust champions. You don't keep your promises, you don't pay your debts, and you don't care who you betray for power."

"What are you talking about?" Brandon barked as Natalie's blood ran cold.

"It was Henry," she whispered. "Henry hired them to

take the castle."

Brandon turned to her. The crease between his eyebrows deepened, as his face flushed scarlet. "Henry?" He released an incredulous breath and shook his head. "No, Henry's an egotistical little sod, but he's no killer."

"No," Walden sighed. "He's no killer, but he's happy to hire people to kill for him. He intended to hire us to stage an invasion which he would then thwart to gain your favor. Sadly, he didn't pay us, and your castle was worth rather more to us than any of you. Rather sad really, isn't it? As far as castles go, this place is a bit of a dump."

Brandon stared straight ahead, his eyes unfocussed and glossy.

"You can't stay here," Natalie snapped. "Leave."

"Why? Being Lord Blackmere is a damn sight more comfortable than what I'm used to," Walden shrugged. "I dare say I'd do a better job at ruling Blackmere than you. Have you seen your accounts?"

His words struck her like a dagger to the gut, twisting and coiling inside her. Heat crept up her spine, burning along her jawline and tightening her hands into fists.

"Fine," Brandon raised his blade and took a step towards the bandit leader. "If you won't leave, I'll make you."

Walden threw back his head and cackled. "You? A washed-up entertainer, whose best days are far behind him? What? Are you so emboldened by this pathetic excuse for a noble lady's attention you'd risk your life to win her neglected castle?"

"I don't care that she's noble," he growled.

Natalie's blood may as well have been boiling oil coursing through her veins as she watched Brandon maneuver around the room. He prowled towards the bandit, like a predator on his prey. The intensity of his glare never wavered, even as Walden mocked him.

"I already took down one of you so-called champions," Walden chuckled. "All it took was a crossbow bolt to the back of his head while he was drinking in the tavern."

A flash of realization crossed Brandon's face. His eyes darkened, and his lips tightened over his teeth.

Walden's face tightened into a menacing grin. "Oh, that struck a nerve. Did you know him?"

"His name was Robert Trevaryn. He was like a brother to me. And you'll pay for his life with yours."

Heart emptying, Natalie could only watch as the man she loved charged.

The bandit assumed an elegant fighting position, one leg poised ahead of the other as he prepared to block Brandon's incoming attack. The Bear struck true to his name.

Natalie winced as Brandon's first bone-crushing blow struck Walden's upper arm. Some part of her almost pitied the bandit leader as his eyes grew wide with the realization that he had fatally underestimated his foe.

Walden blocked the next strike and grinned. His face

shimmered with a fine layer of sweat as Brandon advanced on him, unleashing his full strength.

Desperate, the bandit ducked out of the way of the attacks and rolled across the floor. He leapt to his feet behind Brandon. Natalie's throat shredded as she gasped.

The tip of Walden's blade raked across Brandon's back. The champion roared as he whirred around to face his enemy.

The satisfied smile slid from Walden's face as he pointed his blade towards Brandon. "You'll tire before I do."

"You'll be dead before I tire." Brandon unleashed a new barrage of blows, each falling with the force of a charging bull. He backed the bandit into a corner.

Brandon's eyes were abyssal as a final mighty blow crumpled Walden to the floor. "You took my lady's castle," he panted. "You threatened her life." He thrust forward, spearing the bandit through the heart. "And you killed my best friend, you bastard."

Natalie brought her fingers to her lips as the bandit fell.

Brandon stood blood dripping from his blade. His ragged breath echoed around the hallway. The fight in his eyes still burned as Natalie ran to him, wrapping her arms around his torso and resting her head on his chest.

His heart was a war drum pounding in his cavernous chest. "Goddess forgive me, I want to kill him all over again." His voice wavered as silent tears streaked down his cheeks. "He killed Robert. He was going to kill you."

"He's gone," she whispered, pressing a kiss above his heart. She attempted to soothe him, stroking the vast expanse of his back. His muscles twitched and tightened as he held back his sobs.

"He would've hurt you. I couldn't let him."

"You fought for us all." She melted against him as he brought a hand up to caress the back of her head.

He kissed her hair as his breathing slowed, and he reined in the pounding rhythm of his heart.

"He killed Robert," he said at last, his voice trembling with grief.

"I know," Natalie whispered. "And you did him proud." She pulled back from his embrace and looked him in the eye. The faint sounds of battle still raged outside. "I will hold you for as long as you need me to when this is over, but we need to get out to Viv. She needs us."

"Aye." He straightened his posture, wiped Walden's blood from his blade and sniffed. "Let's go."

CHAPTER THIRTY-ONE

NATALIE AND Brandon, bloodstained and determined, stormed towards the castle's door. The gangly man standing guard held up his hands in surrender.

"Please, I don't want no part of this," he begged, backing away. "I don't even like Walden."

Brandon shrugged and lifted the heavy bolt from the door. "Walden's dead."

"Dead?" The gangly man forced a chuckle in an attempt to hide his fear. "Oh good, that's good. Thank you, sir, and my lady."

The door groaned open, allowing a blast of icy air to enter the castle. Natalie turned, her hair flowing behind her as she regarded the sniveling bandit. "Get out of my castle."

"Yes, my lady, right. Yes." The bandit stammered as he

hurried outside, and scurried across the cobblestones calling out to his comrades. "Walden's dead!"

Natalie stole a satisfied glance at Brandon.

He pressed his hand to the curve of her back and ushered her out the door. "Come on."

The night air was biting as they stepped onto the cobbled courtyard. The men on the walls had retreated, cowering behind the large wooden gate. On the other side, the sounds of cheering and shouting filled the air.

"Sounds like Viv already has them beat." The confidence in Brandon's voice gave Natalie courage as she approached the cowering bandits.

"Gentlemen," she called, rubbing her hands together for warmth. "You've overstayed your welcome. Leave Blackmere, and you may keep your lives."

Something heavy pounded against the gate from the other side. The wood strained inward for a moment, and the bandits cried out in fear.

"Not a chance. She'll kill us," one of the men called. "We can't go out there."

"I'll call her off," Natalie assured them. "Viv won't—"

"Open this gate immediately!"

The voice on the other side of the gate sent a shard of ice through Natalie's heart. The blood drained from her face. "Oh no."

"That's not Viv," Brandon frowned.

Natalie opened her mouth to speak, but found her voice had left her. It was as though her heart had barricaded her throat in fear. Pulses of dread shot through her body, and her knees grew weak, and yet, she could hardly wait to open the gate.

"I will burn this castle to the ground if you don't open the door."

Natalie took a step forward. The bandits parted to let her through, their eyes wide with fear. The doorway bulged as a battering ram pounded the other side, and a cheer erupted from the fighters.

"Nat, be careful," Brandon warned, standing by her side.

"Stop her," the redhead from the gate cried out. "She'll kill us all."

"And I should let her," Nat barked back. "Just because I'm letting you keep your miserable lives doesn't mean we're friends."

The redhead's jaw snapped shut as he backed away. Natalie returned her attention to the gate and took a deep breath, tilted her chin and summoned all the courage she could muster. "Mother?"

"Lady Austwick," her mother corrected, her sharp voice like the crack of a whip. *"Open this damn door at once."*

"Mother?" Brandon whispered. "Your mother? By the Goddess."

Natalie pressed her lips together and heaved the heavy bolt. The gate creaked open just a few inches, and mercifully the hinges stayed intact. Small victories. She quailed at the thought of how expensive the repair work to the castle and town would be.

She stole a glance at Brandon before pulling open the gates. Her mother stood, clad in shining steel armor, a black wolf's pelt across her shoulder, and her sword poised for battle. Her sun-kissed skin was golden in the glow of torch light. The last time Natalie had seen her, her hair was warm rosy blonde, tumbling to her shoulders. Now it was short and silver, the lines around her eyes and mouth had deepened, and she was even sharper and more beautiful than Natalie remembered.

"Lady Austwick," Natalie bowed. Brandon followed her lead in the periphery of her vision. A clatter of weapons, and the soft crumpling and creaking of leather followed as the bandits bowed behind her.

Natalie righted herself, and whipped around to face the bandits as her face contorted in anger. "Get out!"

The men fled, their feet pounding the cobblestones as they picked their way through the crowd of well-armed soldiers at Lady Austwick's disposal.

Natalie held her breath as her mother's cool grey eyes scanned her from head to foot.

Lady Austwick's lips pressed into a thin, pale line.

"Three days ago, I received a ransom note, claiming that my ancestral home was under attack and my daughter's life was in danger. I came as fast as I could."

"Thank you, mother." Natalie's voice wavered as it rode her shaking breath. "I believe the crisis is averted."

Lady Austwick made a curt nod of approval before taking a stride forward. "May I come in?"

Without hesitation she passed through the gate, leading her army into the courtyard, and began calling out orders to her men. The chamberlain followed close behind, bowing apologetically to Natalie as he began to take notes of needed repairs.

Natalie found she could breathe again as a large, warm hand curled around hers. She looked up to see Brandon smiling at her. He rubbed her knuckles with his thumb and brought her hand up to his lips.

"We won," he whispered.

He was worn. The blood splatter and dirt could not conceal his pallid complexion, or the dark circles beneath his eyes. Her eyes drifted down to the bloodied bandage around his finger. She was in no mood for her mother's admonishments anyway.

"Come, we need to find you a doctor."

"I'll be alright."

"Yes, you will be, once you see a doctor." She took his uninjured hand and led him out of the gate, leaving the chaos at the castle behind them.

CHAPTER THIRTY-TWO

NATALIE'S MUSCLES tightened in protest as Brandon screwed his eyes shut. She stood beside his seat in the surgery, lit by a feeble flickering candle, surrounded by dried herbs, bottles and jars of ointments and medicines.

A healer sat before Brandon. She shivered in her night-dress as she worked. A cap covered most of her fluffy grey hair, and her warm, acorn-brown face creased as she pushed the needle through his skin. "By the Goddess, you poor man. I've been busy in here this past week, as you can imagine. Knife wounds, broken bones, horrible stuff." She snipped the end of the catgut with a pair of scissors and wrapped a clean gauze around the stump. "I've saved as much of your finger as I can. You need to keep it clean and dry. Change the dressing in the morning, and again tomorrow night."

"Thank you," Brandon mumbled through shallow, sharp breaths. Sweat beaded on his brow.

Natalie ran her fingers through his hair, massaging his scalp in an attempt to give him some comfort.

He leaned into her touch and sighed. "How long will it take to grow back?"

The healer's brow lowered and her mouth opened and closed. The corner of Brandon's lips curved upwards.

Natalie chuckled and pressed a kiss to the top of his head. "Thank you," she smiled to the healer.

"Anytime. Now if you'll excuse me, I need to get dressed. I expect I'll be busy tonight."

"Send the bill for your services to the castle. I'll see to it you're paid."

"Thank you, my lady." The healer smiled faintly. "It's been a long time since we saw you outside of the castle. I must say, it's a welcome sight."

"Thank you." Natalie bowed and offered her arm to Brandon. "You need to rest," she smiled.

"No time," he groaned as he stood and steadied himself on the arm of the chair. "That bastard Henry could be anywhere by now. I need to get out there and find him, and see that he pays for what he's done."

They stepped out into the street. The town was alive with chatter as the people cleaned up after the battle. Natalie turned around, pressing herself against Brandon and stretching her arms around him. She stood on her tiptoes and kissed his chest through the rough wool of his tunic.

"You need to rest, and so do I."

She watched as his eyes scanned the castle wall, and could almost hear the battle raging between his warrior's heart and mind, and his weary body. He took a deep breath and lowered his head to kiss her. "Aye. Let's rest."

He began to walk, leading her up the hill towards the castle.

"Not that way."

He turned to her and raised his eyebrows. "No?"

"The tavern, if that's alright with you? I can't go back to Blackmere tonight."

She waited, her lungs solid and aching as he considered her request. He bowed his head and smiled. "I think I broke your bed when I flipped it anyway."

Natalie chuckled as he linked her arm and they headed down the hill towards the tavern. "I'm sure Lady Austwick will have fun seeing to its repair, and berating me for the damage later."

"I'll let her know I did it."

"And admit to my mother that you were in my bed-chamber?" Natalie gasped in mock indignation. "Brandon, the scandal you'll cause."

"I can't wait," Brandon smiled as he opened the tavern door and stepped aside for Natalie to walk in.

They were not alone.

Two figures sat at opposite sides of one of the tables, their fingers entwined as they whispered and laughed together. Soft candlelight cast a golden glow across their smiling faces. Natalie could not help but smile with them. The blush blossoming across Jenny's cheeks was contagious.

Brandon chuckled. Genevieve leapt to her feet, her eyes wide and startled. Jenny turned and gasped at the sight of the intruders.

"Bear!" Genevieve growled as she clutched her axe. "I swear by the mountains, if you jump out at me again!"

"Jump out at you?" Brandon laughed and held out his hands in surrender. "Weren't you supposed to be fighting?"

Genevieve held up her hands in frustration. "I was! Until the angry Ice Queen came and told me to get out of her way, so we came here."

Natalie smiled as Genevieve and Brandon fell into a discussion about their battles, the wounds they had both suffered and inflicted.

With a sigh, she went over to Jenny, her heart sinking as she drew closer. A large purple bruise shone on her cheek.

Natalie swallowed her fear and took Jenny by the hand. "Are you angry at me? You have every right to be."

"Angry?" Jenny frowned. "No, I'm not angry. You didn't do anything wrong."

"I sent the guards away and left the castle undefended."

"Why'd you send them away?"

Natalie shrugged. "To stop the bandits."

An incredulous smile broke across Jenny's weary face. "You weren't to know. You're still alright in my book."

"Thank you." Tears brimmed in Natalie's eyes. "Did they hurt you?"

"They pushed me around a bit," Jenny shrugged. "I've had worse at work. Anyway, I clobbered one of them. That felt good. If I ever see them again, they'll regret it." Her eyes flickered towards Brandon and a sly, knowing smile crossed her lips. "Looks like you've been busy."

Natalie pressed her teeth into her lower lip and shot her friend a warning look through her smile. "I owe you a new dress."

"It's a wonder you're still walking."

A loud snort forced its way out of Natalie's nose, rendering the conversation in the tavern silent. Heat spread across her face as she turned away from the tavern's landlady.

"Will you be needing a room tonight?" Jenny chuckled behind her.

"Aye." Brandon cocked his eyebrow as his gaze drifted across Natalie.

"Take your pick. Not sure if any of them even have locks or beds anymore," Jenny shrugged as she inclined her head towards the stairs. "Your stuff might still be up there Brandon."

"Thank you, my lady."

Natalie's heart swelled as Brandon bowed to Jenny. As she followed him up the stairs, she thought of all the fine qualities he had; his kindness, the respect he had for everyone, regardless of their station. She loved how he looked, how he made her feel, the sounds he made when he kissed her, and his eagerness to please her. She loved his strength, his softness, and how even though she had known him only a few days, she felt as though he was part of her, that they were each molded to fit together.

They followed a shadowy corridor lined with wooden doors, until at last Brandon stopped and rested his fingers on a brass handle. "This was my room."

He held his breath as he pushed open the door, and released a sigh as his trunk, along with its contents lay spread on the floor. Clothing, letters, the torn pages of a book cluttered the floorboards. The lock of the trunk had been pried from the wood.

"Well, I suppose I deserve that for breaking open the chest in the cottage," Brandon sighed as he crouched by the debris and attempted to gather his belongings together.

"Did they take anything?" Natalie stooped to pick up a green tunic, a pair of tan breeches, and a bundle of letters from beneath the little window.

As she stood, she glanced outside. Soldiers marched up and down the cobbled street, searching for stragglers, and ensuring the town was free from bandits. The white rose of Austwick Castle gleamed on their shields.

Natalie's blood ran cold at the thought of facing her mother in the morning, but for now, she was safe and hidden. She was with Brandon, and nothing in the world could tear them from each other.

"I don't think so." The bed groaned as he sat down, and his eyes fell to the bundle of letters in her hand. "Oh, we can just throw those away."

"What is it?"

"Nothing," he ran his hand through his hair and smiled. "Just letters. Honestly, I can't really read them myself. I never learned how."

"Oh?" Natalie's interest piqued as she cast her eyes down at the exquisitely scrolled handwriting on the top letter. "May I look at them?"

Brandon's eyes widened a little and a blush spread across his cheeks. "You may."

"Has anyone ever read them for you?"

"Aye, Robert used to. He thought they were hilarious."

"Oh, Brandon. Are you certain you want me to?"

"It's fine. He's no doubt giggling away at the Goddess's side."

She took the top one from the pile and read aloud, "Brandon, my handsome Grand Tourney Victor. I witnessed your battle last week, and have been quivering at the thought of your strength ever since. Please do me the honor of returning to Westgarden someday, and unleashing your legendary power onto me, and my ever longing qui—my word!"

Brandon chuckled and shook his head. "That's not even the worst of them."

"Lady Catherine Luray." Natalie clicked her tongue in mock indignation as she scanned her eyes across the rest of the letter. "Goodness."

"Most of them are like that." The bed groaned as Brandon stood, and stepped over to her, cupping her face in his hands. "Not all of them though."

He took the letters from her, and began thumbing through the pile. At last he gave a satisfied smirk and handed a small handful back to her.

Natalie gasped at the sight of the ram's head embossed in cracked black wax on the back of each of the letters. "These are mine. You kept them?"

"Aye. I carried them with me all these years."

"But they aren't... interesting like those others."

He gave a gentle smile and shrugged a shoulder. "They made me smile, every year when they came, as sure as the seasons. I recognized the sheep. Perhaps some part of me knew."

"Knew what?"

She let go of a sigh as he brushed his lower lip against hers. Her hand slid across his chest, feeling for the steady rhythm of his heart as their kiss deepened.

The letters fell to the ground as her fingers trailed down his body, sliding underneath his tunic, to feel the soft warmth of his stomach. Smiles broke their kiss, as she pushed the tunic up over his head. She turned around, lifting her hair over her shoulder to signal for him to untie her gown. He did so, working free the tight laces, as he kissed the tender skin of her neck, sending tingles throughout her body.

At last, the dress came free, and she stepped out of it. The cool air nipped at her bare skin, and for a moment they were back in the cottage, and there were only two people in the whole world.

She pressed her breasts against his chest, and traced the line of dark hair down his stomach as she bit into his smiling lips. He moaned as she reached his waistband, yanked open the lace, and slid her hands down over the fuzzy, round cheeks of his ass. His erection pressed against her stomach as she held him.

"I want you," she whispered.

He bowed his head, smiling softly. "You have me."

Her heart was fit to burst as she stepped back to the bed, lowering herself onto the soft mattress, and leaning back against the pillows. A thrill tingled along her body as he looked at her, hunger lighting fire in his eyes. He moistened his lips as he lowered himself to her, pressing a kiss to her stomach and trailing his tongue up to her breasts.

A groan escaped his lips as he slid his fingers through the wetness between her thighs. She was ready, and she was desperate to have him. She writhed beneath his touch, yearning for more as he continued to tease her, tugging her nipple between his lips, and flicking his tongue. As he broke away to turn his attention to her other breast, he placed a kiss over her heart.

"I want to spend the rest of my life pleasuring you, my lady, if you'll have me."

"But the Guild…" she panted.

She gasped as he slid his fingers inside her, first his index finger, and then his middle, curling them in a beckoning motion as he teased her clitoris with his thumb. He watched her, measuring her reaction to see which motions earned him the strongest response.

"Let them try and stop us," he growled.

Lifting her hands from the mattress, she trailed them across his body, the rough texture of his body hair tingled the skin of her palms. Brandon moaned as she ground her hips against him, pushing deeper, setting the pace herself. A cry escaped her lips as he slid a third finger into her, and the new sensation tipped her over the edge. She came, burying her face against his chest, and he held her there until she was able to move again.

"I didn't hurt you, did I?" He whispered when at last she opened her eyes.

"No." Her voice was barely a whisper as she lay her head back on the pillow and smiled. Her thighs trembled against his hips.

Brandon looked at her, his expression softening as she sighed. He pressed his lips together as his eyes fell down to her breasts. The prodding at her thigh drew a smile from her.

She brought up her hand to the back of his head, and lowered him gently to kiss her. "I need you."

He lowered his lips to meet hers. He kissed her like it was the last thing he would ever do, his body burning with the need for her. She brushed her hands along his back, pulling him down towards her. Her heart thrummed as she reached between them to guide him, letting out a gasp as he slowly pressed his cock inside her.

"Oh, by the Goddess, Nat."

A shuddering breath worked its way through her as she bathed in the sensation. There had been others before him, but none who filled her with such a strong sense of wanting. He steadied his weight on his hands, before he began grinding his hips against hers.

He moved slowly, agonizingly so, as though she might shatter and disappear beneath him. She wrapped her legs around his hips, pulled him deeper and relished the quivering sensation coursing through her body.

An excited groan sounded in his throat.

His slow, steady rhythm grew. With every thrust he pushed deeper and his pace quickened. As his excitement built, he was unrelenting. A broken sob escaped her lips as pleasure overcame her, rolling and tingling throughout her body.

He froze. "Too much?"

"No. Keep going," she begged, breathless. Pulses of pleasure rocked through her body as she came, twisting her fists into the bed sheets and bucking her hips beneath him.

A deep growl rumbled in his chest as he resumed the pace, and she clung to him as though her life depended on it, her fingertips grasping his strong shoulders.

When his breath grew ragged and he began to tire he rolled onto his side, pulling her with him, until they lay face to face. Every deep and hungry kiss was a promise, that nothing, not Blackmere, nor the Guild, nor any of the world's obstacles would come between them.

She was his, and he was hers.

Desperate for him once more, she rolled on top of him, straddling his hips and pressing him back inside her. His hands drifted across her body, following the curves of her figure, lingering on her breasts, holding them so they bounced against his palms in time with her. Her chest tightened at the way he looked at her, full of hunger, and adoration.

"You're—" he breathed. "I won't last."

His thighs tensed and shuddered beneath her. She longed to hear the same raw, beastly growl he had made in her bed chamber, and she would pleasure him all night if she had to, just to hear it.

"Nat," he gasped as he held her still, gripping her hips as he thrust upwards into her.

He came undone, burying his face against the pillow. She rolled her hips in time with his breath, and was rewarded with the sound she craved, deep and rough and perfect.

Satisfied, she crumpled on top of him, breathless and spent. The rough bristle of his beard brushed against her chest. Soft, butterfly kisses tickled her collarbone. They lay entwined as their breathing slowed, holding each other, basking in the warmth and comfort of intimacy.

"By the Goddess," Brandon groaned as he ran his fingers through Natalie's hair.

She buried her face against his neck as she grinned. "This was absolutely worth twelve years of petitioning for the Tourney."

Brandon's deep rumbling laugh shook her as he pressed kisses to her shoulder and trailed his fingertips along the length of her back. He closed his eyes and sighed. "I wish we'd come here every year."

"You're here now. Without everything which has befallen us, you would have ridden away the day after the Tourney." She watched him as his face softened. The crease between his eyebrows faded as his long dark eyelashes fluttered against his cheek.

"Maybe." His voice was deep and thick with sleep. "Though I never could've left you."

Finally, as the moon shifted across the sky, and the window lost its silvery glow, they fell asleep, bodies entwined.

CHAPTER THIRTY-THREE

"Get up." Lady Austwick's flint-sharp voice snatched Natalie from her dreams.

She squinted, eyes stinging in the harsh daylight as her heart pounded. "Mother?"

"Get up. Get dressed and get back to the castle." The woman turned her eyes to Brandon, casting a disapproving look over his disheveled appearance, and the tumultuous state of his room.

As Natalie squinted at Brandon, she saw he had already dressed in the green tunic and tan breaches she had recovered from the floor the previous night. He cast her a worried glance as Lady Austwick strode out of the room, accompanied by four armed guards. A blood red cape flowed behind her as she left.

"What's happening?" Natalie's voice croaked as she

bunched the bedsheets around her bare chest.

"I don't know." Brandon's eyes fell to the floor as he raked his nails across his hair, pushing it back from his face. "I woke up when she marched into the tavern and started calling for you. She ordered me to follow her."

"You'd better go. She doesn't like to be kept waiting." Natalie stood, her heartbeat quickening as she searched for her rumpled gown. "I'll meet you up there."

Brandon gave a single sharp nod and offered a weak smile. "Don't be long. Please."

"I won't."

He disappeared from the doorway.

Natalie staggered from the bed and stepped into her chemise, wobbling to keep her balance. Without anyone to help her with the laces of her dress, she had no chance of appearing decent. Instead, she took Brandon's worn brown padded gambeson from the floor.

She pressed her nose to the heavy garment, breathing in the scent of him. Her stomach flopped as the memories of the previous night came back to her, and a smile worked its way across her lips.

Pulling the coat over her frame, she fastened the brass clips across her chest to preserve at least some of her modesty. She looked out of the window, to watch Brandon and an escort of soldiers march up the hill towards the castle. A thousand possibilities, none of them good, swarmed her mind.

Her jaw ached from the tension, as she worked up the courage to follow after them. The thought of Brandon left alone to face her mother, drove her from the sill and out of the room.

The walk to the castle was cold, and lonely. Her townspeople did not look up from their work as she passed. Once she arrived at the castle gate, the guards questioned her before letting her pass, hesitant to believe Lady Austwick's daughter would be anything less than immaculate.

Eventually, she was led up the stairs in her own castle, and instructed to wait outside one of the seldom-used guest chambers. The castle hummed with life as guards patrolled the hallways.

Natalie sat on a bench outside the door, desperately trying to decipher the muffled conversation within. Her head spun as her mind navigated a forest of possibilities.

It was entirely possible her mother would forbid Brandon from ever seeing her daughter again. It was also entirely possible she would remove Natalie from Blackmere, and send her back to Caer Austwick to live under parental supervision. Both options turned her belly to a serpent's nest.

She found herself wondering where Henry had run to, and whether Brandon would ever find him. The thought of Brandon leaving to hunt for him caused her chest to tighten. Aldland was vast, and it could take months, if not years to find the traitor.

Her heart bolted as the door clicked open and Brandon strode out, ducking beneath the door frame. His ears and throat glowed red and his eyes were glassy.

Natalie leapt to her feet, and wrung her hands together. "What did she say? What happened?"

"She's… uh…" he lowered his voice and stepped further from the door. "She knighted me." His eyes grew distant and his lips parted enough to allow him to breathe. His silver temples gleamed in the light from the torches mounted on the walls. "She knighted me for killing Walden. I'm Sir Brandon of Marshdown."

Natalie covered her gaping mouth with her fingertips, before a broad smile broke through her shock. "By the Goddess. Congratulations."

"She wants to speak to you too."

The smile fell from Natalie's lips. "I doubt I'll be knighted."

She garnered a little courage as he took her hands and pressed his lips to her knuckles. As far as she was concerned, no man deserved a knighthood more than Brandon.

Brandon smiled and took Natalie's spot on the bench in front of the room. "Boldness."

She steeled her nerve and placed her shaking hand on the doorknob.

"Come in," Lady Austwick snapped.

Natalie cast a last desperate look at Brandon before slipping inside the room. Her mother sat behind a table poring over various maps and plans. Lady Austwick had changed out of her armor, and now wore a deep purple tunic, embroidered with golden roses. Her cropped silver hair was neat and pushed back over her ears.

In the corner of the room, the chamberlain perched, scribbling in his leather-bound book.

Natalie bowed her head, trying to conceal her rapid breath behind pleasantries. "You wanted to see—"

"I know I did. Sit."

Natalie obeyed, casting a wilted look towards the chamberlain as his quill relentlessly scratched against the parchment.

"Mother, I—" She paused in anticipation of interruption. Lady Austwick lifted her eyes from her charts and fixed Natalie in a deathly stare. She felt like a child, drowning in the oversized coat and shrinking in the face of her mother's ire. "Forgive me."

"There's a lot to go over." The lady folded her elegant hands on the table and sat straight in her chair. "How did this happen?"

Natalie inhaled, her breath shaking in her chest. "I made an error in judgement. I underestimated the threat posed by the bandits, and sent the guards to deal with them as quickly as possible. I wanted my people to be safe."

Lady Austwick gave a slow nod. "Very well. I understand you have your townsfolk's best interests at heart. Perhaps a little too much. Your guards were overwhelmed, and tragically, lives were lost. Many of those who did survive have abandoned their posts altogether. Beside the fact you allowed our castle to be taken, you've all but run it into the ground financially. Do you know, Blackmere has the lowest rate of taxation in all of Aldland? Hm? And, coincidentally, the longest list of necessary repair work."

"I… no. I didn't know."

Lady Austwick raised her eyebrows and peered down her nose at the papers. "And your personal accounts are all but run dry. You spent nothing for years, and now all of a sudden, it's gone. Am I to assume it rests in the pockets of the Guild Master?"

Natalie's ears burned as she bit back tears. She nodded, pressing her lips together. A large portion of it now belonged to Henry.

Lady Austwick made a note with the pointed tip of a peacock feather dipped in crimson ink. "I'm your mother, first and foremost, and I know this has been hard for you since Jamie passed. Blackmere is no place to be alone. I lived in these drafty halls before marrying your father, but our home was always busy. Sir Brandon told me the lengths you went to get our castle back. Not many would have done the same." Her mother's features softened. "I am glad to hear that your people think of you fondly, and they never feel wanting. I also hear from your chamberlain, that you've prioritized your people's happiness and education over profit. Your father and I have always been proud that we raised a kind hearted child, if a touch foolhardy."

Natalie bowed her head and took a shaking breath. "Thank you."

"As for this business with the champion." Lady Austwick stood and strode around the table, to perch in front of Natalie. "Chamberlain, be so kind as to close your ears."

"Yes, my lady," the elderly man's rasping voice came from the back of the room.

"Do you love him?" Lady Austwick folded her arms across her chest. "Truly?"

"Brandon?"

"Is it infatuation or love?"

"Mother?"

"It's one or the other."

Her throat ached as she swallowed a lump. "Love. I think. It's only been a few days, but—" Her heart swelled at the mere thought of him. "Love."

Lady Austwick nodded slowly, sinking her teeth into her lower lip momentarily. "He's strong, good looking, built like a warhorse. He is lowborn however, and the champions are sterile. If you marry him, one of your nieces or nephews will inherit Blackmere after you pass. Do you intend to wed him, or simply bed him?"

Natalie felt her eyes widen as her throat tightened. "I... I hadn't given it much thought. I've known him less than a week."

"My mother and father only knew each other for three minutes before they got married," Lady Austwick shrugged. "They adored each other until their last breaths."

"Aye, but you and father knew each other since you were babies."

"Yes, and I can't abide the man."

"Mother!"

"Daughter?"

The air grew thick between them as they stared at each other. Lady Austwick's laughter sliced through the tension and Natalie felt she could finally relax.

Her mother clicked her tongue and gripped the edge of the table with her fingers. "I'm happy you found a match who makes you happy, but something needs to be done about this castle. Short of you raising taxes, marrying another noble or someone wealthy, there's only one option."

"I'll take the other option," Natalie blurted. "Whatever it is. I don't want anyone else."

"Very well. Then I will remain here in Blackmere for a year, and try to get her back in order. The castle needs a well-practiced hand and someone with connections to those who can help us rebuild—and you always thought all those parties were just for fun." Lady Austwick's icy tone withered Natalie. "You've proven how you flourish when you're forced out of these castle walls, so while I stay here, you will work. I'll not have you sitting about idle and moping."

Natalie's heart skipped. "Work? Where?"

Lady Austwick stood upright and smirked at her daughter. "I have been informed that the remaining champions intend to hunt down the member of their brethren who betrayed them and organized the attack."

"Henry?"

"You will accompany the champions, and see to it that they are comfortable and well-tended to while they hunt down the man who wronged you."

Natalie jumped out of her seat, her breath escaping her in a sharp gasp. "I'm going with the champions?"

"You will squire for the champions, to repay them for their aid. And in the meantime, I hope you find happiness."

Natalie leapt forward, embracing her mother's lean frame. She felt a soft pat on her back, and savored the sensation.

"Thank you," she whispered beside her mother's ear. "Thank you."

"Get to know him, then see how you truly feel about him. I advise utmost discretion."

"Of course." Natalie released her mother from the embrace and stood upright. "Thank you."

Lady Austwick's thin lips curled into the most gentle and subtle of smiles as she gave her daughter a single sharp nod. "Do me proud."

"I will," Natalie scuttled to the door and cast another look back. "Thank you."

"You are dismissed."

"Thank you." The door creaked open and Natalie stepped one foot out into the corridor. "Goodbye Chamberlain."

"Oh. Safe travels, my lady."

Natalie's cheeks ached as she stepped into the corridor and closed the door behind her. She pressed her back to the rough wood and wrinkled her nose as Brandon jumped to his feet.

"Are you alright?" He raised an eyebrow and scanned her face for clues. "What happened?"

"Come with me." Pushing back from the door, she snatched up his hand and led him down the corridor. She led him up the spiraling staircase towards her room, her heart ready to burst with excitement and joy.

By the time they reached her chamber, her face ached from the persistence of her grin. She closed the door behind them, briefly assessing the damage done to the room. Her bed was upright, and the tattered, bloody curtains taken down, but one side of the canopy drooped where the wooden frame had snapped. The floor has been scrubbed clean, which gave Natalie a brief moment of unease as she remembered why.

She shook off the feeling and took Brandon's hands in hers, rising onto her tiptoes to kiss him.

"I take it Lady Austwick had good news for you too?" He smiled down at her. The color had returned to his cheeks, and he no longer had the weary, drawn look.

Natalie sunk her teeth into her lower lip and smiled. "Sir Brandon?" The sound of his title made her smile all over again. "I believe you have business hunting down the man who betrayed us?"

His expression hardened a little at her question. "I do, my lady. Viv and I intend to rally as many of the surviving champions as possible, and go after him. We still have brethren who were unable to attend this Tourney, those who are still in training, even some who have retired." He sniffed and gently pulled his hands from hers, before bringing them up to tenderly hold her face. "I don't know how long I'll be gone. It could be weeks, months. I should hope not years."

"Such a long time," Natalie sighed, concealing her delight by casting her eyes down.

"I will miss you terribly."

"You won't."

His brow grew heavy as he looked down at her. He gently pressed his fingertips beneath her chin and tilted her face towards him. "Nat, not a day will go by where I don't miss you. And the second that bastard's in chains, I'll come back here to you."

Unable to hide her excitement any longer, Natalie grinned and kissed the heel of his hand. "I too have received orders from Lady Austwick."

"Oh?"

"She has decided I must work, to understand responsibility. I will no longer be Lady Blackmere, for a year, at least."

"Oh Nat, that's… well, what will you do? Where will you work?"

"My mother has already assigned me a task. I am to accompany the champions on their mission—"

He scooped her up into his arms and kissed her. For a moment there was nothing but the softness, strength, and warmth of his body. Soft lips, hard muscles, and soft skin beneath her touch as she rested her fingertips on the bare skin of his neck. When he broke away, she was breathless.

"So, you're coming with me?" He laughed as he wrapped his arms tighter around her frame, and carried her to the bed. "Please don't tell me this is a jest."

"There's no jest," she laughed as he pushed open the curtains of the bed and lowered her onto the mattress. "I'm coming with you, as your squire."

He lay down beside her, pulling her close to him as he frowned at her borrowed gambeson. "We'll need to get you some better fitting armor."

As he kissed her, she felt like her heart was glowing. It was a burning core in the center of an awaking mountain, swelling and ready to burst. He was hers and she was his, and nothing could come between them.

CHAPTER THIRTY-FOUR

BIG LAD stamped at the ground, eager to get going as Brandon slipped the bridle over his head. Natalie watched him, her arms crossed over her simple, yet well-made armor. She leaned her head against the stable door's wooden frame and sighed.

At the entrance to the stable, Jenny and Genevieve held hands as they whispered their goodbyes. A week had passed since the reclamation of Blackmere, and the pair had grown increasingly fond of each other.

"Poor Viv," Brandon grunted as he hoisted the heavy saddle onto the grey horse's back.

"Seems we're not the only ones keeping secrets from the Guild." Natalie rested her head on the wooden frame around the stall door, smiling as Big Lad nuzzled her. Heat blasted from his large, velvet soft nose. "We'll have to find Henry as fast as possible, and get them back together."

"Aye. Though who knows when the champions next come to Blackmere." His eyes grew distant as he tightened the buckle around the horse's belly. "Perhaps they'll find some way to make it work."

"I hope so." Natalie smiled as Brandon, dressed in heavy steel armor, walked towards her. His eyes were illuminated with the promise of the hunt. His hair was neat and short, and his beard trimmed. He was indomitable, impervious, yet she knew every inch of him, knew the stories behind each of his scars, and the precise pattern of the constellation of freckles on his thighs.

"Nervous?" His lips quirked as he watched her, determining her reactions.

"A little." She gave what she hoped was a relaxed shrug, though within the confines of her chest, her heart was galloping. Though her mother accepted—even welcomed—Natalie and Brandon's love, the Champion's Guild forbade it. They would have to hide their feelings for each other and deceive anyone they encountered during their search for the Dragon.

"I won't leave you. You'll be by my side the entire time, and I will stand between you and all the horrors of the world to protect you." His eyes trailed across her figure, leaving a path of blazing heat in his wake. "The armor suits you."

She placed her hands on the unyielding steel of his breastplate, as a thrill of excitement coursed through her body. As though acting on their own, her fingers trailed across to his sides, where thick leather straps held the armor to his torso. She bit her lip as she smiled at him.

"As does yours, Sir Brandon."

He let go of a shaking, desperate breath, before a chuckle rumbled deep within his chest. "Come, my lady, if we give in to our desires every time they beckon us, we'll never find Henry."

She sighed as she turned on her heel and sauntered towards her own mount. A black mare waited for her, already tacked in a fine leather bridle and saddle.

They led their horses out of the stable, and stepped out into the cool midday sun. The repair work to Blackmere's town was underway. Hammers pounded, saws screeched, and the street was crowded with people working tirelessly to return the little town to its former glory.

Genevieve turned to them as they approached, swiping the back of her hand across her eyes. "Let's just get this over with." She pulled herself into her horse's saddle and bowed her head to Jenny.

"Don't let anything happen to her," Jenny smiled, though her eyes were glossy with tears.

Brandon hoisted himself up into Big Lad's saddle and chuckled. "It's Viv. No doubt she'll be the one defending all of us."

Natalie cast a last glance at Blackmere's castle walls. As glad as she was to be free of it, it was her home. She gripped the reins of her horse in her leather-gloved hands and pressed her lips together.

"All will be well," Brandon smiled as he slid his hand over hers and gave her a gentle, reassuring squeeze. "He's just one man. There are three of us here, and the champions we're meeting on the road. He won't get away from us."

She nodded her head, and hoped her fear did not show in her eyes.

They left Blackmere without any fanfare, riding slowly through the gate, and down the stony road leading from the town. As the vast rolling green hills loomed ahead of them, the wind whipped through Natalie's hair. She breathed in deeply, savoring the scent of the land, her home.

"Are you ready, Lioness of Blackmere?" Brandon smiled.

"Yes. I am." She filled her lungs with the air of home and took his hand in hers. "With you at my side."

———————

ACKNOWLEDGEMENTS

This book wouldn't exist without Brittany Borshell. Your encouragement, passion, and faith throughout the entire process have been invaluable. Not only are you an amazing publisher, but a wonderful friend. Thank you for everything.

Thank you to Ali for your edits and your kindness and to James for proofreading (especially that one unfortunate instance of the word "beasts," that would've been terrible had you not caught it).

I'm so grateful to Crystal for your feedback and to all my beta readers for helping to make this story what it is. Thank you!

A huge thank you to Naj at Najla Qamber Designs for her incredible work on the book covers. It's been months and I still can't stop staring at them. Thank you to Dewi of Dewi Writes for his amazing map drawing skills.

And thank you to you, for reading this book and making my dream come true.

Keep reading for a preview of the first chapter of

HEARTS OF BLACKMERE
BOOK 2
THE CHAMPION'S DESIRE

Coming in January 2021...

CHAPTER ONE

THE CLATTER of galloping hoofbeats stilled Natalie's heart. Her feet pounded the floorboards as she hurried across the room and peered from the window, hope and fear battling for dominance. A rider thundered along the road towards her; a messenger, dressed in red. Brandon was late, and daylight was fading fast.

"Oh, Goddess no." She held her breath, willing him to keep riding. Whatever message he carried had clearly come with the instruction not to spare the horse. If it was from Brandon, it was not good news.

Mercifully, the messenger passed below the window in a flurry of chestnut and flowing crimson, a cloud of dust billowing in his wake as he sped up the road.

Natalie found herself able to breathe again.

Hours earlier she might have entertained herself by attempting to guess where the rider was going and what tidings he brought, but she was only capable of dark thoughts now. She wrapped her arms around herself and fought off a shiver.

"Where are you?" Her question rode on a puff of vapor, out into the rosy-skied evening.

Closing the window, she turned back to the room. After a month of fruitless searching, shivering through the night in wet clothes and drafty tents, foraging for meagre meals, the small, simple room in the roadside inn was practically palatial.

Brandon's armor gleamed in the corner of the room, laid out so Natalie could learn the names of all the pieces. Eager to excel at her new role as squire, she had polished and re-polished it that morning until her arm ached and he had teased that she would wear through the steel.

How she wished he worn it when he rode out to meet the other champions who were joining their hunting party.

Their quarry was one of their own, Henry Percille, the champion who had organized the bandit attack on Blackmere, and fled before his secret was discovered.

There had been no sign of Henry since, but even so, Natalie worried. Every clatter of hoofbeats, every raised voice coming from the bar below, spiked her pulse. Skilled, vicious, and fueled by ambition, Henry Percille was as dangerous as he was cunning.

As Natalie set about straightening the worn grey bed sheets for what might well have been the twentieth time, a sharp knock on the door turned her lungs to iron. She bolted across the room and flung open the door.

"He's not back yet then?" Genevieve asked in lieu of a greeting. Natalie shook her head. The champion's expression remained neutral as she gave a casual one-shouldered shrug. "The Bear never does anything quickly."

Natalie stepped aside to allow Genevieve into the room and closed the door behind her. The champion strode towards the bed, her boots thumping on the wooden boards. She peered down her nose at the sheets, as though assessing whether they were clean enough for her to sit. "I hate this inn."

Natalie fought back a grin. "Not as nice as Blackmere's tavern, is it?"

"No. No it isn't."

Since they had set off from Blackmere, Genevieve's temper had grown sourer and sourer. Natalie knew the cause. She knew why the champion's sullen gaze drifted to the east whenever she thought no one was looking, and why her expression hardened at the end of every unproductive day.

Genevieve, the indomitable warrior known in the arena as the Thorn of The Rose, was in love, and the woman she longed to be with was more than one hundred miles away, a barmaid, working in the tavern in the distant town of Blackmere.

Compared to Genevieve's heartache, Natalie's anguish at being away from Brandon for a day seemed pitiful.

"I think I need help writing Jenny a letter." The bed squawked as Genevieve sat. She braced her elbows on her thighs and let her hands dangle between her knees "I want to tell her we're still searching for Henry but have found nothing, and that I think about her every day. I don't want her to think I've forgotten her."

Natalie could not help but smile. "I don't think you need to worry about that, but I'll help write it."

Genevieve buried her face in her hands and released a weary breath. When she raised her head again, her eyes were glazed. "Do not tell anyone."

"Of course. Your heart's icy reputation is safe with me."

The champion narrowed her eyes. "I'm serious. When the other champions arrive, you can't mention it, and you mustn't let them see you and Brandon together. Don't even let them suspect. If the Guild finds out about Jenny and I, or you and Brandon...There's a lot at stake. Sex is fine, encouraged, even, but only outside the Guild. Relationships are forbidden. They want us focused on the fight, on training, not our hearts."

"Viv, it'll be fine. Brandon's warned me a hundred times already." Natalie sat on the bed beside the champion. Her heart fluttered as she caught Brandon's scent tangled amongst the bed sheets. She glanced back towards the window, to the darkening evening sky. "Goddess, I hope he's safe."

"The Bear's a big boy, he can look after himself. Besides, Henry will be miles away, fleeing for his life after all he did." Genevieve rolled her eyes and leaned back on her hands. "Don't fret. Darius is among the champions that the Bear is meeting with, so most likely they're wrestling on a roadside, or drunk… or drunk *and* wrestling."

Natalie chuckled and fidgeted with the ram's head brooch on the collar of her dark green padded gambeson. Being away from Blackmere was both a blessing and a constant source of anguish. The brooch was a persistent reminder that her time with the champions was only temporary. "I hope so. I can't wait to meet them."

An awkward hum sounded at the back of Genevieve's throat. "Just try not to act like a noble around the other champions."

"How can I—?" The slow, steady rhythm of walking horses silenced Natalie.

She pressed her lips together, suppressing the urge to run to the window. Every hoofbeat coiled a spring inside her, winding tighter, until she felt as though her excitement would burst and send her leaping through the inn's roof.

Genevieve's eyes bore into her, a single eyebrow cocked in mock despair. "You want to see if that's him, don't you?"

Natalie released a strained breath and swallowed. "Not at all. I'm sure it's nothing."

"You're a terrible liar."

"I had you believing I was a barmaid, didn't I?"

"Not for a moment." Genevieve laughed and shook her

head. "You were far too haughty. Rest your noble bottom, my sweet, delicate lady. I'll check the window." The champion stood, casually stretched her long, muscular limbs, and sauntered towards the window. Every step was torturously slow. She threw a grin over her shoulder, enjoying every second of Natalie's squirming.

Finally, Genevieve reached the far side of the room. "Ah-ha."

Natalie sat tall. "It's him?"

"Oh, forgive me, I was looking at my reflection in the glass. I thought I had something in my teeth…"

"Viv."

"…I didn't though."

"You're terrible." Natalie stood and craned her neck to peer at the road below. Genevieve turned, blocking the little window with her broad, well-built shoulders and gripped Natalie by her upper arms.

"Do you want me to check *your* teeth?" The champion teased as the hoofbeats grew louder and came to a halt on the road beneath them.

"It's him, isn't it?"

"Perhaps," Genevieve shrugged. "There is a big hairy man out there, riding a big grey horse."

Natalie's heart fluttered against her ribs, and her stomach flopped like a landed fish. She stood straight, checked the fastenings on her gambeson and brushed the seat of her trousers. "I'm nervous. Goddess, why am I nervous?"

"Because you are a fool, and you're in love, which is why I'm worried." Genevieve smiled and picked an invisible spot of dirt from Natalie's coat. "Before you go running down there and throw yourself into his embrace, remember what I said."

"I won't let them know we're together. It's alright. Stop worrying."

"Don't even let them suspect it." The champion's face hardened, and any trace of amusement vanished. "His family depends on it."

Genevieve's words were anchored in the back of Natalie's mind as she made her way through the top floor of the inn.

One false move could have him banished from the Guild, and people would suffer.

His mother was afflicted with back pain so severe and constant, that for years she had been unable to work, and his father was nearing seventy years of age. Brandon's salary and any prize money he received were sent directly to them, to pay for healers, medicine to relieve the pain, their noble's tax, and the cost of food and housing. Losing his position at the Guild would mean Brandon could no longer support his family.

Natalie side-eyed one of the bedroom doors as she passed. It had been reserved for her, though she had barely set foot in it since their arrival the day before. She wiped her sweating palms against her hips, and ran over the formal greeting she had prepared. "Well met, Sir Brandon."

As far as the other champions knew, she was simply aiding them in their quest to track down Henry, and squiring to repay Brandon for his services to Blackmere.

At the top of the wooden staircase she heard Brandon's deep, thundering laughter cutting through the humming chatter below. She stood for a moment, and closed her eyes as her heart skipped along her ribs.

"Well met, Sir Brandon. Well met, Sir Brandon." She whispered the greeting like an incantation, cementing it in her memory. The formality was paramount. Too informal and the champions may suspect their relationship. "Any news regarding our quarry?"

The heat of a deep pink blush crawled up her neck as she forced a slow breath. Lightly curling her fingers around the stair rail, she ventured down one of the steps. Her soft leather boots padded upon the wood.

"Well met, Sir Brandon. Greetings, Sir Brandon? No... well met."

Candlelight flickered above her head as she passed, casting a squat flickering shadow across the stairs. Brandon's laughter spurred her heart into a gallop as it rumbled from below, accompanied by raised, excited voices.

The voices of champions.

Natalie's head spun. All her life she dreamed of meeting those heroes, renowned across Aldland for their prowess in battle and their beauty. Now she was to live among them, and work alongside them, for an entire year. Even though their task was less than pleasant, she could not suppress her excitement. A giddy smile spread across her lips as she reached the bottom of the stairs, and stepped into the dense swarm of tavern patrons, crammed into the tiny bar.

"Pardon me. Pardon me!" She grimaced as she wedged herself between two chattering men, and began picking her way through the crowd. "Excuse me, sirs."

The air was thick with conversation and the sour reek of ale and sweat. Warm bodies pressed against her, unyielding to her requests to pass. She squeezed through, holding her breath as she passed beneath clouds of curling blue pipe smoke. By the time she reached the center of the crowd, she was exhausted, and there was still no sign of Brandon.

She stood on her tiptoes and craned her neck to find him, wondering how it was possible to lose a man so large.

"Can I help you find someone, my lady?"

Her heart leapt, and her breath froze at the sound of his voice. Every word fluttered against the back of her neck, sparking a fire in the pit of her belly.

She whirred around to face him. His dark eyes widened a little, as though he sensed her desire to fall into his arms, and the danger they faced if she gave in to her urge. Instead she offered him a friendly smile.

Brandon towered above everyone else, and took up so much space with his broad frame that the air around him seemed clearer than the rest of the inn. No matter how many times she saw him she would always be in awe of his strength, the raw, brutal power of his arms, and the tenderness with which he held her when they were alone.

As Natalie composed herself, the lines around his eyes deepened, and a gentle smile curled beneath the shadow of his thick, silver-flecked beard.

"Well...uh... well met, Sir Brandon." She felt as though she was glowing when she looked at him, all strength and softness, a hardened exterior disguising a gentle heart. "How was your ride?"

"Too long." He took a step closer and lowered his head towards her. A thrill coursed through her at his familiarity. His eyes drifted down towards her lips, as though he could barely contain his desire to kiss her.

Heat crept across her cheeks. "You must be pleased to be back."

"Aye." His eyes trailed across her face. "I can't wait to be back in bed."

She sank her teeth into her lower lip to suppress her grin. His voice was deep and dark and full of promise. This flirtation was a dangerous game to play.

"But first, I have friends for you to meet," he said at last, hooking his arm around her shoulders. The companionable gesture snapped her from his spell.

They made their way across the tavern as people parted to let them pass. Every pair of eyes was drawn towards Brandon, trailing up and down his body as though they could not quite believe his size. A few people turned to whisper to their companions, but no one said anything directly to him. No one would dare.

Though those who knew him knew he was kind and gentle, Brandon looked intimidating. He was a hulking mass of scar and muscle, renowned all over the land for his fighting skill. His glory days in the Tourney were years behind him, but word of his brave defense of Blackmere seemed to ride ahead of them wherever they went.

An ache rolled through Natalie's body as she pressed her side against him. She longed to steal him away, even if just for a moment.

She was burning up as they reached the far corner of the tavern.

"There he is!" A man held out his arm to Brandon and clapped him on the back, pulling him into the fray.

He was young and strikingly handsome, with warm brown skin, long, black dreadlocks, and kind, dark eyes which sparkled with excitement as he talked. "We thought you were lost forever."

Natalie's heart swelled as she looked around the small gathering. There was no denying they were champions. It was obvious from their stunning appearance, strong physiques, and the confidence with which they carried themselves. They were chosen because they were as beautiful as they were brutal.

"I hope you didn't miss me too much, Darius." Brandon's cheeks rounded as he gestured towards Natalie. "May I introduce you to Natalie, my new squire."

"A squire?" Darius's eyes lit up. "You have a squire this year? Goddess, you must be taking it seriously."

"Darius?" Natalie's breath hitched as she held out her hand. "You're the Storm, aren't you?"

"Why, yes I—" The smile dropped from the man's lips. His eyes narrowed as they fixed on the broach at her throat, a glare so fleeting Natalie might have missed it were she not hanging on his response. Her pulse fluttered anxiously as he stiffened and tucked his arm behind his back. "Lady Blackmere." The slight was so subtle that Brandon did not notice. He gestured to a young woman, whose pale white skin, prematurely silver hair, and slender, muscular frame made her seem as though she was a statue carved from ice. "This is Sara."

Natalie bowed her head, restraining her enthusiasm. She knew the young woman as the Snow Fox. Both she and Darius were fresh out of their debut season, and riding high on a wave of expectation. They had not qualified for the Grand Tourney at Blackmere, but hopes were high for the following year.

Sara's features hardened as she looked down at Natalie. "Brandon told us about what happened at Blackmere."

"Oh," Natalie felt herself redden. She wondered how much Brandon had told them. Her stomach coiled at the thought that they might know about her deceit, and her failure to prevent the attack at Blackmere. "Yes, it was truly terrible. I'm so sorry for the loss."

Darius raked his eyes across her face, leaving behind a

trail of blazing heat. "We lost good people in the attack."

Shame weighed heavy in Natalie's chest as she searched for something to say. It was her carelessness which had led to the deaths of champions and squires. Among the list of the dead was Robert Trevaryn, a man beloved by Brandon, his best friend. His death still stung.

There had been many nights she noticed Brandon staring into the flames of their campfire, his dark eyes glazed with unspilled tears.

Now the eyes of all the champions were on her, burning into her, as though they could see the weakness of her heart, and the stain of death on her soul.

"Aye, it was a tragedy." Brandon's voice came as a relief. His arm brushed against Natalie's elbow as he shifted his weight, grounding her once more. "I'll introduce you to everyone else later, when it's less noisy. What say we share a drink?"

"I knew there was a reason I liked you," Darius's wide smile spread across his face. His eyes creased into a grateful smile as he turned his back on Brandon and Natalie, and his dreadlocks swung behind him like a pendulum. "I'll find somewhere to sit and you get them in."

VIOLET GAZE PRESS

Violet Gaze Press was born out of the desire to see Romancelandia flooded with diverse, sexy, romance. When readers ask "Help, where can I find characters like me?" the answer should always be "Where do I start?"

We are a small indie publisher, with a passion for romance novels and the community that has sprung up around it. Entrenched in it, we were dismayed to see readers struggling to find recommendations for romance that encompassed all the beautiful variations of relationships and the people who enter into them.

We want to bring books into the world that people have been yearning to read; books that foster a sense of being seen and that make people feel loved and lovable.

At Violet Gaze Press we believe that all love is valid, that all people deserve to see themselves represented in romance novels, and we strive to make that a reality

VISIT US AT

www.violetgazepress.com

Twitter @violetgazepress

Instagram violetgazepress

Facebook https://www.facebook.com/violetgazepress

9 781838 203702